Scourge of the Granny Cartel

Scourge
of the
Granny Cartel

David Harrison

A RedDoor book
Published by Ember Press 2023
www.emberprojects.co.uk

© 2023 David Harrison

The right of David Harrison to be identified as author of this Work has been asserted by him in accordance with sections 77 and 78 of the Copyright, Designs and Patents Act 1988

978-1-7392844-1-1

All rights reserved. No part of this publication may be reproduced, stored in a retrieval system, copied in any form or by any means, electronic, mechanical, photocopying, recording or otherwise transmitted without written permission from the author

A CIP catalogue record for this book is available from the British Library

Cover design: Clare Connie Shepherd

Typesetting: Fuzzy Flamingo
www.fuzzyflamingo.co.uk

Printed and bound by Severn, UK

To Sarah and Monica

God is a comedian playing to an audience too afraid to laugh.

Voltaire

ONE

It was the first time that anyone had heard of a pack of Maltesers being responsible for the deaths of two people. Especially while waiting for a bus. It was a sad little tale, and doubtless it would have remained just that, if it hadn't come to the attention of two of the most divisive forces in Britain.

The seeds of tragedy germinated in a bus queue in a town called Swillington on a hot June day. While the mercury crawled up, so did the tempers in the queue as the minutes passed with no bus in sight. All eyes were focused on the shimmering road ahead, so no one in the surly queue noticed Bernard Drain lumbering up to the bus stop.

Driven by the notion that Swillington's old-fangled bus timetable could reliably predict when one of the veteran fleet of buses would actually arrive, Bernard had rushed to the bus stop and was now puffing away like a wretched old steam engine.

To clarify, rushing for Bernard was never more than an animated shuffle, however it was enough to leave his face awash with sweat and his clothes clinging uncomfortably to his frame. He was by no means the only one in the queue carrying a goodly store of fat, but his sheer size marked him out from the rest. He was a mountain surrounded by chubby hills, but in increasing isolation as the others sensed his presence and began to sidle away as his presence increased.

While waiting for the inevitable cluster of buses to arrive, Bernard searched in his bag. In his haste he had only managed to lay his hands on a large bag of Maltesers and a bottle of cola. He opened the bag of Maltesers and sunk his fingers in.

With a mouth full of sticky brown balls, Bernard became aware of a growing disturbance around him and looked around for the cause of the unease. Something was making the queue skittish, as though it could stampede at any moment. The growing sense of fear was palpable, animalistic. It reminded him of those herding beasts in Africa that the lions and hyenas were so mean to. Scanning the horizon above his fleshy foothills, he spotted the reason for the unrest. His jaw dropped, his eyes grew wide, and a Malteser hopped out of his open mouth.

'God help us!' Bernard cried in a rather muffled falsetto voice. He heard somebody else in the queue begin to mumble Psalm 23.

The Willoughbys were coming. Count Dracula with an iron deficiency would have been a more welcome sight.

Everyone knew Molly Willoughby and her son, Jason Willoughby. The issue with Molly was mainly auditory in nature and could, in large part, be negated with careful breathing and some tissue stuffed in each ear. It was Jason that posed the serious threat: Bernard wouldn't have rated the chances of a troupe of baboons (he was quite into nature programmes) in a fight against him. Jason was a wiry ginger-haired, freckled skin, sugar-fuelled eight-year-old alpha predator who would have given Satan a nervous tic.

Molly's guttural cry drifted down the street on the warm breeze: 'Ge' ba' 'ere ya litta fecker! I swer I gona sal' yer oggans.'

That's a new one, Bernard thought as he watched in growing horror the pedestrians scatter away from the oncoming Jason.

Sandra, the manager of Pound Heaven on the high street and a No.456 regular, managed to gather her wits and yelp, 'We've got to stick together or else we are done for. If we stand back-to-back in a circle, we may just have a chance. Don't use anything as a weapon. The little brat will only nick it and use it against us. Anyone with false limbs, keep to the middle, for all our sakes. Everyone, prepare to defend yourselves!'

This plan of defence was standard operating procedure when a bus queue in Swillington was faced with a Jason attack. There were no amputees present. So, to give the defensive circle some structural support, the queue reluctantly pressed in around Bernard. He was left looming out of a squashed mass of humanity's lower-hanging fruit. It reminded him of a documentary he had seen about the sinking of the USS *Indianapolis* where the survivors had to band together for days to fight off the sharks.

Molly had no idea who Jason's father was. In fact, she was pretty sure she hadn't been conscious when Jason had been conceived and no one had come forward out of any fatherly curiosity. A small shaft of insight had led her to form the hypothesis that the father might have ginger hair. This had prompted her to search the town for a ginger-headed procreator, in the hope of some maintenance money. Once she had even mentioned paternity tests in her local boozer, The Knackered Dog, while keeping an eye out for anything ginger bolting for the front door. This hadn't gone down so well with the landlord, who had been left with a heavily depleted pub.

Given the nurture society had afforded her, it could be said that Molly had never had a chance. Most of her days were regulated by her available supplies of fags and cheap booze. Sometimes she would run out of money before the month was up and would either try to avail herself of the charms of one of Jason's many uncles or send him out foraging with a stern warning to keep an eye out for the boys in blue. This week, Molly had run out of cash, and because she was too hungover to face the outside world, had sent Jason out to purloin some provisions. This typically involved him preying on the weak and infirm as they left Penny Heaven, which was the local corner shop; unfortunately named, given its close proximity to a rowdy pub called The Whippet. This time Penny Heaven's proprietor had called the police the moment he had spotted Jason, forcing Jason to return home empty-handed to a less-than-motherly reception. This all meant that Jason was now in desperate need of a sugar fix which, with his upbringing, was interchangeable with hunger. And he was ready to rain terror down on anyone to get it.

The bunched bus stop queue watched the ginger terror home in on their position. He slowed down as he drew closer, like he was trying to sniff out the weakest of the pack, inhaling the panic he had induced.

Jason used his marshy top lip like a bloodhound to search out the delicate scent of confectionery. His large freckled nose roamed around the petrified crowd, drawing him closer to his prey. His brain matched the chemical compounds to a specific confectionery and the image of a red pack of Maltesers – yes, opened today and still three-quarters full – appeared in his mind. Quite how he knew that could have been a subject for scientific study, if only Jason had survived the day.

Then Sandra cried, 'Look! The 456, 457 and the 078 are coming.' All eyes turned to the convoy of buses rolling down the road, bar two sets of wide eyes that were locked onto each other. Jason's increasingly wolfish smile left Bernard in no doubt about the situation. The crowd huddled around Bernard soon realised the same and removed themselves, leaving nothing between Bernard and a ruthless foe.

'Give him the sweets, you damn fool, and save yourself.' This was from another No.456 regular called Amy, who ran Amy's Winehouse off-licence on the high street.

'Leave me alone,' Bernard whined. He could feel the stress building in his chest, as Jason growled in response and began to crab around him, looking for the best angle of attack. By now, the first bus had stopped and the doors were opening behind him. Bernard backed towards the doors, ready to parry any attack. Just as he stepped between them, Jason leaped into the air and landed like a ginger bat on Bernard's heaving chest. The others in the queue turned away in shame, too scared to come to poor Bernard's aid. In no time, Jason's hands had grabbed the bag of Maltesers, but Bernard wasn't going to give up his snack without a fight. He clung to the treat bag with all his might, flicking his head from side to side to avoid the gnashing, filling-packed teeth and absorbing the pummelling of the small feet into his stomach.

Realising that he was going to have to be a bit more persuasive, Jason kicked his legs up and planted them on the door frame, then pulled with all his might. It would prove a fatal mistake. Bernard's hands lost their grip on the bag and Jason fell to the ground, landing in the crab position with the Maltesers in one hand. A look of glee beamed across Jason's face, but when he glanced back up to sneer at his towering victim, he frowned. What was the fat git doing, wiggling his arms around like that?

With all the majesty of a giant redwood, Bernard's 190-kilos bore down on Jason. By the time Jason realised he was going to be squashed like a bug, it was too late. With a sound few would wish to remember, Bernard descended directly onto Jason's stringy frame with such force as to cause a sickening snap, crackle and pop. Jason had been crunched like a Malteser underfoot.

Bernard found himself lying on something sticky and prickly. His chest was now a tight, dense ball of pain. Cries of 'oohh' and 'aagghh' rose up from the crowd around him as he rolled this way and that over an increasingly flattened Jason, in an effort to rise. The rolling was to be the final straw for Bernard's ailing heart as it finally succumbed to all the exertion. With his last gasp of breath, he watched the Maltesers roll gently from Jason's dead hand, before his own head hit the pavement with a fatal thud.

Now, this bizarre turn of events would have remained a local fascination but for one man. William Hanock. (He had changed his surname from Handcock by deed poll.) He was a hack who wrote for the *National Mail*. He wouldn't ever have set foot in the dingy town of Swillington but for the fact that his dying spinster of an aunt had lived there. He didn't give a fig about his Aunt Louise, but as her closest living relative he thought he had a fair crack at a notable mention in her will. However, moments before she croaked, she had voiced her opinion that his rightful place was in a toilet bowl and that he wouldn't receive so much as a penny from her will.

Charmed by this deathbed response, Hanock had delivered some shrivelled flowers to her funeral and was on his way back to London when, as chance would have it, he noticed the commotion at the bus stop. He wouldn't have been much of a hack if he couldn't sniff out a story to pervert, and his curiosity was piqued by the sight. So he parked up and made his way over.

He reached Bernard about the same time as Molly. She would have been there sooner but had stopped to scrounge a fag off some nearby children. Now she stared at Bernard in confusion as the crowd stared at her. It seemed unnervingly quiet, which made her wonder where Jason had gone. Then she saw his small crushed hand poking out from under Bernard's bloated frame. She looked up at the sombre crowd, who shook their heads in unison. With a breaking heart, Molly descended to her knees and let out an excruciating wail.

What sympathy she had managed to garner in those few moments dissipated when she revealed the true basis of her grief. 'Little bugger lost me 'is child 'lowance. That were me fags an' booze.'

William Hanock was faced with an embarrassment of riches. Another online article denouncing Britain's grasping hoi polloi seemed on the cards, before he looked at the small hand and the Maltesers lying close by and a diabolical idea came to him.

He stepped over to the prostrate body of Bernard, picked up the Maltesers and placed them between Bernard's and Jason's hand. He then stepped back, got his camera out and started taking pictures. Molly, ever the one for an opportunity of self-promotion, thrust her face out of a curtain of blond locks and squawked, 'I wan' money for 'em!'

'Of course you do, dear,' Hanock responded before wandering off through the crowd to take interviews with the assembled throng of bemused onlookers. Molly nearly leaped after him, intent on forcing the issue, but thought better of it and descended back into her faux grief. By the time the police and ambulance had arrived, Hanock had got what he wanted and left. To his surprise, his diabolical idea had turned out to be pretty close to the truth. Printing something that was actually true was going to be a novelty for him.

Even though the two police officers were inured to the creative ways people managed to kick the bucket, this one seemed destined for the local force's hall of fame. With the help of two paramedics, the two officers succeeded in rolling Bernard over, to reveal that most of Jason had been squashed into two dimensions.

They considered the situation. Finally, one of them decided that the best people to deal with the sad occurrence would be the local undertaker. 'Frank, best send for Wish, Bone and Ash,' muttered George, 'and tell them to bring a jumbo and a...*hmm*. There's the rub.' He looked down at the boy, pressed like a dried flower onto the pavement.

'D'ya reckon they do flatpacks?' Frank asked.

'I wouldn't know,' George replied, running his tongue over his top lip. After some thought he cocked an eye at Frank and said, 'I reckon a child's coffin will suffice, as long as they bring a shovel, being that there will a bit of scraping to do.'

George remembered that Jason had a mother. He looked around, but she was nowhere to be seen. 'Where'd she go?'

'It almost looks like one of those street paintings, don't you think?' Frank remarked.

George looked back down at the redistributed Jason and, after a pause, replied, 'Yeah, I know what you mean.'

'The pub,' Frank murmured, still fascinated by the gruesome street art. 'That's my guess, at least,' he added.

'You've lost me,' George murmured back, who was also unable to pull his eyes away from the florid paving slabs.

'Molly.'

There was silence for a few seconds before George replied, 'She's a rare flower.'

'That she is,' Frank concluded as he cocked his head at the pavement.

*

'MALTESERS FIGHT ENDS IN DEATH' ran Hanock's headline in the *National Mail*. Realising that they actually had a true story for once, the paper felt compelled to balance the scales with an accompanying article about the pernicious effect sugar was having on society. Even the paper was surprised by the reaction the contentious article provoked.

The country, already concerned about the rise of sugar-addicted, malnourished children and the lipid wave of obese, diabetic adults squashing the National Health Service into submission, gave a collective jerk of the knee. Naturally, the unpopular government saw an opportunity in the upcoming election and, with almost evangelical fervour, began to beat the drum of change, denouncing the corrupting influence of the saccharine substance. The newly formed Sugar Temperance League took to social media to push home their message, using righteous indignation to silence all opposing voices. Tweets and social media posts of support came rolling in, with it transpiring that a surprising number of Russians seemed to be concerned with the nation's health. When the government edged past the winning post in the general election everyone was surprised, not least most of the government. A baffled world then looked on as the prime minister made good on his promises and rushed through a bill to heavily restrict the sale of all sugar-based products.

'MAD DOGS AND ENGLISHMEN!' ran *Le Monde*'s headline, while *The Scotsman* demanded release from the 'yoke of the Sassenach fools'. Eyebrows rose when *Der Spiegel* sardonically called it 'Britain's *Kristallnacht*' and predicted the imminent destruction of the British corner shop. *The New York Times* questioned Britain's commitment to NATO. All the Russian newspapers supported the British government's visionary stance, but made no call for Russia to follow the same example. China barely raised an eyebrow at the result, in public. Buckingham Palace said that the queen was indisposed for comment, with rumours that the news had left her speechless.

Despite the criticism, the British government stood firm. Sugar restriction was here to stay. But there was one thing the government hadn't considered. That was the law of unintended consequences.

*

In a bucolic corner of Surrey, Maude Appleby sat quietly in her kitchen as she tried to come to terms with the destruction of her award-winning cupcake business. As the full reality of the news hit home, something snapped in her mind and a weird light began to enter her eyes. In an unearthly whisper she spoke to the teapot in front of her: 'My name is Maude Appleby, prize-winning cupcake maker, chairperson of the Surrey Women's Institute, loyal servant to God and queen. I have been a wife, a mother and a grandmother. And I will have my vengeance, in this life or the next.' In the surrounding forests and fields, animals turned in fear, or irritation, as a blood-curdling howl rose up from within the stone-built cottage.

When Maude opened her front door the next morning, she was no longer the sweet, amiable granny she had once been. With lips curled, she began to plot her revenge.

TWO

Godfrey Fairtrade gazed absentmindedly at the brick wall opposite his second-floor office in Westminster's Portcullis House. He pondered the series of events that had led him to be gazing out at a brick wall opposite a second-floor office in Portcullis House.

He had never intended to be an MP. He had been quite happy working for the diplomatic service and, despite an internal appraisal describing him as 'amiably maladroit', he had been slowly moving up the ladder. This was entirely down to his willingness to be posted to any squalid, flyblown, gun-toting, despot-mincing hellhole that other candidates would hospitalise themselves to avoid. Then, unexpectedly, he was offered his first ambassadorial position…of Mongolia. It later proved to be a clerical error, which happened in August when most of the foreign office was, in effect, abroad.

But that had still left the problem of Godfrey's wife, Lillian. After years of being bitten, burrowed into and subjected to violent bowel venting, not to mention being traumatised by sectarian violence and Soviet-style architecture, Lillian had become a rather ill-tempered diplomatic appendage. Her bridal aspirations of status had never envisaged such a hellish route and now she strongly suspected her dreams of being a socialite would remain just that.

Her response to Godfrey's ambassadorial position in Ulaanbaatar had certainly been spirited. She had fallen on their bed in a quite unseemly display of wailing and sobbing. His speech about the honour of representing your country at the highest level had only induced further hysteria. All she had done was thump her pillow harder in time with her frenzied utterances of 'Ulaanbaatar', prefixed with a most unladylike sexual expletive.

Godfrey turned from the window, creaking as he did, took a sip of his El Maestro Sierra and shuddered at the specific event that had led him back to his leafy suburban home in Ewell, Surrey.

His ambassadorship of the Mongolian embassy had only lasted a few weeks. The first clues of impending disaster came when the increasingly inebriated Lillian refused to leave the isolation of their embassy's drab accommodation. Things had eventually, horribly, come to a head at a welcome reception held in his honour at the Mongolian Chamber of Commerce in Ulaanbaatar. Godfrey was left with no choice but to cajole a surly Lillian into attending.

Despite his whispered protestations, her first port of call had been the port, at the bar. Duly fortified, she had begun to wasp her way through the crowds of Mongolian dignitaries and foreign diplomats. Despite his attempts to keep her in check, every blasted person in the room had seemed intent on ensnaring him in a web of interconnected and quite incomprehensible conversations. In quiet desperation

Godfrey had watched Lillian with her dishevelled beehive, and tipsy toddle, lurch through the crowd like an upper-class zombie aboard a storm-tossed cruise liner.

His diplomatic career ended when she careened into the Mongolian minister of agriculture, sending his canapés and both their drinks down his front. The astonished minister, who was now covered with a wet mass of food, red wine and a large gin with a dash of tonic, accused his paralytic assailant of being just that. Lillian's obscene two-syllable suggestion that he should go somewhere else needed no translating. If that wasn't bad enough, she had quickly concluded her insult by describing him as…well, let's just say that he most certainly wasn't unwashed (before she got to him) and nor was he bow-legged or Chinese. She then splashed the not inconsiderable contents of her stomach over his beige chinos.

The Foreign Office offered Godfrey early retirement.

Over time, Godfrey's night terrors about that dreadful evening had subsided and he no longer came out in a cold sweat every time he heard the sound of splashing. He especially remembered the murderous look in the Mongolian minister's eyes: it had been referred to by those in the know as the Genghis Stare. It was a glance Godfrey would soon see again, but from a quite unexpected quarter.

Godfrey sighed. All water under the bridge, he thought. It would be fair to say that their marriage had been a little strained after that. When they returned to Ewell, Godfrey felt he needed a hobby, so he joined the Progressive Conservative Party. At meetings he was somewhat left behind by the political cut and thrust, but was happy to follow the chorus of grunts and be rewarded with tea and biscuits at the end. Never would he have imagined the dangerous waters this light bit of social interaction would lead him in to.

While Godfrey had been enjoying his weekly hob-nobbing and Hob-Nobs, the MP in the bordering constituency of Vole Valley had been slowly moving towards his maker after a long battle with Alzheimer's. The Progressive Conservative Association of Vole Valley had, of course, taken great pains to find a suitable heir. That meant an individual who would epitomise the progressive nature of the party without advocating anything of detriment to their own existence. Once they had found a suitable candidate, they informed the incumbent MP, in a moment of lucidity, that his parliamentary duties had finally come to an end; whereupon he promptly and very gratefully expired. The candidate, a certain Vincent Burton, was a clear departure from the previous MP, not least because he was in full possession of his faculties. He was also slim and fit, being an avid cyclist, which fitted better into the official party image. This was basically anything that would displace the fat, broadly unfit and gouty image the metropolitan masses seemed to associate with the Progressive Conservative party.

The road ahead looked clear, but fate was waiting with an IED. On a sunny Sunday morning, heir apparent Vincent was cycling in a peloton from Guildbury to Dorsham. Over the last few years, the Vole Valley had become something of a Mecca for cycling enthusiasts, much to the ire of the local community who found themselves regularly trapped at twenty miles an hour behind a mass of wheels and Lycra. On this particular Sunday morning one particular local, in the full throes of the male menopause, finally snapped. In a fit of rage, he had swung his Nissan Micra with all the force he could muster into the body of the peloton.

In the carnage that followed, the prospective MP was forced off the road only to find himself airborne over an embankment. The physics of Vincent's departure from the road caused the bike to rear up like a startled mare, with his chest and the handlebars forced into embrace. Man and bike then began their descent, with precious moments being spent parting his shoes from their peddle clips. Then time slowed to one long mind-crippling moment for Vincent Burton when he realised his buttocks and the slender seat were horribly aligned. The back wheel hit the ground with devastating force, causing the pointy saddle to plough mercilessly into his inner sanctum.

With bike firmly attached, Vincent was airlifted to Guildbury Hospital where, after five hours of fiddly surgery, the saddle was finally removed. The doctors said his gait would never be the same again.

With the traumatised prospective MP in uncommon traction, it was clear that he wasn't going to be running for anything. This left the Vole Valley Progressive Conservative Association with no viable candidate for the impending election. That was until they heard of a recently retired diplomat living in Ewell. Discreet enquiries were made. Contacts in the Foreign Office were contacted. Unluckily for Godfrey, his affable nature combined with the F.O.'s warped sense of humour meant that the reports that came back were largely sanitised of his shortcomings. So apart from some nebulous comments about something referred to as 'Mongolgate', Godfrey was given a clean bill of health and became the frontrunner in the contest to be the next MP of Vole Valley.

Godfrey was blithely unaware of any of this, of course, until the morning he opened his front door to find the entire Vole Valley Progressive Conservative Party Selection Committee on his lawn. While Lillian had kept them entertained, Godfrey had gone to change out of his dressing gown, wondering why the VVPCPSC were in his living room. When he returned, he found Lillian and the VVPCPSC talking through the details of his election campaign for the Vole Valley constituency. Godfrey could see that Lillian and the others had already got the challenge by the scruff of the neck and were too busy to ask his opinion. All that was left for him to do was serve the tea and biscuits, as Lillian plotted to get her husband just where *she* wanted to be.

Godfrey became something of a bewildered bystander in his election to the House of Commons. His 'advisory team', of which Lillian was chief whip, were always on hand to tell him what to say and do. Vole Valley was a secure Conservative seat, so the drudgery of canvassing was dispensed with. The only problem was Godfrey's shape, which was very much old Conservative. Again, Lillian provided the solution, and ever since he had been creaking around in a corset, which also doubled as a torture device when his sedentary grazing got out of hand. Six months after he won the by-election, a general election was called.

Godfrey had been vaguely aware that one of the Progressive Conservative Party's new flagship manifesto commitments was its heavy restriction on the sale of sugar-based products. Senior Progressive Conservatives buried the public in a blizzard of sound bites on the subject until the public were so befuddled with righteous quotes, blue-sky thinking and twisted truths, that they were fearful of voting for anything else. The manufactured consensus was that only forthright (but undefined) legislation could save the day. With the PCP in full moral crusade mode, the bulk of the newspapers in full scaremongering mode and the newly formed Sugar Temperance League in full marching mode, the opposition didn't stand a chance. Godfrey had watched it all with a certain detachment as the PCP sailed to victory, helped along by the terrified shrieks of warning that emanated from the sugar industry. On the day of his election victory, Godfrey and his team celebrated with mid-range champagne, but it had seemed that Godfrey was alone in seeing the irony.

*

Four years later the government-enforced sugar restrictions had certainly produced a marked improvement in the nation's health, but the country had grown to despise its medicine. A licence to sell sugar was beyond your average retailer and the sight of boarded-up corner shops had become commonplace. The result was that anything with high levels of sugar that was not considered an essential food item, had become luxury products beyond the reach of a normal household spend. In an attempt to lessen the hammer blow to the sugar industry, the government gave out handsome tax breaks on their vanishing profits. It only served to galvanise the anger and resentment towards the government, from all sides. Nor was the rest of the economy immune to the effects of sugar restrictions. This had prompted the opposition to quip that the government was getting its just desserts. It didn't help when Horace Karloff, the gaffe-prone foreign secretary was caught on tape likening the government's popularity to that of a jihadist at a bar mitzvah. The government was in trouble.

Its biggest concern, though, was the black market. A new criminal cartel had emerged to circumvent the cost of the punitive licencing system by taking control of the illicit trade in sugar-based products. Anything containing sugar could be purchased off the street or in clandestine 'Sweet Easy' establishments, accessed from side doors down dark allies. But the most startling thing was where the power actually rested within the cartel.

The existence of the cartel first came to light when an investigative journalist broke the news in an article in *The Guardian* called, 'The Dark Side of the Women's Institute'. In it she said that the venerable institution had become a front for a very secretive, and very unusual, criminal organisation. She called it a 'granny cartel', because all the power brokers happened to be grannies. She said the Granny Cartel had now become by far the largest criminal organisation in the country and was rapidly growing in numbers and influence. Somehow this matriarchal monster had spread its tentacles into every aspect of society, right under the noses of the authorities. The article proved to be a severe embarrassment for the government and caused a plenitude of marital problems at the same time.

Suddenly, talk of the Granny Cartel was on the nation's lips. Social media adored the Cartel, painting them as heroic outlaws fighting against the system, or the patriarchy, depending on who was talking or ranting. The fact that the Cartel remained as silent as a tomb only enhanced their allure.

And it wasn't just in Britain that the Granny Cartel was causing ructions. A new genre of music – Sugarcorridos – emerged to take the internet by storm with songs eulogising the real or imaginary exploits of the Granny Cartel. This prompted the Mexican drug cartels to complain that their own Narcocorrido culture was being misappropriated. Which in turn prompted the head of the U.S. Drugs Enforcement Agency to suggest where they could shove their misappropriated culture. That triggered the social justice warriors to get involved, organising large rallies in the name of the culturally suppressed Mexican bandits.

The existence of the Granny Cartel was a nightmare-in-waiting for Godfrey. He was haunted by images of old biddies wearing sombreros and gun belts. Indeed, many of Godfrey's fellow MPs were convinced that Surrey was now the British equivalent of Mexico's Sinaloa. And therein lay the problem for Godfrey, for the stronghold of the Cartel was indeed in the Surrey Hills, which just happened to be in his constituency. It was not a happy position to be in, and his loathsome constituents were fond of pointing this out at his dreaded weekly MP surgeries.

The Cartel had already proved it would not tolerate any intrusions into the rolling forests and meadows of their private fiefdom. This had been made abundantly clear by the Russian incident, which had so horrified Godfrey: seeing the bounty of the illicit sugar trade, the Russian Mafia had decided on a bit of regime change. Maybe it was a sign of respect that the hit squad they sent into the Surrey Hills was a large one. Unfortunately for the Russians, what happened next became the stuff of Sugarcorrido legend. The stories of the cartel's giant enforcer, Pippa Blackwood, and her homicidal band of female mercenaries – the Baker's Dozen – were true. And the Russians ran straight into them. They didn't know the woods and were quickly overpowered. It is then speculated that one of the Russians got a bit lippy with Pippa. What was almost as astonishing as the injuries he received, was that the Russian in question managed to survive long enough to get transported to Dorsham hospital, where he swiftly expired. The government had used the incident to try and blacken the Cartel's name, but, if anything, it had only enhanced their appeal. It was like fighting Che Guevara and Robin Hood combined, with the muscle of a pet giant that would send the likes of Gregor Clegane running.

Of course, none of it could be proved from the one recorded murder. Nor were the authorities having any luck tracking the river of money flowing into the black market. The National Crime Agency suspected links between the Cartel and a cryptocurrency called Cupcake (CAK), but again, nothing could be proved. Paranoia filled the hole that the lack of progress made. Suspicion between government agencies was on the rise. Allegiances were questioned. Talk of fifth columns was rampant. It was widely assumed that the Surrey Police had become a mere puppet of the Cartel.

And the government was running out of time. Another election was around the corner and a confrontation seemed inevitable. It had occurred to Godfrey that this was what the Godmother of the Cartel, that shady figure presiding over her fiefdom in the Surrey Hills, might want. Even in the corridors of parliamentary power the name of Maude Appleby was whispered in nervous tones as though the very name was cursed.

Lillian was under the delusion that Godfrey should be at the centre of any government initiative aimed at tackling the Cartel. By contrast, Godfrey was much more concerned about his own passion, that of staying alive. He'd heard all the stories about what had befallen the Russians on his own patch. This had left Godfrey with only one choice: hiding in the long grass of the backbenchers and hoping no one noticed him. So far it had worked. But that was about to change.

THREE

A few days after Godfrey's brick wall gazing, Paul Symes, private secretary to Mervyn Nipper, was just getting ready to leave Portcullis House for home when his phone rang. Paul saw that it was Nipper's line and muttered, 'Bloody typical,' before picking up the handset. 'Paul, could you come into my office?' The line went dead before Paul could say a word. He dropped the handset into its cradle and gave it a slow two-fingered salute. Paul was the sugar tsar's second private secretary. The first one had disappeared without a trace, leaving Nipper without one of his closest confidants. After a bit of clandestine manipulation from Paul's 'secret backer', Nipper had been persuaded that Paul was the perfect one to fill those vacant shoes. Paul could well imagine Nipper's reaction if he ever discovered that his arch rival had a cuckoo in his nest.

Paul knocked on Nipper's door. The grandfather clock in the corner ticked down several seconds before he heard: 'Enter.' He opened the door and stepped into the frugal, lifeless space that was Nipper's office. There was a desk, some shelves and filing cupboards, a bare bulb cupped by a zinc shade and a few chairs to welcome visitors. A shadowy figure rested his elbows on the desk. He eased his face forward and a lofty nose cut through the frugal curtain of light, followed by a brow and cheek.

'I'm glad I caught you,' Nipper said. His chin came into view and then the light caught the moist top of the angry haemorrhoid that served as his bottom lip. 'Would you like a nightcap?' Nipper's bulbous eyes slid over to the drinks tray and his 'vintage' selection of mineral waters. Paul gave up all hope of getting to his fiancée's parents' that evening. 'I have this rather intriguing little number from the foothills of Kangchenjunga in the Himalayas.'

Mervyn Nipper didn't smoke or drink. He was an intense, humourless man; traits, which, along with the body he was housed in, had ensured a celibate existence. Nipper had no family that Paul knew of and seemingly no friends outside the Sugar Temperance League. As the architect of the government's loathed sugar policy, and then in the capacity of sugar tsar, its implementer, he was regarded as the most hated politician in the land. But for Nipper it was all water off a puritanical duck's back.

Paul accepted the Kangchenjunga tipple, which tasted like tap water.

'I assume the British Dental Association are still lobbying the government to provide aid to fill the hole in their member's finances?' Nipper said as he sat back down.

'That they are, minister,' Paul replied, wishing that Nipper would get to the point.

Nipper scoffed, 'Well, they can just crawl back into the cavity from which they came. Their complaints only show the magnitude of our success.'

Due to the sugar ban, divorces across the nation were

up, as were drug addiction and domestic abuse. Murder was also on the rise, and suicide. Paul didn't point any of this out.

'Exercise and clean living, that's what people really need. You can't start pandering to people's whims. I didn't get where I am today by pandering to people's whims. My dream is one day to know that the only thing people cherish is the zest for life and what they can bring to society. Think of the utopia the country would be then. We are carving out a brave new world.' Nipper took a sip of mineral water and rolled it around his mouth to savour the as-advertised electrolytes. 'The problem with people is that they don't know what's good for them,' he continued. 'It is our duty to give direction to the herd. And at the vanguard of change is the Sugar Temperance League.'

Paul had heard this all before. 'They were certainly at the vanguard when they were marching through Liverpool at the weekend,' he replied with restrained dryness.

'A courageous display if ever I saw one,'

'They narrowly escaped with their lives,' Paul retorted. 'It was a stroke of luck that the Dean of Liverpool Cathedral was on hand to stop the lynching.'

'Where were the police, that's what I want to know?' Nipper complained, shaking his head.

'There were two football matches going on at the time and, to be fair, Saturday shoppers don't generally turn into spontaneous lynch mobs.' Paul suspected a few of the Merseyside police had been more than aware that Liverpool's main shopping drag was about to be adorned with some strange fruit, but he kept his own council.

'We have to root out the subversive influences within society that cause this seditious behaviour, and its taproot is this insurgent Granny Cartel. We have to crush these geriatric delinquents once and for all,' Nipper exclaimed with a euthanistic gleam in his eye.

'That poses some unique challenges.'

'That they all look the same?'

'That wasn't what I meant.'

'Same cardigans, same blue hair dye, same wrinkles. You can't tell one granny from another. Bit like Labradors.' Paul tried to banish an unwanted image of Labradors dressed in tweed from his mind.

'There are strong suspicions that Surrey Police are in bed with them. Who knows what depraved things are going on in those hills?'

'Figuratively speaking,' Paul found himself saying. 'It's a delicate situation and could easily result in a public backlash if we do something...*heavy-handed*.'

Nipper grunted. 'We just have to make our case better and be tougher with these subversive elements within society. Because of the sugar restrictions people are healthier, fitter, and less of a burden on society. People should be applauding our success. If we can just remove the temptation, then society will grow to see the wisdom of our sugar policy.'

'Not if the opposition wins the next election.'

'The British people haven't elected a prime minister with a beard for well over a hundred years, Paul,' Nipper retorted. Nipper's pogonophobia was well documented, although the reasons were still obscure.

Nipper then did something he rarely did. He smiled. It was a hideous sight. 'Anyway, we transgress. These subversive elements must be crushed!' Nipper banged his fist hard on his desk, with his fist coming off worst. 'To that end, I am going to propose the creation of a small, hardened, professional, incorruptible special police taskforce to bring down the Cartel's ring leaders,' he said, wincing.

Paul wondered if Nipper had recently watched *The Untouchables*. 'I would suggest that's a conversation you need to have with the home secretary,' he ventured, knowing how that would go down. Sir Cecil Mandeville-Blythe and Nipper got on with each other about as well as Stalin and Trotsky.

'What, only for that snake to try and squash my idea!' Nipper snapped. 'I'll be going direct to the PM, preferably after my yoga class tomorrow morning. That's why I called you in. I want you to check to see if the PM will be around.'

'I'll try to book an appointment with Florence, but it is a bit short–'

'Don't book an appointment, he'll only find a reason to cancel it. I just want to know if he will be around,' Nipper barked. The PM had made an artform of avoiding Nipper.

'As you wish, Minister,' Paul said as he rose up to leave, thinking that his upcoming holiday couldn't come too soon.

Nipper had often stopped to wonder how the home secretary was so often one step ahead of him. But he had never stopped to wonder if there might have been some intelligent design behind it. Once Paul got back to his desk and was sure he couldn't be overheard, he gave Sir Cecil a call.

★

The next morning, Prime Minister James Houston was grappling with some policy proposals for a third term: handing over portions of the welfare state to charities and floating off chunks of the NHS to venture capitalists. There was a separate proposal from Nipper called 'Welfare by Weight', which relied on a sliding scale of how much benefit a person could receive, depending on their level of obesity. Houston made a mental note never to make Nipper health secretary. In fact, he had come to see Nipper as a serious health risk to his own legacy.

The anti-sugar campaign had worked on the population like a snake charmer's *pungi* in the last election. When the electorate had eventually spat out its dummy at its own sugar excesses just before the election, it was Nipper who had come up with the 'visionary' plan to heavily restrict sugar. Reducing the burden on the NHS would more than make up for any fiscal shortfall, he promised. There would be economic downsides, but they would be manageable, he promised. The Sugar Temperance League had made itself large on social media, deriding any opposing voice as being socially corrupt. For Houston it was just a case of selling the best route to victory. After all, elections were about manipulating hearts and circumventing minds, not about democracy as most of the electorate believed.

Four years on, the government's sugar policy was threatening to become Houston's greatest regret, for all the trouble it was causing. But, like Captain Ahab, he was well and truly tethered to his nemesis, unable to free himself without a fatal loss of political capital as an election loomed. And with the nemesis came Mervyn Nipper, who was dug in like a tick and just as tricky to remove. Things weren't helped by the fact that the PM's wife, Eleanor, was a member of the Sugar Temperance League and seemed to think that Nipper had been sent from God to save the nation.

Luckily, the Labour Alliance Party were still yanking each other's beards about the best worst direction to take the party in. It was down to the resurgent Social Liberal Party to be the biggest threat at the next election, with their terrifying pledge to bring in proportional representation. So far, the government had kept them at bay with a variety of dirty tricks and smear campaigns, but one PR disaster could change everything.

Houston pushed the proposals aside and was preparing to consider his other source of angst, the vacant position of the chief of the armigerous Houston clan, when he heard a knock at the door. Florence, his private secretary, popped her head around the door and said, 'The home secretary is here to see you.'

'What for?'

'Matters relating…to…policing.'

'What, *again*?' Houston leaned his head on his palm with a grimace. 'You'd better let him in.' The door opened and the gaunt figure of the home secretary appeared. He was a tall man with a stoop, obtained through many years of looking down his nose at others. He always reminded Houston of an ageing vulture wearing an ill-fitting suit. In comparison, Houston had a high forehead below a crest of slick black hair, with thin lips and eyes snuggled close to the bridge of his nose. With his youthful appearance and crisp dark suits, he always reminded Sir Cecil of a salesman of expensive cars, or properties. Or policies.

Sir Cecil drifted in and placed himself in the chair opposite Houston, putting a rather grandfatherly look on his face.

'Sir Cecil, what an acquired pleasure this is.'

'Very droll, Prime Minister, coming along nicely,' Sir Cecil replied. 'You wanted a meeting to discuss the concerns raised at our last meeting regarding policing.'

'I did?'

'Yes, Prime Minister.' Sir Cecil nodded with a melancholy smile. Houston was always irked by how the doddery old coot could make a man twenty years his junior feel senile.

'Ah, yes, slipped my mind what with…anyway, um, how are these concerns, going?' Houston said, casting his attention back to the policy proposals.

'Badly. The chief inspectors are revolting.'

'You mean revolting, as in, not happy?'

Sir Cecil wagged a hoary eyebrow. 'Yes, Prime Minister. They are unhappy about interference from Whitehall. They feel they need more autonomy in dealing with the law enforcement issues before them.' He promptly launched into a droning monologue of said issues.

Houston drifted back to his chiefdom problem. Because of equality laws, his claim to be Houston clan chief was now being challenged by some seedy ex-stripper from Baltimore. Furthermore, her lineage suggested that her claim was stronger. Worse still, she was gaining ground; partly because of his present reputation, and partly from her tactics of swishing the equality banner. She also was wafting money around the noses of clan members. Apparently, in her stripper days, some geriatric fart had taken a liking to her tasselled mammilla and undulating gluteus maximus. The old goat had turned out to be a canned goods mogul, who promptly married her body and was ridden into his sunset, but not before she had become the main beneficiary of his will.

Houston was thinking of ways to discredit his grubby pond-hopping relative when Sir Cecil concluded, 'So I have assured them that we will not pursue any more operations without their consent.'

'I didn't know we had.'

'And we mustn't start.'

'You're the home secretary, so any interfering, as you say, would be done by you.'

'And that is the way I want to keep it.' A knock at the door cut through Houston's confusion. He raised a finger as Florence entered.

'We've got Mervyn Nipper here,' Florence said, as though it was a job for Rentokil.

'Well, tell him to be here someplace else. I would have remembered it if I had arranged a meeting with him. No offence, Sir Cecil.'

'None taken, Prime Minister.'

'Apparently it's important,' Florence said, looking unconvinced.

'Anybody would think I was running some kind of

ministerial drop-in centre. Florence, tell him I'm in a meeting with Sir Cecil discussing policing and cannot be disturbed.'

Nipper barged past Florence into the room. He stopped and his eyes veered towards Sir Cecil before flicking over to Houston.

Houston sighed, 'That will be all, Florence. What is it, Mervyn?'

'Can we talk privately?'

'As you've walked in on a private meeting, you can privately tell me now or I'm going to privately tell you to get a private appointment and leave me to my privacy.'

'It's OK, Prime Minister,' Sir Cecil said affably. 'We can start again later,' and he began to stand up from his chair, letting out a deep grunt as he did so.

'God, no. Mervyn, speak,' Houston said with a little more urgency than he would ideally have wished.

Nipper stifled a growl. 'Sorry, Prime Minister. I have an idea regarding the Granny Cartel.'

Sir Cecil settled back down in the chair, letting out a deep grunt as he did so. 'Ah, Prime Minister, a subject on which I may be of service.' Nipper bristled at his incumbent form.

'Well?' Houston said impatiently.

'I have thought of a way to bring them to justice.'

Houston's eyes narrowed as they floated over to Sir Cecil. 'Why do I feel I know where this is going,' Houston said. 'OK, out with it.'

Nipper grudgingly outlined his idea and reasoning, while keeping a watch on Sir Cecil from the corner of his eye. 'A small, hardened, professional, incorruptible special police taskforce to secretly go in and quietly decapitate the snake,' he said.

'Mervyn, have you been watching *The Untouchables*?'

Sir Cecil tutted and said, 'As fate would have it, this is exactly what I feared, Prime Minister,' shaking his head slowly with a soupçon of sorrow in his eye.

'It's a strange thing, fate,' Houston replied with his own soupçon of wryness. 'Unfortunately, Sir Cecil, I'm inclined to run with it.'

Sir Cecil sat bolt upright. 'But, Prime Minister, this is exactly what I was talking about.'

'I know, I know, but I need to be rid of this Granny Cartel before the next election. They're making this government look like a bunch of even bigger twits. Extremely risky though. Any action we take will need to be highly classified,' he continued as he rose up and turned toward the window, assuming a Churchillian stance. 'Naturally, I will need a minister to be held accountable if the plan fails. A person who is prepared to put the party before their own political career. The type of selfless individual who will sacrifice all to protect the party, of which I am the embodiment.' Both Sir Cecil and Nipper were about to volunteer the other, but Houston cut them off. 'We need a junior minister who is politically expendable. I'm just not sure who.'

Neither Houston nor Nipper noticed the sly smile creep over Sir Cecil's face. He said, 'Why not promote Godfrey Fairtrade to some relevant junior ministerial position?'

'The MP for Vole Valley?' Nipper sneered. 'He's a

buffoon. Remember his maiden speech?'

'Yes, perfect, isn't he,' Sir Cecil replied, suddenly a lot brighter. 'If things go pear-shaped, we can just drop it all on him.'

'Yes, not a bad idea,' Houston said, looking out of the window, stroking his developing second chin. 'Not a bad idea at all. OK, let's flesh out the plan and get things in motion. Then you can tell Fairtrade the good news, Sir Cecil.'

Sir Cecil, resigned to his employer's command, shuffled out the room. When he arrived back at his office, he took a burner phone from his briefcase and dialled a number. When an elderly voice replied, Sir Cecil whispered, 'Hello, Maude. There have been some…developments.'

FOUR

As Harold Wilson once said, a week is a long time in politics. Within a week of Godfrey's fate being secretly sealed, he found himself being bumped into an impromptu local government fact-finding junket to Wolverhampton with Clive Katnipp, MP for Runnymede and Weybridge. Why Wolverhampton was the destination, he never discovered. What he did discover was the career-destroying way Katnipp liked to relax.

Godfrey was furious for allowing himself to get plastered. That in itself was odd because he could only remember having two drinks. Then Katnipp had manhandled him into that horrendous 'private club', which he was now pretty sure must have been a brothel. He vaguely remembered being accosted by that frighteningly young girl, all sneaky fingers and sucking lips. Before he knew it, she was stark naked, his pants and trousers were at his knees and she was trying to push him down onto a bed.

Luckily, his animal instincts had given him the presence of mind to escape before things had turned really ugly. He stared at the now-familiar brick wall out of his office window in Portcullis House. What had that Katnipp been thinking, he thought? If the press ever got a whiff of it…

the thought made him shudder. Then he thought of how Lillian would react and he picked up his bin and hugged it until the nausea passed. Godfrey looked at his watch and saw that Prime Minister's Questions were starting soon. He stood up, put on his jacket and made his way to the door. Best show his face and, once he was settled, he could have a quiet nap at the back.

*

Godfrey was dreaming that he was in the House of Commons listening to Prime Minister's Questions. The PM was replying to a question about the lack of nursery places for the over eighty-fives when a flock of cooing doves marched into the chamber. Before Godfrey could hear what the doves were cooing about, a huge skeletal hand came down, grabbed the lead dove and unceremoniously flicked it through the doors of the chamber. The other doves then turned into hideous black carrion birds with long gnarled beaks and demonic eyes. The birds then proceeded to take their places on the front benches and began humming 'The Girl From Ipanema'.

Suddenly the girl from Wolverhampton and one of those hideous birds were standing in front of him. The bird kept kicking him and saying, 'Wake up'. But his eyes were on the girl. She slowly bent down, fluttered her eyelids and whispered in his ear, 'So you like underage prostitutes.'

Godfrey woke up with a yelp. One of those hideous birds was still in front of him. No, it wasn't a bird, it was the home secretary and he was kicking him. He looked around blearily to discover he was indeed in an emptying House of Commons.

'Wake up, will you.'

'Huh…hmm…yes, er, sorry. I must have dropped off. Been working really hard, what with–'

'Shut up and follow me,' Sir Cecil ordered, then stalked off.

'Right, yes… OK,' Godfrey replied to no one in particular. He stood up with a creak and followed Sir Cecil, still haunted by his nightmare. Godfrey trailed along behind Sir Cecil as he weaved his way through clusters of muttering members to the Terrace Pavilion and headed for an isolated table. Godfrey creaked down next to him and looked around nervously. Sir Cecil then produced a well-crafted smile and said in a voice laced with menace, 'We've been watching you.'

'Has this anything to do with Wolverhampton?' Godfrey replied, feeling his stomach lurch.

'Wolverhampton? What's Wolverhampton ever got to do with anything?'

'Nothing!' Godfrey quickly replied. 'I'm just not very keen on the place.' The home secretary gave him a quizzical look, before his expression changed to one of mild amusement.

'We're making you deputy assistant parliamentary undersecretary of state with responsibilities for rural law and order.'

'You are?' Godfrey replied, mentally reading the title back until he finally got to the *rural law and order* bit with a cerebral thwack. 'You are!' A waiter came over but Sir Cecil shooed him away.

'Yes, and you know what that means.'

'Can I think about it first before I turn it dow…decide?'

'No trade, Fairtrade.'

'I'm quite happy on the back benches.'

'Was.'

'So you are saying I have no choice?'

'In a nutshell.'

'But why me?'

'I'll give you one guess.'

'I can't be held responsible for the behaviour of all my constituents.'

'Want to bet? It's your constituency that's causing the problems. We can't have safe seats turning into lawless ghettos. It's embarrassing for the government and embarrassment equals poor poll ratings. As you're their MP you can take the lead in getting rid of them.'

'But surely that's a problem for Surrey Police?' Godfrey replied, trying to keep the pleading out of his voice.

'Are you purposely trying to be obtuse?' Sir Cecil growled. 'You know as well as I do where the Surrey Police sympathies lie. All they have done so far are search and avoid missions. So the Metropolitan Police are going to set up a special taskforce to go in and sort out the mess once and for all. Your job as minister will be to coordinate with them, provide whatever support you can and generally show a ministerial presence.'

'Do I get bodyguards?'

'Oh come on. We're talking about grannies here. What do you think they're going to do, stab you with their knitting needles?'

'Yes.'

'I heard you had a bad back, but I didn't realise you were completely spineless,' Sir Cecil quipped. 'Anyway, the taskforce will be going in under cover, working independently of Surrey Police, reporting directly to Sir Archibald Punchard, the Metropolitan police commissioner. Everything is being arranged as we speak, so all you have to do is not get in the way.'

Godfrey concurred. He didn't want to be anywhere near in the way. Like the Easter Island kind of not in the way.

'Sir Punchard will be in contact with you shortly to explain the details of the operation. Any questions?' Godfrey opened his mouth. 'No, good, must dash.' Sir Cecil stood up and was about to leave when he stopped abruptly. 'If things go south, we will expect you to do the honourable thing.'

'Which is?'

'Take full responsibility for the failure and fall on your sword. We don't want the government further tarnished by this nonsense, as I'm sure you understand.' Sir Cecil walked off without waiting for a reply.

Godfrey sat back in a sweaty pool of misery. He felt a few drops of rain and looked up to see one solitary black cloud hovering over his head. How very fitting, he thought to himself. Oh for the halcyon days of North Korea.

FIVE

Some miles from the urban sprawl of south London there lay a bucolic land largely untouched by the ravages of the twenty-first century. In this peaceful world were the two rival villages of Okney and Nokney. Nokney lay on the undulating plains, surrounded by meadows and slow flowing streams, whereas Okney commanded the timbered heights and looked down on the lowly dwellings below. To reflect this, the generally dissonant musical evenings at the Whortleberry Arms always finished with a rendition of 'The Folks That Live On The Hill', with the guiding voice of Peggy Lee rising above the cacophony.

There was only a sunken single-track lane from Dorsham to Okney that climbed up between mighty beech trees to the hilltop village. The postwoman drove slowly and meditatively up the lane as she listened to Vaughan Williams' 'The Lark Ascending' while she glimpsed vistas of sylvan valleys and paddocks through the sun-dappled trees. The post van passed Revd Graham Massey as he looked up from between the gravestones at the crooked bell tower of St Morwenna in Okney. The fretful vicar, unlike his folly-building ancestors, didn't possess the expertise to correct the tower's dangerously misshapen geometry. He did now have the necessary funds, although the philanthropist responsible was another source of anguish to him. He looked at the wisteria- and rose-clad cottages that surrounded the church. It was hard to imagine this rustic idyll was the lair of the Granny Cartel. Nestled in the woods was the philanthropist's cottage, named 'Judges 14', a biblical allusion the vicar felt best left to a Tate & Lyle tin. He hoped that God would forgive his servant for accepting her donation.

Apart from some feline windowsill watchers the chocolate-box cottages were empty, barring the few menfolk who weren't yet marinating in the ground or sitting on the mantlepiece. He looked aghast when he came to the ancient lychgate. A Harley Davidson was parked amongst the souped-up mobility scooters. The mural on the petrol tank strongly suggested an ungodly owner. Opposite the Harley Davidson was a smart green Range Rover. Revd Massey scowled when he read a sticker on the back window which read: 'Land Rover, a great Indian company'. He saw that the roof was decorated with stripes of white, saffron and green. He dreaded to think what was happening in the crypt. The reverend missed Pippa Blackwood's henchwomen, the Baker's Dozen, hiding in the graveyard, watching him as they kept guard over the crypt. The Baker's Dozen were a breed apart in the granny community. They were composed of grannies from the wrong side of the tracks, hardened women who had cut their teeth on the seafront benches of Eastbourne. Pippa had taken their raw skills and, between naps, had honed them into a fearsome fighting force versed in the martial arts weapon, the nunchuck.

The reverend looked up at the crooked bell tower of St Morwenna one last time before heading for his retreat, the garden shed. Once he was in his retreat, he locked the shed door and uncorked one of his parishioners' treacherous homemade wines. When he had recovered from his first sip, Revd Massey began to lament his quarrelsome parishioners. Cutbacks from the diocese had meant the recent amalgamation of St Morwenna in Okney with St Damien in Nokney. With distress he recalled how 'Stir-up Sunday' before Advent had become more like 'Dust-up Sunday' as his pugnacious congregation had descended into hostilities over the assertion that the best Christmas puddings were created at altitude. As he had spoken the words of the Collect, his flock had taken to hurling hymn books at each other across the nave. He only wished they would lay down their village rivalries as they did for the owner of Judges 14. Revd Massey retreated into the Pre-Reformation world of Early English arches and misericords and reflected mournfully on the idea that if only he had an anchorite's cell possessing a hagioscope, he wouldn't have to rely on his Mafiosi parishioners. Alas, St Morwenna had nothing of interest to draw the faithful in from further afield, and closer to his collection box.

Meanwhile, the bull-necked piggy-eyed owner of the bike was in the crypt, sporting a sleeveless patched leather jacket and arms covered with biker gang ink. He was standing uncomfortably in a horseshoed row of grannies. His name was Alf.

In front of Alf the biker were two ladies of advancing years, but that was all they had in common. One was small, crisply dressed in a Barbour jacket and tweed skirt with a deceiving air of grandmotherly sweetness. She sat in a composed position, like a feudal lord. This was the owner of Judges 14, Maude Appleby.

There was nothing deceiving about the woman on Maude's left, but that didn't prevent her from being astonishing. She was so tall and powerfully built it was easy to imagine her as another species or an individual from some wild evolutionary fork. Her long grey hair, the eyes and craggy face gave her the look of a berserker at rest. Despite her age, she still looked capable of choking a polar bear, let alone any living human being. She liked her drink. And she liked men. The problem was when the two came together. Her name was Pippa Blackwood and she was the reason Alf the biker was there.

'Look 'ere, Maude,' Alf began to complain. 'Every time Pippa comes to the clubhouse, she causes trouble. The lads are fed up with her coming over when she's 'ad a skinful and treatin' us like pieces of meat. It's gotta stop.'

'Are you saying, young man, that she's showing you no gender respect?' Maude gently replied with an enigmatic frown.

'Gender respect?' Alf grimaced at the notion. 'Not sure I'd use those words, but…well…' His words died to an untranslatable mumble.

'You must speak up, son. Our hearing isn't what it used to be.'

'I guess,' Alf said and snorted. He then turned to the Pippa, who had a gothic tattoo of the word 'MARS' on her arm, and in a moment of reckless manly defiance, sneered,

'Besides, ain't she gettin' a bit old for it now.'

Alf just had time to register the general sharp intake of breath and a blur of movement before he found himself hoisted up from the neck by five strapping leathery digits, leaving him flailing impotently in the air. As the biker clawed at the meaty hand, and his face reddened to a rather alarming burgundy, Maude casually said, 'Pippa, put that poor boy down. I simply refuse my guests to be man… sorry, woman-handled.' Pippa dropped him in a crumpled heap on the floor and thudded back to Maude's side.

Once his windpipe had recovered, Alf croaked, 'You could have said that a bit earlier.'

'I'm curious as to why the…' Maude hesitated. Pippa bent down and whispered in her ear: 'Why the club president isn't here to represent the club?' Rubbing his neck, the biker staggered to his feet and said rather sheepishly, 'We drew straws. I lost.'

'I see,' Maude replied, and looking up at Pippa. 'I will have a quiet word with Pippa. If she desists in her passions, would the problem be resolved?'

Alf hesitated before replying, 'If that means she'll stop all the rough stuff, yeah. It's so…'

'Demeaning?'

'Hair-raising. Especially when she laces the drinks.' Maude caught the scowl that Pippa threw at him.

'Pippa has promised to be good in the future, haven't you, Pippa?'

Pippa's eyes moved over to Maude and were met with a chilling stare. In a voice about as deadpan as her face she said, 'Yes,' and gave a few reluctant nods.

Maude patted her hand. 'Now, I hope this has cleared the air,' she continued, smiling sweetly at the biker.

'We're all good.' Alf nodded and made to leave, tripping on the stone steps of the crypt when Pippa caught his eye with a sly wink.

Once the biker had left, Maude turned back to Pippa and said, 'Who was he again?'

'Member of the Hell's Rejects, Dorsham chapter.'

'Oh, I see. Anyway, I want you to leave them be, OK?'

Pippa scuffed her foot over the ground and muttered, 'OK'.

'I *mean* it.'

Pippa cowered back and replied, 'Yes, Maude.'

'Good. The Cartel has a reputation to keep. You have a new family here that accepts you for who you are. Keep your womanly predations in check.'

'Sorry, Maude.'

'Now, what's next?'

'We have Mr Mukhergee here to see you,' said a lady sitting closest to Maude. Her name was Deirdre Wotheringspot.

'Ah, Mr Mukhergee, are you there?' Maude said.

A svelte man appeared from the shadows and gave a short bow. He had thought about curtseying. He wore a double-breasted, pin-striped three-piece with patent winkle-pickers and slicked-back hair, all giving the impression of a 1940s spiv. He glanced nervously at Pippa, the giant that had just made a rag doll out of a biker, who could have made a rag doll out of him.

'My good lady, my wishes from all at Mithai Associates

of Harrow.' This was followed by another short bow. 'Please accept this small gift of sweets from my outlet in Drummond Street. I hope one day we may see a branch in these beautiful hills. It evokes cherished memories of my Darjeeling.'

As Mr Mukhergee spoke, he moved forward and placed a large box at Maude's feet. With one eye on Pippa, he pushed back a stray strand of hair and retreated to what he hoped was a safe distance.

'And how is business?' Maude asked with an edge of weariness. There followed a rundown of just how badly his business was doing. It ended with, 'So, I come to you with grievous news.'

'And just what would that be?'

'I am most sorry, but because of the various perils of smuggling and subsequent costs incurred we feel we will struggle to honour our sugar shipments at the cost agreed.'

'Really?' Maude said with a sardonic edge in her tone.

'It grieves me to say it.'

Maude smiled but there was no warmth behind it. 'Maybe you should cut back on the gambling, drugs and other paid pleasures which your wife doesn't know about…yet.' Mr Mukhergee stiffened like he had suddenly encountered a knife where the sun rarely shone. 'Don't think I don't know how well you're doing. I know the level of all the illegal imports you are bringing into the country, on top of all your other shady ventures. Do you want to remain a favoured supplier?'

'You seem well informed,' Mr Mukhergee replied casually, but was betrayed by the beads of sweat on his brow.

'I have eyes and ears everywhere, which you would do well to remember,' Maude responded with an edge of menace. 'You warm yourself at my fire, Mr Mukhergee. Move away from my fire and you will find the shadows cold and dangerous, especially as a previously favoured supplier.'

Mr Mukhergee dropped his eyes. 'We will sacrifice the food from our children's mouths to honour our bargain.'

'Good, that's settled.'

With undisguised haste, Mr Mukhergee backed away and disappeared up the crypt steps. Maude sighed and said, 'Deirdre, I think it is the time for the M&Ms.'

The M&Ms consisted of two types of summarised monthly report. The first related to Marathons and the second related to Milky Ways. A Milky Way was a smuggling method using mass drones, often employing what they called Starbursts, being drone parachute drops. A Marathon used all other traditional forms of transportation. The vast majority of this bootlegging was done by the Cartel's affiliate gangs, making the Cartel a form of criminal franchisor that provided the strategy, tactics and logistics for the smuggling networks the Cartel had developed with the help of the affiliates. It was a fluid model glued together by trust and shared aspirations, selling anything sugary that they could get their hands on, from booze to bourbons to barbecue sauce. And given that it was all considerably cheaper than any of the officially licenced outlets, it was no surprise that the Cartel was exceedingly popular.

These affiliate gangs covered pretty much the entire country. There were the Beeties in East Anglia, run by a

Boudicca-like figure called Ma Simms, who had forced the sugar beet farmers to employ armed guards. In Yorkshire there were the Fat Rascals and, in Sussex, the Brighton Rockers, who the previous year had forced a Sugar Temperance League rally to retreat into the sea.

Both smuggling methods relied on sympathisers: people from all walks of life and function, ready to throw a spanner in the works of the authorities attempting to enforce the sugar restrictions. They were the eyes through which the Cartel looked. They were the midnight runners on the slippery end of a Marathon Run. They were the people playing with knobs in the dark amidst the drone of drones, delivering treats from the skies. The Cartel used cutting-edge technology and ink on paper to communicate. It even had its own private postal network thanks to sympathisers in the Royal Mail.

There were forty-eight grannies in the inner circle of the Cartel, excluding Maude, Deirdre, Pippa and the Baker's Dozen. These forty-eight were Maude's consigliere. The M&Ms were their reports in summary. The crypt couldn't fit them all in, so there was a rota, with those in attendance disseminating the business of the day to those that were not present.

Mavis, Gladys and Mildred were typical members of this matriarchal cadre. Mildred was a lowlander from Nokney, whereas Mavis and Gladys were from Okney. Gladys was sitting between them, to stop any squabbling between the other two. Gladys' nephew happened to be operations director for the port of Felixstowe, and as each granny was like an account manager for one or more affiliate, her focus was the affiliates in Suffolk. Mildred had links in Essex; Mavis, in Norfolk. This made them a kind of regional team, albeit a grumpy one.

Maude's chief intelligence officer, Deirdre, stood up and stepped into the circle. If Pippa Blackwood was Maude's 'shock and awe', Deirdre Wotheringspot was her stealth fighter. When it came to strategy and tactics, it was Deirdre that Maude turned to. But Deirdre also had some extremely useful contacts in the field of covert operations: in a previous life she had been a senior MI5 spook. She was tall and slim, but not thin, and conservative in her dress with an austere face that would have sat well on a cruel Victorian headmistress. Which all belied the fact that she was compassionate by nature, while knowing when to be ruthless.

'Our spies in the police force have updated us on all ongoing operations. We have modified our shipments accordingly,' Deirdre began. After speaking for a number of minutes she concluded, 'Last month our affiliates delivered a total of a nineteen thousand tonnes of product, excluding managed losses. We can also confirm that all the branches of the Women's Institute south of Middlesbrough have now come into the fold, apart from Derbyshire, but they can't hold out for long now. CAMRA also wish to meet with you. That's it.'

'Very good, Deirdre,' Maude replied. 'Unless anyone has any other business, I move to close the meeting.' They all stood with hands linked and began to sing their own personal variant of 'Jerusalem':

And did those hands in ancient times
Knead upon kitchen worktops clean
And was the blessed Mary Berry…

The hymn ended with the words, 'Freedom for sugar in this land again'. Pippa began to help the less able out of the crypt until only her, Maude and Deirdre were left. Maude fished in her pocket and produced a small electronic box with one button on it. She pressed that button. A tombstone lying on the floor began to tilt up, revealing steps. At the bottom of the steps was a filing cabinet. Deirdre descended the steps, filed the reports and came back up. The tombstone slowly descended back to the floor. This modest cubbyhole of secure storage had been built when the vicar had been on holiday. The previous occupant of the tomb was now residing in a cardboard box at the back of Maude's garden shed.

'Have you heard any more from Sir Cecil?' Deirdre asked Maude.

'Not as yet. I assume your contacts still haven't heard a whiff?'

'Nothing from the Met or *Box 500*,' Deirdre replied, using the colloquial name for M15.

'They're keeping it close,' Maude said, looking thoughtful. She shrugged. 'It doesn't matter. Our contacts in the Met will let us know in good time.'

'Do you trust Sir Cecil?' Deirdre said.

'I trust that old reptile will do anything he can to rid his party of Nipper and Houston.'

'And Godfrey Fairtrade?'

'That was quick thinking on Sir Cecil's part. With Fairtrade in our pocket, we have the potential to make a laughing stock out of this police taskforce. At least that was Sir Cecil's thinking. I'll be paying Mr Fairtrade a visit when the time is right, and, thanks to our friend Clive Katnipp, it should now prove a fruitful one.'

Deirdre glanced over at Pippa who was standing motionless, listening to the conversation. Maude read her thoughts.

'I'm afraid the Baker's Dozen might have to sit this one out, Pippa. We're not playing by Russian rules this time. I want to humiliate the government, not send back body bags.' Pippa looked disappointed, but unsurprised.

'It will be interesting to see who will be heading up this police taskforce.'

'We have to assume they will be a worthy adversary,' Maude replied. 'If it were me, I'd want someone with a long pedigree. Someone who's as hard as nails.'

SIX

Inspector Tancred Punchard was slowly sipping his third noggin of Old Reliable in the Elusive Fox. He wore a Harris Tweed gilet that blended seamlessly in with his wavy blond locks; all finished with a face that hinted at an overbred 'noble' gene pool. *He* felt his appearance as country squire was *comme il faut*, given his Norman ancestry and the gently mouldering Wolfestone Manor with its sadly retrenched estate, which he and his parents inhabited in the remote Dorset village of Winstead. Yet here he sat, alone, in a snug, a victim of his own woefully inadequate social skills as well as being the law, nominally. Having been fast-tracked (and carefully side-lined), Tancred was now a more common sight in Winstead than in New Scotland Yard.

Even so, he considered his (carefully considered) post at the heart of the strategic cut and thrust of the police force. Through various committees, working groups, focus groups and policy units he helped steer the future of the force through a raft of recommendations that were slowly strangled as they percolated up the chain of command.

In the past, when Tancred was more compelled to venture up to the big smoke, he had always tried to travel up with his father. He greatly preferred the chauffeured experience to the abhorrent cattle carts of British Rail. However, Sir Archibald Punchard had shown less and less appetite for his only son's company. Tancred had put this down to the pressures of being Metropolitan police commissioner. That weight of responsibility was a heavy burden for such a person, Tancred knew. A burden that, due to his medieval mindset, he expected to shoulder one day.

As he sipped his Old Reliable in comfortable silence, Tancred's thoughts drifted with the effects of the Fox's ale. His mind wandered into an avenue that always gave him a feeling of self-worth; his family's glorious history. He stretched his tweed plus fours towards the glow of the flickering gas fire, yawned and allowed his imagination free rein.

Yes, he was there, clad in his knightly armour looking down at the Saxon serfs whose descendants were the usual recipients of his derisive glance on entering the pub. Of course, Sir Thurston Punchard was a hero in Tancred's imaginings. In 1066, Sir Thurston had helped bring King Harold and his motley crew to an understanding that Normans were a breed apart, even down to the superior cheeses they brought with them.

As the official guardian of provisions, Sir Thurston Punchard had known his cheeses intimately. However, Tancred's imaginings of his warrior ancestors bore little resemblance to the truth. The reality was that the heat of battle had not been for Thurston, who preferred the avoidance of said heat. From the safety of the cattle train he had watched the gruesome battle, ready at a moment's notice to become the vanguard of retreat. But that was never to be. Instead, the victory was theirs, and, in a rare moment of befuddlement, William the Conqueror mistakenly rewarded Thurston with a knighthood that came with land, serfs and the *droit de seigneur* which could be applied whenever the sexual urge took him.

Tancred drifted up to the bar for his fourth tepid noggin. Ignoring the landlord's mumbled complaints about his lengthening tab, his thoughts moved to the War of the Roses. It was a time when the choice of rose could have dire consequences. The Punchards had, quite inadvertently, created a family crest – a bunch of white feathers on a red background – that served them well through those turbulent times. Their ability to switch sides was summed up by the family motto, '*Liberat animas cogitandi*' (Thinking saves lives). It also fitted in with a strong genetic trait that spurred any Punchard into a run at the first sniff of danger.

Next was the time of Sir Mordecai Punchard. Mordecai was the keeper of the royal horses, a role for which he had a marked fondness. Several of his assistants could have been described as horse whisperers. But even then, Mordecai was known as a horse worrier. The royal horses that knew the sound of his footsteps shied away from his presence using every scrap of available hay to hide their behinds. His conduct on entering the stables is best left to the imagination. Nevertheless, he was skilled at silencing the beasts and training them to use every inch of cover to hide. Mordecai's inclinations and skills would ultimately save his life. At a field called Bosworth, he was tasked with keeping in reserve the king's only spare horse, unfortunately for Richard the Third.

At the crucial moment in the battle Richard's horse decided it was home time and dumped the hapless king into the dirt. Meanwhile, Mordecai was behind a hedge worrying the king's spare horse. According to that Elizabethan scribbler, the king cried out, 'A horse, a horse, my kingdom for a horse!' What he, in fact, said could be roughly translated as 'Where the fu–' but he was cut down before he could finish the sentence. Mordecai, satiated and sensing the weather vanes of history had shifted, mounted the traumatised steed and quietly trotted over to the other team, and somehow managed to be rewarded for this. Buttressed privies were subsequently added to the bedrooms of Wolfestone Manor.

Tancred carried down the centuries of heroic imaginings that his ancestors had nurtured to hide the cold historical facts. His musings were interrupted by the call for last orders before he could recall the family's great feats for empire and their exploits in the two world wars, which had been just as significant for all the wrong reasons. He wound the few hundred yards back to the manor, aching to emulate his forefathers. As it happened, Tancred would soon get his chance, but there was one thing that marked Tancred out from the Punchards of old. They had all been blessed with luck.

*

The next morning Tancred was consuming a breakfast of boiled eggs and marmite soldiers in the conservatory. It was promising to be a nice day and he was thinking of taking a morning stroll. Afterwards, he would put the finishing cosmetic touches to his report appraising the choice of lockers available to replace the ones presently being used by the police. It was titled 'Police Lockers For The Twenty-First Century'.

He heard the Bakelite phone begin to ring in the hall. 'I'm not here!' he shouted at the housekeeper. He heard the ancient phone being picked up and then the distant voice of the housekeeper saying, 'Good morning, Sir Archibald… I'm sorry, but Tancred says he is not…'

Tancred jumped out of the chair and dashed to the phone.

'He is having breakfast…yes, breakfast…I couldn't say, sir, zoology isn't my strong point.'

Tancred slid into the hall and grabbed the phone off the housekeeper. He flicked some blond locks out of his eyes, composed himself and said, 'Hello, Father, how can I help you?… Yes, it is a little late, but I…you do…*this afternoon*?… Oh, certainly. Message received, this afternoon in London.' The line went dead before he could ask why he was being summoned. He looked around to see the housekeeper still standing there.

'Don't you have something to do?' he said, looking down his nose at her.

'Are there any other secretarial services you require?' she replied.

'No, you have done quite enough.'

'I'll get back to being a housekeeper then,' she said with a contemptuous stare, before walking away.

'Leprous witch,' Tancred muttered under his breath

and stomped off to his room to choose a more suitable attire, wondering as he did what was important enough for him to be dragged up to London. An hour later, he set off, clad entirely in Dubarry Bramble Tweed from Farlows.

It was mid-afternoon by the time Tancred parked his Morgan Plus 8 at his father's flat in West London and boarded a bus. He was thinking about pheasant sexing when something black sat down next to him. He glanced over to find a stud-encrusted Goth looking him up and down with clear distaste. Tancred felt more than justified in doing the same. They carried on doing this for a while like a couple of courting penguins until the Goth made a break for the high ground by turning away.

Half an hour later, Tancred pushed through the double doors of New Scotland Yard, signed in and then took the lift to the executive floor. It was rare for his father to even take an interest in him, let alone summon him to the sacred top floor. He breezed into the outer office where the rather fetching Ms Pettigrew was sitting.

'Hello, Miss Moneypenny,' Tancred said, greeting his father's secretary in an execrable Scottish accent as he took a perch on the side of her desk. It was a running joke that Tancred thought hilarious and Ms Pettigrew knew to be puerile.

'Good afternoon, Inspector Punchard. I'll let the commissioner know that you have finally arrived. Please take a seat,' she concluded, looking pointedly at where he was perched.

Tancred laughed and said, 'Very prim. OK, so I shall.'

Ms Pettigrew picked up the phone and punched a

button. 'Sir, Inspector Punchard is here to see you.' She put the phone back down. 'He'll be with you presently,' she confirmed without looking at Tancred.

Tancred sat down and started patting his legs – much to Ms Pettigrew's irritation – as he tried to think of something worthy of saying. Ms Pettigrew studiously avoided any eye contact and concentrated on the screen on her desk.

'Er, Jenny,' Tancred ventured, resorting to her first name, 'I must say you look ravishing today.' She looked up at the ceiling then cast her eyes at him. A penurious smile managed to fight its way into existence on her face. 'The commissioner will be with you in a second.'

Tancred frowned and tried again. 'I would wager that you are quite the popular girl with the young beaus.'

Jenny stopped typing, counted to ten, decided to add another ten, and then looked at him again with weary resignation. 'Actually, if you really must know, I'm in a same-sex relationship.'

Tancred looked at her dumbfounded for a few seconds before saying, 'What a waste.'

While Tancred was delving into Ms Pettigrew's more violent side, Sir Archibald was sitting at his desk trying to decide how best to verbally tackle his son. When it came to the male line of Punchards, Sir Archibald was something of a fluke. He was mildly competent, with a cunning that had served his unconscionable pursuit of position and power well. He largely put this down to his mother's genetics; although she was not without her own genetic foibles. Her favourite phrase had been 'Spare the rod, spoil the child,' and she had taken every opportunity to express her sadistic tendencies on him and on his cowering father, or indeed anyone who was childish enough to cross her path. She had eventually been committed to Broadmoor after taking a nine iron to a couple of Jehovah Witnesses who had pressed their luck at the front door of Wolfestone Manor. Other than these homicidal leanings, she was a fine figure of a woman.

What Sir Archibald's less roadworthy genetics lacked, his expensive education and the old boy network had made up for, allowing him to become a person of consequence. In Tancred, however, the genetic tug of war had been savagely pulled in the Punchard direction. He was a spineless idiot of a fop that Sir Archibald had no time for, but the family name unfortunately rested with his only child. The traditional routes for the Tancreds of the world now mostly required a degree of competence or, at least, a strong streak of self-preservation. Tancred had neither. That had meant Sir Archibald had been forced to abuse his influence and even resort to blackmail to smuggle Tancred up to the ludicrous position of inspector. But if Tancred had any hope of finding safer pastures at the top, he needed some demonstrable success and Sir Archibald believed he had just found the solution to that thorny problem.

Despite all the evidence to the contrary, Sir Archibald was still convinced that the Granny Cartel would be easy to bring down. They were just a bunch of old women that, up until now, the government had been too scared to confront. There are lots of old woman voters, after all. He was confident that, once pushed, the whole Cartel would come down like a house of cards. Even a half-wit like Tancred couldn't butcher this opportunity. But Sir Archibald was not about to leave Tancred to his own devices. He had just the person to keep Tancred in line.

He buzzed Ms Pettigrew. 'You can send in Tan… Inspector Punchard.'

'Gladly,' Ms Pettigrew snapped back. Sir Archibald pressed his fingers to his temple, sensing her irritation with his only son.

Tancred came in looking a bit ruffled. He closed the door and said, 'I can only assume it's Jenny's time of the month.'

'You assuming anything is a truly terrifying thought,' Sir Archibald growled. 'Sit down and shut up.' Tancred did as he was told. Sir Archibald thought about pouring a couple of glasses of AnCnoc Cutter, then thought better of it. Instead, he sat back in silence and studied the vacuous face of his offspring. He sighed and said, 'I'm giving you the chance to prove yourself, Tancred. To the outside world, at least.' One of his eyebrows seemed to be trying to distance itself from the belligerent eye below. 'We are setting up a new covert police taskforce of which you are going to be – theoretically – in command.'

Tancred's eyes brightened and he straightened up: 'I won't let you down, Father. May I inquire as to the purpose of this taskforce?'

'Its purpose is to bring down the leaders of the Granny Cartel in Surrey. And to ensure that you don't let me down, I'm putting a seasoned police office in as your number two. Your job will be to follow the advice he gives you and take credit for all success in the operation. Do not, on any account, follow your own advice, because this will almost certainly lead to disaster. Do you understand me?'

Tancred started to object, but his father's index finger intervened. 'Do you understand me?' Sir Archibald slowly repeated.

'Yes,' Tancred grunted and in a sulky tone asked, 'Does this mean I won't be able to work from home?'

Sir Archibald gave Tancred a look which Tancred was familiar with: for some reason it always reminded him of Hannibal Lecter. In an even tone Sir Archibald replied, 'Yes. You will have a briefing in a few days' time by the Organised Crime Intelligence Unit and then you will remain in Surrey until these wayward old crones have been put back in their place.' He handed Tancred a document. 'This is an outline of your team and your objectives. Remember, this is a covert operation. I would prefer it if every man and his dog wasn't aware of it. Can you do that?'

'You can rely on my utmost discretion,' Tancred said, trying to pull back a bit of dignity. His eyes then brightened. 'Can I name the taskforce?'

Sir Archibald looked to the heavens. 'Call it what you like. Just keep it to yourself.' He returned his focus back to a confused-looking Tancred. 'The reputation of the family is on your shoulders here. So, don't balls it up. Just follow the advice of your number two, Inspector Richard Fleming. And, believe me, he has a particularly vested interest in seeing you succeed.'

SEVEN

Sir Archibald's confidence in Inspector Richard Fleming was based on an incident from a couple of weeks earlier.

For Richard, that fateful day had started with a trip to London Zoo, or more specifically, the lion enclosure. There was clearly a victim and there were some clearly unabashed perpetrators. Pieces of evidence included a licked-over camera on a selfie stick, a pile of disassembled bones, and one severed hand still grasping a tuft of reddish fur, which was considerate of the lions. Fingerprints were run, an adolescent past of minor criminality was found and...

To cut a long story short: a drunken man had broken into the zoo the night before with the obvious intention of taking a selfie of himself with a lion. His reasons hadn't been ascertained, but a psychiatric disorder or sheer stupidity were the obvious possibilities. This could be said with some certainty because the first shot was of him leaning over the fence backwards, grinning of course, just as one of the cats was rearing up to wipe that grin off his face. What was surprising were the subsequent pictures, which could only have been taken by the lions. This could be said with some certainty, because of the number of mouth and paw shots, interspersed with a few pictures confirming that the man was otherwise engaged.

Then Richard got hooked into a case involving a traumatised pedestrian whose coffee cup had been violently knocked out of his hand, along with a man with serious genital discomfort, plus a ragged and naked woman who had nothing whatsoever to say on the matter.

It transpired that the man in such discomfort was a serial adulterer, with a vengeful wife. It had taken several times for his wife to successfully inject his condoms with enough cruel chilli juice to her satisfaction. She knew him from old. He would not check; his eye trained, as she knew, on the view.

While practising his infidelity, hubby liked to look out at the London skyline from his eighth-floor apartment and his secretary was required to point her eyes in the same direction. His haste was fatal. Taking the burning sensation for burning passion, he sheathed and dove in with gusto, housed in a punctured condom.

The secretary's tearful flatmate later told Richard that she had a bad case of thrush, which explained why she torpedoed straight through the plate-glass window. Richard could only imagine that she had been very ambitious for something. She knocked the coffee cup out of the pedestrian's hand on the way down, covering his shoes with coffee, amongst other bodily fluids. The cheating husband seemed much more concerned about being publicly embarrassed than the fate of his poor secretary. Having dealt with that case, Richard came to his last case of the day. The one that would change his life.

This involved a man who liked children very much. As

he lived on a high-rise estate, the pervert didn't have the kind of protection that the privileged could rely on. So he was looking at a long stretch under her majesty's roof and board where punishment would doubtless be served up in many different ways. As a seasoned police officer, Richard had conducted many interviews with criminals in which he had had to hold his emotions in check. When, at the police station, the man started outlining his justifications for what he had done, Richard's resolve and patience with humanity finally broke. He stopped the recording and quietly asked the other officer to fetch some coffee, leaving him alone with the offender.

He knew why he did it, he just wished he hadn't.

The paedophile was taken to hospital to repair the extensive damage Richard had done and Richard was suspended pending criminal charges. He realised his career was at an end. He also knew he would soon be bunking up with some of the men he had helped put behind bars.

His suspension was stretching into its second week when he was summoned to meet Chief Superintendent Phillip Barrington. It was then that Richard discovered his fate.

*

'You realise your actions have brought the whole force into disrepute?' the chief superintendent lashed out.

'I know what I did was inexcusable, sir, and I deserve all that is due to me,' Richard replied quietly. He was feeling sincerely contrite and apologetic and was just waiting miserably for the hammer blow to land.

'Yes, it was. Your career should be over and by the letter of the law you should be facing a custodial sentence. That's what should happen,' was Barrington's cryptic reply. Richard looked down and frowned. He could see that Barrington's body language was all wrong. He seemed tentative, conciliatory even, and not at all at ease.

'*Normally...*' Barrington shot Richard a meaningful stare. Richard was totally baffled. He was becoming wary himself now.

'Of course, we would much prefer that all of this just went away. I'm sure you would like that too?'

'I, as a police officer with a duty of care, beat a suspect to near death?' Richard replied, looking quizzical. 'I can't see how it can, sir.' But he knew he was about to find out.

'What if I said it...could?'

'Sir?'

'I want you to imagine this scenario. A certain suspect is compelled, through means which I won't go into, to withdraw his complaint against a serving police officer. The extremely lucky police officer shows his appreciation by joining a newly formed police taskforce run by...' Barrington coughed at that moment, '...by an up-and-coming police inspector. That extremely lucky police officer then moves Heaven and Hell to ensure that the taskforce is a success, with the up-and-coming police inspector taking all the credit for all the extremely lucky police officer's...' another cough, '...*extremely* hard work. And if the extremely lucky police officer fails in this task, he ceases to be an extremely lucky police officer and becomes an ex-police officer in jail. Do you see the scenario?'

'I see it,' Richard responded. 'I just can't believe it.'

'Well, you better start. This is not *my* scenario, you weren't *my* choice,' Barrington replied with some chagrin. 'Richard, you are a fine police officer, one of my best. But you made an unfathomable mistake. Something I mourn, because this wasn't…' Barrington stopped and paused, before saying, 'I wish it weren't this scenario you were being offered and I'm furious with you for putting me in this position.'

Richard opened his mouth to insert some words into the air.

'I haven't told you who the up-and-coming police officer is,' Barrington intercepted.

'That sounds ominous.'

Barrington was about to reply when Richard said, 'Does the suspect being compelled get favourable terms for withdrawing the complaint?'

'Most definitely not. Other…' Barrington hesitated. 'Other ways were found to compel him.'

Richard was faced with a dichotomy of emotions. What Barrington was suggesting was corrupt. Richard clearly deserved to go to jail and that jarred with his principles. He felt ashamed; not of what he had done, but that he had done it so while on duty. Even so, his principles wouldn't protect him in jail.

'As long as that bastard receives no benefits, I would be prepared to go along with this scenario.'

'You might first want to know who this inspector is,' Barrington said. 'It's Tancred Punchard.'

Richard shrivelled into his own body. 'Oh hell, I should have seen that coming.'

'Sir Archibald has pulled you out of the frying pan. But with Tancred Punchard as your new boss, it will be a marvel if you're not dropped straight back into the fire.'

'What choice do I have?' Richard replied with an edge of bitterness. He looked Barrington directly in the eye. 'Why did *you* agree to this?'

Barrington shifted his gaze and, in a loud whisper, replied, 'Believe me, I didn't want you to be a part of this, but I wasn't given a choice. Sir Archibald wanted an officer with an edge, as he put it; someone he could...*control*.'

'Blackmail, you mean,' Richard retorted. Barrington offered no reply. 'I'm afraid to even ask what the taskforce is supposed to do.'

'To bring down the Granny Cartel. For some reason Sir Archibald thinks that will be easy and wants his son to take the praise for it.' Barrington looked sympathetically at Richard.

'I can already feel the fire licking at my feet,' he said.

EIGHT

Deirdre found Pippa finishing off the new footbridge to Maude's cottage. She dismounted her bike next to Burt, who was lying on the verge. When she bent down to scratch his ear, he bared his teeth and began to growl. She ignored him, and soon the growls of the old bullmastiff turned into grunts. He looked every inch the junkyard beast, with his one shredded ear and a single savage eye that glared out from the folds of his scarred face. (As it happened, Burt now self-identified as a pacifist, although a couple of Russians would have begged to differ.)

Deirdre shaded her eyes against the shafts of evening light as she watched Pippa pick up a large oak railway sleeper one handed and climb down into the stream. She placed it next to three others and gave it a mighty thump, before waving Deirdre forward. Deidre stopped when she came level with Pippa. Looking back at Burt, she asked, 'Where did you get him from?'

'Last owners kept dogs for fighting.'

Pippa loathed cruelty to dogs, which didn't bode well for the last owner, as Pippa's next comment confirmed: 'Should've fed them better. Should've taught them not to play with their food, either.'

Maude was sitting by the patio table tapping away on her iPad. When a slightly disturbed-looking Deirdre walked up, she said, 'Have you been talking to Pippa again?'

'You'd think I'd know better by now.'

Maude looked down at the sheets of paper in Deirdre's hand. 'Is that the intelligence on this police taskforce I requested?' Deirdre nodded and handed her the details of the taskforce and an analysis of its composition before walking off to the kitchen. Thanks to their contacts in the police force, the information they had on the taskforce was considerably more detailed than the information the police had on the Granny Cartel. When Deidre returned, she wasn't surprised to see the peevish look on Maude's face.

'It doesn't take a psychic to know what Archibald Punchard thinks of us,' Maude snapped before throwing the papers onto the table. 'Putting his inbred invertebrate of a son in charge has made that clear.'

'Given Tancred's reputation, he might just turn out to be our best asset. He is a narcissistic, delusional imbecile. I would say this is a result.'

'Yes, you're right. I should be pleased,' Maude said, looking at the comprehensive file that had been compiled for her, 'but Richard Fleming could be a problem. Sir Archibald has ensured that he can't afford to let Tancred fail.'

Deirdre took a sip of peppermint tea, and then said, 'You know we've pushed the government into a corner. We've made the cost of a political climbdown on the sugar restrictions too high. In my opinion they now have no choice but to bring us down before the next election. We poked the Gummi bear…'

'How were we to know social media would react the way it did? I suppose the Russian incident didn't help, either.'

'You don't say.'

'When push comes to shove, you'll be glad Pippa's by your side,' Maude replied a little defensively.

'I won't be if she treats the police like she treated that Russian gangster.'

'It was self-defence.'

'She pulled his arms and legs off.'

'He called her a fat slag and Pippa gets defensive when she's called fat. Anyway, getting back to what we were saying, we need an endgame.' Maude knew that Deirdre felt a line had been crossed with the Russian incident. And, privately, Maude had to agree.

'Which was what I was coming to, and preferably before they discover who I am,' Deirdre said, looking up at the blush contrails crisscrossing the wispy cirrus clouds above. Deirdre had been friends with Maude since childhood. In addition to her contacts from her time at MI5, she also just so happened to be the aunt of the Andrew Harrington, the current director general of said organisation. These were facts that Maude and Deirdre were keen to keep hidden. Deirdre didn't know how Pippa had come into Maude's orbit or how Sir Cecil had become Maude's collaborator. All she said when asked was that it was best left unsaid.

'Yes, that would be awkward,' Maude replied. 'In the meantime, we need to prepare a welcome for this taskforce. And I think it's time Pippa and I should pay our newly promoted constituency MP a visit. Just for a chat.'

★

Godfrey Fairtrade sat in his sitting room huffing and puffing while he read his ministerial guidelines. Lillian came in buttoning up her coat and then stopped to look at him.

'Does one have a problem?' she announced with perfect elocution.

'One does,' muttered Godfrey. 'These ministerial guidelines when meeting the public, that's what. For example, I've been given guidelines on how many hands to shake, how many babies to pick up or young children to crouch down to.'

'Well, image is everything, my dear,' Lillian replied, fussing around in her bag.

'I'm a minister, not a nursery worker. I had enough of that with my own children,' Godfrey said, looking despondent.

'Yes, I remember you being such an asset.'

Godfrey looked at her sour face. 'Where are you off to?'

'I'm going to the choral society. It's Wednesday night, remember,' Lillian said. She leaned down and gave him a dry peck on the cheek. 'It's the responsibilities of the job, darling.'

Godfrey huffed and said, 'A job I didn't want.'

'Just think about where it could lead to.' She squeezed his cheek.

'A&E?'

'Stop it. You're being melodramatic.'

'It's Indian country out there and I'm the pony express with a lame message.'

'I've told you before about metaphor abuse,' Lillian replied. 'Are you coming to the history society tomorrow?'

Godfrey and Lillian had become members of the Dorsham History Society after Godfrey was elected. As they both enjoyed learning history, Lillian had thought it a good way to connect with the local community. It was about the only place now where he could expect a pleasant welcome.

'Aiming to,' Godfrey uttered into his chin.

After another tussle with her bag, Lillian waved goodbye and left. The girl from Wolverhampton briefly flashed through Godfrey's mind and his mood dropped further. He put his papers down and turned on the television for some distraction. He watched *Embarrassing Bodies* for a while but found it too embarrassing. He flicked over to a fashion show in which models were prancing around, but he found their emaciated bodies disconcerting. He flicked channel again to *Celebrity Big Brother* which seemed to have no celebrities in it, as far as he could tell. He turned the television off and picked up the book he was reading, but was instantly interrupted by a knock at the front door.

Godfrey opened the door to find a well-dressed old lady standing there, beaming sweetly. Then he noticed something massive standing behind her in the shadows. The old lady held out her hand and said: 'Maude Appleby.' Godfrey nearly fainted.

'*The* Maude Appleby?' Godfrey gibbered. He put his hand on the doorframe to steady himself and staggered as a beefy finger came down from above to push him back. Maude walked in before he could object. The massive bear-like thing behind Maude ducked under the door frame and began to push Godfrey into the sitting room with a hand the size of a baseball glove.

'Wh-why are you here?' Godfrey spluttered as he was pushed back into his armchair.

'While Lillian is at her choral society, we thought it would be a good time to have a quiet word with you,' Maude replied, sitting down slowly in a chair next to him.

'How did you know... I am not sure I have anything to say to you,' Godfrey said in a quivering voice, glancing between Maude and the female Goliath glaring down at him.

'That's no way to talk to one of your constituents,' Maude admonished. 'I'm sure you can remember the girl from Wolverhampton.' She held out some pictures. 'Does this jog your memory?' Beads of sweat began to mushroom over Godfrey's brow. Instead of trying to snatch the pictures, Godfrey buried his head in his hands and, deflated, let out a moan.

'Now, I'm sure you are thinking that these pictures were taken with the express purpose of blackmailing you into doing what I want,' Maude said. Godfrey peered between his fingers at her and squeaked, 'Should I?'

'Oh, very much so,' Maude cheerfully replied. 'Excuse my manners, I haven't introduced you to Pippa. You've read about Pippa from the police reports, I assume?' Godfrey peered up at Pippa from behind his hands and began to quiver at the behemoth before his eyes. Pippa leered at him salaciously and said, 'I like him.' Godfrey squeaked again and shrunk back further into the chair.

'See, Pippa likes you. Although I have to say her passions are bit too much for most men. She doesn't know her own strength; it's a bit like Lennie and the rabbits.'

'Lennie and the rabbits?' Godfrey murmured, head still in his hands.

'*Of Mice and Men*, I'm sure you've read the book.' Godfrey nodded, looking up at Pippa in terror again, peeping out between his fingers. She stepped behind his chair and placed her ham-like hands on his shoulders and squeezed. It was like being clamped by two fully grown crocodiles. Godfrey shuddered and dropped his hands to his knees, moaning under the bone-bending pressure. Pippa relaxed her grip to allow him to speak.

'What do you want?' he asked, surprisingly clear.

'In a few days this newly formed police taskforce will be descending on our peaceful corner of the world. You being, what was the title – oh yes, deputy assistant parliamentary undersecretary of state with responsibilities for rural law and order – quite a mouthful, isn't it – you will be liaising between them and the government.'

Godfrey heard the horrid sound of Pippa licking her lips when Maude said the word 'mouthful'.

'Which leaves you well placed to know exactly what is going on, doesn't it?' Maude slapped her hand on her knee before carrying on, 'And you will tell me everything. And you will do everything I tell you to do.'

'But… I can't,' Godfrey replied.

'Godfrey, you disappoint me, because you know you've no choice. Maude picked up an offending picture and showed it to him. 'What do you think Lillian would say about that? She does look very young, shame on you.'

Godfrey looked at the picture, mortified. 'We never did that!'

'Isn't Photoshop great? We would have made you manlier, but, well, Lillian may still remember.' Maude withdrew the picture. 'A number of things will happen to you if you don't do as I ask. You will lose your job and be ostracised from society. The police will also be anxious to talk to you for abusing an underage girl. Prison would be hard for somebody like you, but I'm sure love, of a sort, would be found. That's assuming you ever made it to the prison. Lillian may just fillet you first. And then there is Pippa; needy, passionate Pippa. I can see it now, a romantic moonlit night in some isolated forest glade; two lovers embracing; the sound of a rabbit squealing under the moon. What do you think, Pippa?'

Pippa squeezed Godfrey's shoulders again until his arms became numb. 'Sexy talk, that is,' she replied and pushed his face up and stared down into Godfrey upturned eyes and gave him terrifying wink.

'Are you going to disappointment me again?' Maude said, looking at Godfrey with sad eyes. Godfrey shook his head.

'Excellent,' Maude said, 'Let's shake on it.'

'I can't lift my arms,' Godfrey pointed out. Pippa picked one of his arms up and proffered his hand to Maude and they shook, or rather Maude did. Pippa dropped his arm back down as Maude got up to leave. 'And remember, Godfrey; don't put yourself through the abject misery of disappointing me. Here's a number you can reach me on.

I'll be in touch.' Maude handed him a number, wrinkling her nose as she did so. 'You may want a shower before Lillian gets back, my dear. Pippa tends to induce that pungent perfume in others. Can hang in the air for days. Just a suggestion. Anyway, toodle-oo.'

Maude and Pippa left, leaving Godfrey to ponder his descent into Hell.

NINE

Tancred was still smarting from the meeting with his father when he came back to New Scotland Yard for the police briefing. He especially resented having to take his cue from that oik Richard Fleming, someone he knew of only vaguely. How was he to receive the deference from the team his rank warranted if somebody else was calling the shots?

Tancred was about to round the bend to the conference room when he caught his name being mentioned and stopped.

'Putting Punchard in charge of this taskforce is insane,' someone said in a hushed tone.

'Completely barmy if you ask me. The guy's a complete idiot. He only got the shout because of his father. Bloody nepotism, that's what it is.'

'We'll be all right with Richard though. You heard the rumours?'

'Who hasn't? Makes you wonder why he's on this gig.'

'Do you know what I think, he's...'

Tancred heard a voice behind him say, 'Tancred?'

He spun round to see Chief Superintendent Barrington standing behind him. Barrington saw the look on Tancred's face: an odd mixture of fury and self-pity. 'Are you OK?' Barrington asked.

'Er, ah…bit of, of…indigestion,' Tancred muttered, backing up to crane his head around the corner to see the conference room door slowly closing.

'Shall we go in?' Barrington ordered.

Tancred pulled himself together and said, 'Yes, lets.'

They entered just as an officer standing by a whiteboard uttered, 'Oh, I see what you mean,' as he looked down at a document in his hand. There were eleven other people in the room. Barrington introduced Tancred to the officer by the whiteboard. His name was Michael Jackson and he was from the Organised Crime Intelligence Unit. Jackson was short and balding, with a birthmark on his cheek in the shape of Vietnam that changed to Peru when he smiled. As Jackson shook Tancred's hand he said, 'We spoke on the phone about the name of the taskforce.' Jackson then gave them both a copy of the briefing document. Barrington looked at the title of the document: Taskforce for Illegal Trade in Sugar. Only Tancred could have chosen that name, Barrington thought as he turned to the others in the room and announced, 'Tancred, this is your team.'

Tancred looked over to them with a haughty gaze, then slowly swung round to stand square on in front of them. Barrington introduced them in turn: Matthew, Mark, Luke and Thomas, followed by Alwin, Joan and Jenny, Emmeline, Muhammad and Rosie.

Barrington finally came to Richard at the end of the line and caught his eye. He paused before saying, 'This is Inspector Richard Fleming, your second in command.'

Richard offered his hand to Tancred, who shook it limply and with obvious disdain. This is going to be a painfully long assignment, Richard thought. Tancred, dressed once again in tweed, looked Richard up and down: a cheap suit, worn shoes, dog-eared tie and shirt. There was no breeding to the man. He was the type his ancestors would happily have had horsewhipped for the most minor infringement.

Barrington and the others looked at the two of them. He briskly said, 'Let's sit.' Tancred chose to sit apart from the team. Once they were all in place, Jackson began.

He put a grainy picture on the board. Eyelids rose and there was a sharp collective intake of breath. Before them was an image of a huge creature with long grey hair and small flinty eyes boring out of a flat, round, pugilistic face. Their chest suggested that they were female.

'Before we get onto Maude Appleby, we should start with Pippa Blackwood. This is what we know from the intelligence we have been able to gather about her, which is unfortunately a bit patchy. Blackwood can be best described as a force of nature. She has uncommon size and strength that few, if any, men could match. And her upbringing was unusual, to say the least. From what we can gather she was abandoned as a baby in the woods near Tunbridge Wells where she was adopted by a pack of wild dogs, circa 1951. After a while the travellers, who owned the dogs, realised she wasn't one of their own children and took her in. Her childhood was nomadic, as they moved around the country, living off the land and allotments and stealing anything that wasn't bolted down and generally being the scourge of the countryside.'

Richard interrupted him, with irritation in his voice: 'I'm sorry. Where exactly did you come by this information, because it sounds particularly prejudiced to me?'

'We have it on good authority from certain respected residents living in the home counties along with accounts from the traveller community; with a bit of extrapolation. I'm quite sure it is all reasonably accurate,' responded Jackson.

'Kindly keep your personal feelings to yourself,' said Tancred, glaring at Richard. Chip off the same block, the two of them, Richard thought. He let it go and refrained from rolling his eyes.

'Anyway, by all accounts she was a fearsome bare-knuckle fighter even as a child. Her predatory sexual nature first came to light in her teens when she was ostracised from the community after a number of sexual assaults against their menfolk. There are medical reports to back this up,' Jackson said, looking pointedly at Richard. 'She also didn't like dog fights, which put her at odds with some in the community. She has a passion for dogs and they have a thing for her, which we will discuss in due course. The next time she popped up was in the mid-1970s in the French Foreign Legion, of all places. In those days they didn't ask many questions, accepting murderer and mammary alike, as long as the recruit was happy to die in a dubious hat. Despite being an exceptional warrior, the *esprit de corps* took a nosedive in her battalion and desertions soared. Do I need to draw the dots?'

Jackson looked at his stunned audience, who had clearly connected the dots, so he carried on, 'The French grudgingly allowed us to talk to an old French colonel who was her commanding officer. Poor man went white as a sheet when we mentioned her name. All he said was that she was dishonourably discharged for, in his words, undisclosed emotional and physical atrocities. He wouldn't elaborate, saying it was too painful to recall. We have pretty firm evidence that Blackwood then became a soldier of fortune, fighting in conflicts in both Africa and South America. There are also unsubstantiated reports that she was involved somehow in the CIA's shady relationship with organised crime, although the CIA has specifically denied any association with her. Eventually, she gravitated back to Europe. Interpol is convinced she still has connections to organised crime, although they have never been able to prove anything. Intriguingly, there is strong evidence that she had a sadomasochistic affair with the former Italian PM, Emanuele Bernardini.'

'My God, we knew he had unusual tastes...' Barrington muttered, looking horrified.

'Well, his proclivity for a bit of carnal rough and tumble didn't end well. It ultimately landed him in hospital. The official line was that he had been involved in a serious road traffic accident, although the nature of his injuries was suppressed. What we do know is that Blackwood is here now, with the Granny Cartel. Quite how or why we don't know, but we suspect she gained a sweet tooth when she was in the Foreign Legion. In the two years since she has been associated with Appleby, she has set up a paramilitary wing and the Cartel has become much more brazen in their criminal activities. Whether this is down to Blackwood's influence or Appleby's despot aspirations, we can't be sure.' Jackson looked around the room. Everyone's mouths were agape.

He continued: 'Going back to my previous comment, Blackwood has an unearthly sway over canines. We can guess where she gained that ability.' Again, another pointed look at Richard.

'Which means?' Richard asked, drearily.

'The German police found this out to their cost in 2001, when raiding a counterfeiting operation which she was suspected of running in Düsseldorf. They went in after the dogs only to find them hurdled around this mountainous individual wearing a gimp mask. An improvised concealment, I'm assuming. Next thing they knew, the dogs were attacking them. Although they weren't able to make a positive identification, they were pretty sure it was Blackwood. So, no police dogs in any operations. Understood?' Again, Jackson looked around the room. He saw only shocked expressions. 'Any questions?'

Jackson was confronted with a sea of pale faces. Someone gulped.

'She must have a weakness?' Richard ventured.

'Only for brutalising men. Her libido and strength haven't appreciably diminished with time, and, of course, she has access to Viagra now.'

The men in the room looked horrified. Tancred looked as though he was about to retch.

Jackson took a large glug of water and mopped his brow.

'Of course, to bring down Appleby you may have no choice but to bring Blackwood down first.' Jackson stared at the picture of Pippa and murmured, 'There's something to be said for being office based.'

Richard waited for Jackson to smirk, but he didn't. Instead, he put another picture on the board, this time of a sweet elderly woman.

'OK, moving on. Maude Appleby. In some ways Appleby is a bigger enigma than Blackwood. Born and raised in the Vole Valley, she had by all accounts led an exemplary life up until four years ago. She ran a successful cupcake business, was Surrey's chairperson of the Women's Institute and an avid church goer. Not even so much as a speeding ticket. She's had two children, adults now, one lives in Scunthorpe, for some reason, the other in Edinburgh. We can find no connection between them and their mother's criminal enterprises. Appleby was married to the revered restaurant critic Abraham Appleby, who some of you may have heard of?'

No response.

'Anyway, he died a few years back of food poisoning, which was a pretty damning review for the restaurant he was visiting. And here is where it gets interesting.' Jackson paused to let the anticipation build.

'Before the restaurant proprietor went to trial, he disappeared. His son visited him one day to find a half-eaten sandwich, a cold cup of coffee and the radio on. Nothing, including his wallet, was missing. He just vanished without a trace. That makes Appleby's recent activity a little more questionable...and disconcerting.' Jackson drew a breath. 'So, on the surface, at least, Appleby was a model citizen. That is, up until four years ago when the government restricted sugar. Overnight, her award-winning cupcake business was no more, and nor was the model citizen. In the four years since, she been highly effective in developing her influence and connections to build up a sugar-based criminal organisation with more than a passing resemblance to the Cosa Nostra. She hasn't lacked support: The Women's Institute is now considered a criminal organisation in most of England. Her main power base is centred in the Surrey Hills: the Cartel's lair. We believe Appleby now effectively controls the local council and police and that her corrupt tentacles have spread throughout most of the UK, *even* into central government and the Church. Quite an achievement in four years. In other words, do not underestimate her.

She may look small, sweet and frail, but she's highly intelligent and completely ruthless, with a dedicated and fast-growing following numbering in the thousands, alongside the mainstream of the UK population who see her as an elderly Robin Hood figure. Blackwood may pose a physical threat, but we believe Appleby poses a greater threat: to the very foundations of our society. Simply put, she must be stopped. You will be given further background information in the briefing document.'

Richard couldn't help but admire Appleby. But that wouldn't stop him from trying to bring her down.

'Are there any other questions?' Jackson said with a sip of his coffee.

'What is the size and composition of their paramilitary wing?' Jenny asked.

'We believe it to be quite small at present – somewhere

around a dozen. Their speciality is the use of nunchucks. Not to be treated lightly, I can assure you.'

'A bunch of old grannies wielding nunchucks. Hardly a paramilitary force,' Tancred laughed as he looked around the room. Jackson gave him a look of contempt.

'As I'm sure you remember, six months ago the Russian mafia tried to muscle in on the illicit sugar trade. There was a turf war with the Granny Cartel. The Russians were roundly beaten by this stick-wielding paramilitary force.' Tancred scoffed, but said nothing.

'Does anybody have any questions?' repeated Jackson.

As Tancred leaned back in his chair with his hands behind his head, Richard listened to Jackson answer various questions while sizing up the task they were facing. By the time the meeting broke up, he was in a thoroughly despondent mood. As the team were shuffling out, Barrington grabbed Richard's arm and pulled him to one side.

'I know what you are thinking,' Barrington said.

'If you did, you would look more worried.'

Barrington saw that Tancred was coming over. He whispered to Richard, 'Just watch your back.' Barrington turned to Tancred as he came up to them. 'Ah, Tancred, I assume you will want to sit down with *your* team.'

'Indeed,' Tancred replied coldly. Barrington had brazenly chosen to talk to Richard first. Surely the slight was obvious to everyone else, Tancred thought. He resolved at that moment to defy his father. He was going to make damn sure that he, not Richard, was the one calling the shots.

It was also clear to Richard what Tancred was thinking.

He could feel the resentment. 'Where are we meeting Godfrey Fairtrade tomorrow?' Richard asked, breaking the awkward silence.

'It's to be confirmed,' Tancred replied, looking away. 'Organise a team meeting for this afternoon. I'm going to sort out our accommodation in Dorsham.'

Then he smiled.

TEN

Tancred had seen fit to billet the team in a particularly squalid guest house next to the town sewage plant in Dorsham. Meanwhile, he had booked himself into the most expensive hotel in town. But Tancred would soon be regretting his choice of accommodation.

'What do you mean I have to pay in advance for my stay? What are you running here, some seedy flophouse?' he said gesticulating all over the place.

'I'm sorry, sir, but the sign clearly states that you must pay in full in advance,' the manager declared, having shooed the receptionist out of the way.

'This is utter rot. I refuse to be treated like this!'

'I'm sorry, sir, but really, my hands are tied,' said the manager with an obsequious superiority crafted through years of dealing with insubordinate customers. Tancred had met his sort before and he wasn't going to stand for it.

'You listen to me–'

'I am, sir, I truly am. But rules are rules. I can endeavour to secure you with alternative accommodation, but with the Medieval Fair in Nokney this weekend it may prove quite the challenge.'

With this sort of character, Tancred always ended up

with a feeling he was about to be placed onto a sticky wicket. He growled snootily, then backed down. 'OK, I will pay the blasted bill in advance. But mark my words, you'll pay for this on Trip Advisor.'

The manager responded with an infuriatingly unctuous smile. He said, 'That is your prerogative, sir.'

Tancred, pointing to the wheeled trunk beside him, snapped, 'Where's the porter?'

'On leave,' replied the manager.

'What?'

'In the Outer Hebrides I believe, bird-watching.'

'Are you seriously telling me there is no porter available?' Tancred snarled as various parts of his brain mustered themselves into a scream.

'That is indeed the case.'

Tancred looked around the deserted foyer and back at the underemployed manager. 'So I am to haul my luggage up by myself?'

'I do apologise for the inconvenience.'

'Now you look here, you jumped up–'

'I should point out that the hotel has a zero tolerance policy to abuse of staff,' the manager pointed out, firming up his chin. Tancred admitted defeat, but he wasn't going down without the last word. But before he could say anything the manager slid the bill across the reception desk.

'If sir is not staying, I can organise a taxi to wherever sir wishes to go. Otherwise, I shall require payment now.' Tancred paid without another word and proceeded to drag his trunk up the stairs. Once Tancred was halfway up the stairs, the manager stepped into the back office and picked up the phone.

'Hello, Maude. He's arrived and is just heading up to the room we prepared for him.'

*

After much searching Tancred eventually found the door to his room down a dark, dingy hallway. A Jammy Dodger had been glued to the door. He looked at it, pulled back, and then leaned forward again to look at it more closely. A noise down the corridor caused him to turn around. A maid was parking up a housekeeping trolley. Tancred stomped up to her and said, 'What is the meaning of this?'

'*Qué?*'

'That thing on my door.'

'*Qué?*'

'Do you speaky English?' Tancred bellowed indignantly.

The maid paused to hunt down the right words. 'A little, *señor*,' she said, squeezing an invisible pea with her thumb and index finger. Tancred, in response, wiggled his finger in the direction of his door.

She raised her eyebrows and spoke in Spanish: 'They have given you that stinking room? They must really hate you. I'm not sure I like you much either.'

Tancred raised his eyes to the ceiling and pulled her down the corridor. 'This,' Tancred said, pointing to the Jammy Dodger. She looked at it, wide-eyed, and did the sign of the cross, before saying in Spanish, 'It is the mark of the Granny Cartel, which I'm reasonably certain means you are seriously screwed.' Then, in English, she said, 'I pray,' pointed a finger at Tancred, 'you.' Tancred curled his lip and said, 'What the devil are you talking about? Just get the damn thing off my door.'

'*Qué?*'

'Remove!' Tancred demanded, making a rubbing movement with his hand. This didn't seem to go down too well with the maid. She flung her hands up in a gesture: there was no need to understand Spanish to see her meaning was: 'Sod off, it's your Jammy Dodger. I'm buggered if I'm touching it.'

She backed down the corridor, dragging her trolley with her and made one more sign of the cross before she disappeared.

A dismayed Tancred watched her shuffle away. He raised his arms in despair, glanced at the Jammy Dodger and chiselled it off the door with his room key. 'This is the hotel from Hell,' he said to himself. He opened the door. It was the hotel room from Hell. Tancred blinked; walked up the corridor and back down again before peering into the room once more in the hope he had imagined it.

It was just about wide enough to house a small single bed. The smell of cigarette smoke and rotting food hung in the air. Tancred edged past the bed to look into the 'en suite'. There was a shower attachment pushed onto one of the taps of a tiny stained sink, and a grubby toilet with a treacherously loose seat. There wasn't enough room for a cat to squat, let alone be swung. He sat down on the bed and immediately regretted it. He hopped back up and massaged his behind from where the spring had struck. He stretched over to the window, which wasn't much of a stretch, and opened it in the hope of dispersing the rank smell in the room. The smell of rotting food got worse. Easing his head out of the window, he discovered the source of the problem. The room was right above the kitchen bins, which were ripening and rising in the warm air. To top it all, the kitchen fan was clattering away only a few feet away from the window. Seeing that a cloud of flies was marshalling their forces for an all-out assault on the open window, he quickly closed it again. He went to sit on his trunk in the corridor.

Tancred couldn't believe how badly he was being treated. He thought about confronting the manager again, but even he could see that was a futile act. He toyed with the idea of finding a hotel in London and travelling down by train every day. It was undeniably tempting, but it might bring down the wrath of his father, so he dropped the idea. Besides, he had already paid and trying to get his money back would only involve further humiliation. For the moment he would have to accept his reduced surroundings. Tancred saw the Jammy Dodger on the floor and wondered again what the maid had been rabbiting on about.

*

Richard had to put down a minor revolt when he and the others arrived at the entrance of Tancred's hotel.

'I'd like to take a cricket bat to him,' Joan said. She was a cricket fan.

'While we're stuck in that crap hole, he's living it up like a king,' Jenny complained.

'Yeah, it stinks,' Alwin spat.

'OK, guys, just calm down,' Richard said, 'I'll talk to him about the accommodation.'

'It's like he's got it in for us,' Alwin piped up.

Richard led the disgruntled team into the hotel. The moment he walked up to the reception desk, the receptionist disappeared – to be replaced by Tancred's tormentor.

'Good afternoon, sir,' the manager said with a twinkle in his eye that Richard didn't much care for.

'Good afternoon. We are here to meet a Mr Tancred Punchard,' Richard replied.

'Ah, off...' the manager paused, and then continued, 'off to the right, down the corridor. You will find him in the Laurence Olivier suite. Mr Punchard has ordered some lunch. Will you also be eating with us?'

'I think we will be,' Richard replied, sensing the nodding heads behind him.

'And could you kindly ask Mr Punchard not to stand on the furniture.'

Richard gave an involuntary shake of the head. 'Come again?'

'We have already caught him twice climbing over the furniture.'

'Why?' Richard wasn't sure what else to say.

'It would seem that he is looking for something, although what he was expecting to find on the chandelier is a moot point.'

'I will speak to him,' Richard responded as he speculated

about what Tancred was up to. The team moved off under the unwelcome gaze of the manager. They entered the suite to find Tancred busily unscrewing a plug socket.

Richard watched for a few seconds, before saying, 'Tancred, what are you doing?' The others had by now made a semi-circle around their leader. Tancred looked up between the legs of Muhammad and Rosie and said, rather haughtily, 'I would have thought it was obvious.'

'You have to excuse my mental incapacity.'

'Huh?'

'It's not obvious to me, Tancred. But a theory is forming as I speak.'

'Bugs.'

'That was the first part of the theory. Do you remember the speech you gave us about being ever vigilant to the dangers of surveillance, and when you took a breath, I said we would bring a bug detector, rather like the one Luke is now brandishing?' Tancred looked around to see Luke brandishing a bug detector like a cudgel.

'You did? I don't recall.'

'That was the second part of the theory.'

Tancred stood up, pulled his tweed down and pushed through his sullen-looking team. At that moment, the door opened and a waitress came in and started handing out menus.

'Can you please explain what you are doing?' Tancred said, glaring at the waitress.

'I'm not sure if there is a technical term for it, but I call it handing out the menus,' was the waitress's sarcastic response.

'Don't be impertinent!'

Seemingly in anticipation of his reaction, the waitress produced a complaint form and slid it across the dining table towards Tancred. Tancred smiled and gave a knowing nod. 'Well, you can take them away.'

'Tancred, can I have a quick word,' Richard said, holding up his hand to the waitress. He beckoned Tancred over to the corner of the dining room.

'What?'

'Do you mind if I do a bit of begging?' Richard said.

'Oh, beg away.'

'Unless you intend for this team to comprise of just you and me, I would suggest you let the others have some lunch. This is the begging bit.'

'Hmm. Oh, very well, as a special treat.'

'And I would also say that the accommodation is causing some resentment among *your* team.'

'Why, I checked all the reviews and it seemed quite the perfect place,' Tancred said with a malicious grin. 'Whatever could possibly be wrong with it?'

'If I were to describe anywhere as a stinking hovel, it is our lodgings,' Richard replied, putting as much pleading into his face as he could muster.

'It's too late now. Everywhere else is booked up, apparently there is a medieval fair on. Believe me, this place is no picnic either.'

'Just what I was thinking when I walked up to the hotel,' Richard replied in a flat tone. The pair returned to the table to find the waitress had already gone, leaving the menus behind. Richard said to the others, 'When the waitress returns, we can order some lunch.'

'And the accommodation?' Jenny asked.

'I don't want any more bleating about the accommodation,' Tancred cut in. 'I really can't believe it is any worse than what I'm having to put up with,' he said waving his hands around. Richard fancied that the Bolsheviks had probably looked at the Romanovs in a very similar way to how the rest of the team was now looking at Tancred. Tancred tilted his head over to Richard, 'What's that woman doing?' he whispered.

'Joan?'

'If you say so.'

'Practising her cricket strokes.'

'Well, she won't get anywhere playing like that. You're meant to knock the ball into the air, not bury it into the ground.'

'Quite.'

Everyone drifted over to the table, apart from Luke, who was still scanning the room. As they thumbed through the menus, Tancred whispered to Richard, 'Godfrey Fairtrade should be with us shortly.'

Just then, the waitress returned and placed the croque monsieur Tancred had ordered in front of him. Complete with suspicious brown smears, long hairs and floor dirt, the croque monsieur managed to look like roadkill. Everyone stared at it and then put their menus down.

'Will there be anything else?' the waitress said. Tancred stared down at the abomination in front of him and slowly pointed at the toxic mush. She pulled out a complaint form. Tancred waved her away without looking up.

Richard looked at the others before saying, 'No, I think that will be all.' The waitress left. Richard could imagine Tancred being showered with such service in some places, but he was suspicious that it was so blatant in such a fancy place. Could it be a greeting card from the Cartel?

'Actually, our accommodation isn't so bad,' Joan said. The others murmured their assent.

They were all still looking at the croque monsieur in shocked silence when Godfrey walked in.

Richard stood up. 'Godfrey Fairtrade?' Godfrey nodded. 'Richard Fleming. Quite the town you have here.' Richard shook his damp hand, noting his uneasiness.

'If you say so,' Godfrey replied in a subdued tone. Richard nudged Tancred. 'Tancred Punchard, the leader of the pack,' Tancred said, getting up to shake Godfrey's hand. 'Although I would say the lodgings in this town are an acquired taste.'

'That's frontier towns for you. I've seen a few,' Godfrey replied. He looked at the croque monsieur. 'My God, you're not going to eat that, are you?'

'Absolutely not,' Tancred replied. The rest of the team were introduced and they all sat back down. Godfrey didn't bother with any preamble.

'The situation we have here is very politically sensitive. So, for that reason, you will need to tell me everything you intend to do so that the government is prepared for any fallout. And I mean everything. We just need to know. The government doesn't want to get in your way, so don't regard this as meddling. Consider it nothing more than…staying in the loop.' He pulled at his collar and gave a nervous look around the room. 'I would suggest that you start by visiting the Medieval Fair at Nokney.' Maude Appleby had demanded the taskforce attend the fair, and Godfrey felt like every sweaty pore was pumping out his treachery. He subdued a shudder and carried on, 'Everyone will be there, including my poor self. It will give you a good taste for what the locals are like, weak constitutions permitting. Personally, I would use tactical nuclear weapons on the county rather than sending you lambs down to slaughter.' They all gawped at him.

'I take it you are not overly fond of your constituents?' Richard said.

'Nor would you be in my position.'

'I think I have a pretty good idea what the locals are like,' Tancred said. Godfrey looked at him as though he had brought a knife to a tank battle. 'No, you don't,' Godfrey said in an ominous tone.

Tancred chose that moment to take a comfort break and told Richard to fill Godfrey in on how they were going to conduct the operation, which Richard assumed was because he didn't have a clue. When Tancred returned, it was his turn to say something ominous. 'Do they dress up for the Medieval Fair?' This earned him some alarmed looks from the others.

'Apparently. Just make sure that whatever you wear, you can run in it,' Godfrey replied, before standing up with a creak. He said goodbye and left. When Godfrey was gone, Richard said, 'I really don't think dressing up is a good idea.' That wasn't the only thing concerning Richard. Something was off with Godfrey; he was on edge and his body language was sending out signals that Richard's honed professional instincts quickly identified. Fairtrade was hiding something.

Tancred said, 'I know just the place where we can get some costumes.'

Richard rolled his eyes and let out a sigh.

ELEVEN

The unmarked police van trundled along, causing an unwelcome tinkling amongst its occupants each time it hit a pothole. The only other thing that broke the peeved silence was Tancred's resonant humming of 'Greensleeves'. Richard had a premonition that he was going to end up being haunted by that song in prison. He tried to tune out the ballad and thought about their plans.

One of the problems for the authorities had been to get hard evidence against the Granny Cartel. Promising leads had fizzled out like mist in the morning air. It was like trying to put handcuffs on a shoal of fish. Without doubt the Cartel had allies who had the power to protect their interests, not to mention widespread support from the general public. The government wasn't fighting a traditional criminal organisation; it was fighting an unknown enemy, an insidious revolution. And here the taskforce was in the middle of it all, dressed up as court jesters and being tormented with 'Greensleeves'.

The taskforce entered Nokney village and were funnelled down a rough track to a field being used as a makeshift car park. Eleven gloomy court jesters and one chirpy knight emerged from a large unmarked white minibus. As the others quietly grumbled amongst themselves, Richard moved over to Tancred, who flicked up his face plate and yawned, 'Trunks don't make good beds.'

Richard decided not to go there. 'I would recommend that we don't do anything to draw attention to ourselves,' he said, feeling compelled to state the obvious. Tancred noticed the pained look on his face and became petulant.

'That is the whole point of our attire, if you hadn't guessed.'

'I bow to your logic. Can I at least ask that we split up?'

'Of course we are going to split up. What were you expecting, eleven court jesters trailing around behind a knight?' In fact, that had been the image in Tancred's mind, but on closer inspection he saw how it could cause unwanted attention.

'At least we are in agreement on one thing,' Richard said.

'You and the others should break up into smaller groups,' Tancred announced. 'I intend to wander around by myself and see what snippets I can pick up.' Tancred stretched his arms to relieve the soreness to his elbows caused by the couters in his armour.

'Is that such a good idea?' Richard asked, as someone might say to a person who's about to wash a cut in a piranha-infested pool.

'I'm more than capable of looking after myself!' Tancred bellowed. Maybe trussed up in a padded cell, Richard thought, but there was no point arguing. The team split up into groups and made their way through separate entrances into Nokney's Medieval Fair.

At about the same time, Godfrey and Lillian Fairtrade were arriving at the Medieval Fair through another entrance to the tents and stands and medieval razzmatazz.

'Start smiling, Godfrey. Everyone will think you don't want to be here.'

'It would be disingenuous.'

'Well, you'd better start being disingenuous. Politicians are ethical clothes horses dressed with expediency, after all. I really don't know what has got into you in the last few weeks. And in the last few days you have been a complete misery. Come on, we've been in a lot worse places than this. In fact, I would say most of the constituents I've met have been perfectly agreeable.'

'And therein lays the danger. They're not to be trusted.'

'Enough,' Lillian demanded. 'Stick a smile on your face and shut up.'

An undernourished smile began to secrete itself over Godfrey's lips.

'Come on, put your back into it,' Lillian insisted.

Godfrey's lips strained upwards until Lillian nodded her approval.

'I can't see anyone smiling at me,' Godfrey said, studying the faces in the crowd. Lillian brought his attention to a smiling family walking towards them. 'You were saying?' As the family passed them, they greeted Godfrey and Lillian with a hearty, '*Guten morgen*.'

Neither of them noticed Deirdre swim up to them in their slipstream. 'Godfrey Fairtrade?' Godfrey spun round, ready to defend himself. Deirdre took a step back. Godfrey, seeing that there was no imminent danger, replied, 'Good morning.'

'Deirdre Wotheringspot.'

'What?'

'Wotheringspot. On behalf of the Vole Valley Women's Institute, I would like to welcome you to our humble fair.'

'You would, would you?'

'She would,' Lillian said, giving him a hard stare.

'We are so pleased you could come. This is your first time, I gather,' continued Deidre.

'Yes,' Godfrey forced out.

'Well, I am here to ensure that you make the most of your visit.'

'Meaning?'

'That is most kind of you,' Lillian said and squeezed Godfrey's hand so hard his fingers buckled.

'That is indeed most kind,' Godfrey said by way of submission.

Godfrey looked around at the gaudy banners hanging from ropes across the trees which surrounded Nokney village green. Sunlight filtered through the branches, sending gentle waving patterns across the whole affair. A bunch of medieval minstrels somewhere in the melee were trying to take the visitors back through the centuries, although the sight of medieval peasants holding mobile phones and taking selfies wasn't particularly helping the cause. The whole thing was making Godfrey come out in a nasty misanthropic rash.

'We have the tug of war,' infused Deidre enthusiastically.

'I can see that.' Godfrey grimaced.

'The jousting display is always a crowd pleaser.'

'I'm sure.'

'And you must try our medieval refreshments.'

'Must... I must,' he said, wincing with pain.

'And, of course, there are many people who would like to meet you,' Deirdre said. Lillian squeezed his hand before he could reply.

'I am looking forward to it,' was his flat response. As they began to walk, Deirdre asked what the creaking sound was. *This blasted Lady Trim corset, that's what*, Godfrey nearly said. 'It's the support for my bad back.'

Deirdre nodded. 'Oh.' And she raised her eyebrows.

*

While Godfrey was getting his dread in order, at the other end of the fair, Tancred was feeling at one with his ancestors. He noticed a rather fetching milkmaid doing what milkmaids did to cows. Tancred strode up to her in manly fashion.

'And what may your name be, young wench?'

She looked up from the udder line. A stable boy standing next to her bent down to whisper something in her ear. Whatever he said produced a spirited response.

'Bugger off, creep.'

Tancred staggered back as though he had been poked with a halberd and quickly moved on. As he moved through the crowd, he noticed people whispering and pointing at him. Tancred smiled generously, assuming they were impressed by his knightly attire. He saw a group of frocked children, cross-legged on the grass up ahead, and decided to have another go at making contact with the natives. He strolled over and placed his feet firmly in front of them. The children looked at his feet and then looked up at him.

'Kneel before your knight,' Tancred said, feeling a tingle of pleasure running down his spine. He was truly a man born into the wrong age, he thought. In response, the children jumped up, shouting 'stranger danger' and 'perv', then legged it. In panic, Tancred dropped his visor and scuttled off in the opposite direction.

*

Godfrey was now walking straight into the lion's den: the food stalls. Every one of them possessed, or was possessed by, a hoary-haired, flint-eyed lady. Here, there were plenty of smiles, which Godfrey found deeply unnerving, although Lillian seemed blithely unaware of the portent of this.

'Now, you don't want to offend anyone by not trying their wares, do you?' Deirdre said with an evil glint in her eye. Godfrey looked at the line of stalls that seemed to stretch down to the coast. Godfrey looked at her with saucer eyes. 'Hope you are hungry,' Deirdre said. Godfrey cast a fearful eye down the stalls again as wild boar drifted not so enticingly on the midday breeze. Sod that! he thought.

Next to the swinging pig was a stall advertising 'Becket Burgers'. Next to that was a confectionery stall advertising 'Chaucer's Crumpets', subtitled 'The Miller's Tasty Bit'. Behind it sat the Princess of Darkness herself. Maude Appleby smiled sweetly at Godfrey and summoned him over with a flick of her head.

Like a wary serf fearing the retribution of their capricious master, Godfrey creaked over to her stall. She stretched across the table to clasp his hand. He glanced around for the Blackwood ogre, but, thankfully, she was nowhere in sight. 'Godfrey, Godfrey, Godfrey, I despair of you,' Maude said, smiling and shaking her head up and down to give the public impression that all was well, although Godfrey sensed the opposite was true.

'What have I done?' Godfrey tried to pull his hand away, but Maude was having none of it. Godfrey looked over to Lillian, who had been ensnared in conversation by some silvery goblins dressed up as old ladies.

'You didn't tell me that *they* would be in disguise. And I was very clear when I told you I wanted to know everything. As it was, Tancred wasn't difficult to spot.' He had seen that look Maude gave him once before, in Ulaanbaatar. There was no mistaking the Genghis Stare.

'But–'

'No buts. Let this be a lesson for you. Your punishment will be trial by stall. After a crumpet you must try one of my cupcakes,' she said, pushing a crumpet forward. Godfrey looked down at the punishment crumpet. Maude slid a retributive cupcake next to it. Godfrey picked up the crumpet, took a bite, put it down and was just reaching for the cupcake when Maude said, 'Uh-uh, you eat everything offered you.' Godfrey was about to plead for mercy, but the slow shake of Maude's head extinguished any hope of clemency.

'Time to face the feast,' she said.

Once Godfrey had begun his journey down the stalls of

Hades, Deirdre sidled up for a quick word with Maude. 'I almost feel sorry for him.'

'Just wanted to make sure he is fully motivated in the future,' Maude replied.

'The young lads have found their van,' Deirdre said. 'Bit of luck that Inspector Punchard decided to come in a suit of armour. Although it's not quite as dashing as what we had lined up for him. And he's decided to walk about on his own, which is helpful. I just hope Pippa doesn't get too carried away with him.'

'She's been told to just humiliate him.'

'You're forgetting Richard.'

'Hopefully, by the time he realises what is going on, it will be too late for him to stop it. If we can just get Tancred to screw up a few times, the government may lose its stomach for the fight.'

Deirdre looked over to Godfrey and said, 'I wish I could share your optimism. I'd better get back to the minister. Make sure he doesn't skip any stalls.'

'And I think it's time to make myself scarce,' Maude said.

*

While Godfrey and Tancred were doing their best to be seen to be enjoying themselves, Richard and Joan had calmly walked around the entire fair. At various points they had bumped into the others from the taskforce doing the same, compared notes on suspicious old ladies and moved on. As they walked, Richard was beginning to appreciate what it was like to be the wife who was the last to know.

'Do you feel it?' Richard said to Joan as they meandered along.

'That we may as well be wearing our uniforms?' Joan said, eating a wild boar hotdog.

'That's the one.'

They walked on for a bit. Joan finished her hotdog and bought a cone of chips. 'You know the other feeling I'm feeling?' she said, shoving a chip into her mouth.

'That we have all walked into an ambush?' Richard said.

'Yep. There's something of *The Wicker Man* about all this.'

'Have you also noticed that we are literally being tailed by the Grim Reaper?'

'Yep.'

'The scythe, a little worried about it.'

'Yep.'

They came across two policemen. These ones were wearing uniforms and sitting in a police Smart car (due to cutbacks). Richard strolled up to them.

'We've certainly been lucky with the weather,' Richard said in typical British fashion.

'We certainly have, my court jester,' the officer in the passenger seat replied. Both officers were smirking. They happened to be called George and Frank.

'Where do you put people when you have arrested them?' Richard asked, appraising the Smart car and the officers. Looking at their girths, he reckoned they would be hard-pressed to catch anyone in the first place.

'Oh, we don't have much crime around here,' George replied.

'I'm glad to hear it. Good to see that this crazy sugar

restriction hasn't affected the fair too much.'

'People muddle through,' George replied. Richard and Joan bade farewell and moved along. Once they were out of earshot, George said, 'Richard Fleming, I presume.'

'The very one,' Frank replied and turned to the young woman who had just walked up to his window. 'Sally, you're an angel,' he said as she gave a look at the receding backs of Richard and Joan and passed the tray she was holding through the window. It had two mugs of tea and two doughnuts on it.

'If you want anything else, just holler,' Sally said and slunk off with her eyes still on Richard and Joan.

Once Joan had finished her chips, she bought a venison burger. As Richard watched her devour it, he said, 'The local bobbies knew exactly who we were as well.'

Joan swallowed and said, 'Oh yes.'

'Joan, are you running a boarding house for tapeworms?'

Joan looked at her burger, then at Richard, then at her burger again. 'I've just got a big appetite.'

'I don't know where you put it. You should be as big as a house, but you've got a…' Richard stopped. 'Sorry, I didn't mean…' Richard flushed as his words faded.

'Didn't mean what?' Joan blushed.

Richard examined the grass and unconsciously rubbed the back of his neck, missing the flash of amusement that passed across her face. At that moment he was saved when Jenny and Luke walked up.

'How's it going?' Richard asked, noticing that Luke was eating a flapjack and Jenny's face was buried into a large balloon of candy floss.

'If it were narcotics instead of sugar, this would be the place to get off your face,' Jenny said. Luke followed Richard's gaze to his flapjack and said, 'To help us fit in,' and gave a timid look. Richard couldn't help smirking in response.

'Just keep going. Oh, and I suggest you steer clear of the Froggy's Fate in the beer tent,' Richard said. He grimaced. 'And the Trench Foot.'

'I quite liked the Trench Foot,' Joan said. 'And they sell pints, not those bloody noggins.'

'What are we actually looking for?' Luke asked.

'Suspicious-looking old women, I guess,' Richard replied.

'That's all I see.'

'Oh, I don't know,' Richard said. 'If you see twelve wizened vagabonds led by a giant, you know you're getting close. If she's here, Blackwood will stick out like a sore thumb.'

'We were thinking of heading over to the cow pie tossing,' Jenny said.

'Can we go as well?' Joan asked.

Richard lowered his brow and said, 'I'd be suspicious of your motives.' He then turned to the other two. 'Have you two seen Tancred?'

'We saw one knight and a bunch of kids running away from each other so we reckon that must have been him,' Luke said.

'Maybe you could find him and keep on his tail,' Richard said.

'Will do, boss.'

They broke up the jesters' conference and went their separate ways.

★

By now Godfrey's Lady Trim corset had sprung some teeth and was slowly gnawing into his flesh. If he ate any more, he feared a black hole might appear in his stomach into which he would disappear. Lillian had been allowed to forego some of the stalls, but she was also beginning to suffer. Their dutiful persecutor, Deirdre, was now leading them to the beer tent. The banner proudly proclaimed, 'traditional homebrews'. Last time Godfrey had tried a homebrew it had caused a brutal evacuation. In his present distressed state, the thought of drinking homebrew was thus a trifle distressing. They walked into the yeasty gloom to examine the concoctions lined up before them. Godfrey made a mental note of the location of the portable toilets they had passed and went to study the barrel labels. Most of them smelled capable of bringing down a sprinting elephant.

'All the fun of the fair, eh,' mocked Deirdre. Lillian was staring, mesmerised, at a label for an ale called Froggy's Fate. The one next to it was called Agincourt.

'Have you no pity?' Godfrey whispered to Deirdre.

'You really must try the Pre-Reformation, a fine Trappist tipple, and the cheeky little brew the locals call Ale Mary,' Deirdre said.

'Imp.'

Lillian waddled uncomfortably up to them and said

to Deirdre, 'You'll have to excuse us, but I think we both could do with a sit down.' She looked around. 'Somewhere else.'

Godfrey's pained eyes shuffled over to Deirdre with a little beg in the corner of his eye. There was no pity in Deirdre's expression. 'Don't worry, dear, I shall carry on by myself,' Godfrey said to Lillian. She gave him a look that suggested he needed psychiatric help, but after a few shakes of her head she waddled away. As she left the tent, she noticed that everyone was holding pint glasses, which didn't bode well for Godfrey.

Forty minutes later, Godfrey emerged from the tent. He shielded his eyes from the sun and staggered. Then he made a wavering beeline for the portable toilets. There was a nesting queue in front of every makeshift cubicle. Godfrey waited with his knees firmly together and his buttocks clenched until his turn came. He toddled towards the plastic door, but just before he got there an old woman appeared from nowhere and nipped in before him. In desperation, he edged over to the next toilet as the door opened.

'There's a queue, you know,' the elderly woman at the front of the queue said, barring the entrance with her arm.

'But I'm desperate and some woman pushed–'

'Piss off,' she said as she went in and closed the door behind her.

Godfrey edged his way back to the first queue.

'There's a queue, you know,' said another elderly woman, who had been behind him.

'But I was in front.'

'Do you see a reserved sign on this bog? You can't just

wander off and expect to step back to the front of the queue any time you want.'

'But I was just over there.' Godfrey pointed at the other queue, which was a metre and a half away.

'Get lost, unless you want a kick in the walnuts.' Godfrey wasn't at all keen on that outcome.

He looked down the expanded line of women, all glaring back at him, and began his painful waddle to the back. He eventually managed to get into the toilet cubicle without mishap but was soon wondering if Maude was a real demon, because despite his body's desperate state nothing was budging. He was completely bunged up. After about ten minutes of being pounced on by the flies – they seemed to be doing relays between the toilet bowl and his face – he achieved a modicum of success and got out. Deirdre was sitting on a hay bale waiting for him.

'We're on the home stretch now,' Deirdre said. 'Just a few more chores and then we're done.'

Godfrey felt a wave of relief, despite his pressurised state. 'Give it to me,' he said with a mild slur.

'We were rather hoping you would introduce the joust.'

That didn't sound too bad. He could do that. A short speech of meandering and meaningless eloquence and maybe no one would notice he was half cut. 'OK.'

'But first there is one more tent that we *must* pop into.' Deirdre noticed the hunted look on his face and said, 'Oh, don't worry, no food or drink is involved. In fact, you will be able to sit down.'

The ordeal was nearly over. Godfrey could see why people could be so grateful to their torturer when a scrap of mercy was tossed their way. He followed behind Deirdre like a badly treated dog. Wondering where Lillian had gone, he looked around for any upside-down crosses where she might be hanging. They reached a tent with a banner that read 'Medieval Crèche'.

'What is this?' Godfrey asked.

'I would have thought it was obvious.'

'What's in there?'

'Babies, you silly goose.'

Godfrey didn't appreciate being called a goose. He decided that if he was sitting, there wasn't too much they could do to him. Stick a few babies on his knee maybe, while he lied to their parent about their hideous offspring. When they entered the tent, he was confronted with a line of babies in medieval garb in various stages of crying, vomiting, dribbling or straining. Their peasant mothers were lined up behind the babies, with a burly male peasant also in attendance. Surrounding this lot were a jocular mob of modern-day villains in various stages of medieval regress. Some looked to be making bets, though on what Godfrey had no idea.

'We are all honoured that the minister has manfully volunteered to help,' Deirdre said. All the mothers smiled their appreciation, or rather smirked it.

'What have I manfully volunteered for?' Godfrey asked, suddenly on guard.

'Why, the baby weighing. Hope you have strong arms.'

Godfrey froze in horror. 'You want me to weigh babies?' he said very slowly, looking at the twenty or so chubby infants.

'You hold each one up in turn, get a good gauge of their

weight,' she said with sadistic cheerfulness, 'and then you go on to the next one.'

'Whatever for?' Godfrey blurted, looking at her as though she had gone mad.

'To see which one is the heaviest, obviously.'

Godfrey looked down the line of at least ten babies and pointed to a child that reminded him of Jabba the Hutt. 'That one. It must be.'

'Now, now. That would be cheating.' The stare Deirdre gave him was unequivocal.

Godfrey realised what the betting was really about, and it had nothing to do with baby weighing. He was placed on a bale; a large bean bag was placed in front of him and a man's hands were placed on his shoulders. He couldn't even plead safety concerns. The first blubbery weight was placed in front of him. It looked up at him in a sinister way. He was forced to stretch down, with the blood rushing in his ears, and heave the revolting specimen up.

'Arms stretched out.'

Godfrey stretched his arms out.

'Hold it, hold it.'

Godfrey held.

'And, and…and…and…aaaannnnd…down.'

Godfrey dropped the creature onto the bean bag. He would have fallen headfirst into the bean bag as well, but for the man's hands on his shoulders. He was straightened back up, panting.

'Excellent.' Deirdre clapped her hands and said, 'Next!'

By the time Godfrey got to the last blubbery lump, his arms were like jelly. He was also aware of some worrying pinging sounds coming from the back of the corset and the danger signs of gas building inside him. The flash of a few SLR cameras started to disorient Godfrey further.

Then Jabba the Hutt was placed in front of him.

'I must say, you have exceeded expectations,' Deirdre said. Godfrey was vaguely aware of some disgruntlement in the betting community.

'Just this wee chap left.' She pointed to Jabba the Hutt. 'His name is Bernie.'

Godfrey looked down at the little beast. It looked back up expectantly and belched a glob of mother's milk. With a huge hyperventilated effort Godfrey stretched down and snatched Bernie onto his lap. The baby, seeing how he was suffering, took pity on him and, in a compassionate attempt to lighten the load, belched its half-digested lunch over Godfrey's trousers.

Godfrey stared at his sodden milky crotch in disbelief.

'I'm not sure Bernie is the heaviest anymore,' Deirdre quipped.

★

Tancred was increasingly feeling out of sorts. The Medieval Fair was proving to be no fun, nor was being in a suit of armour on a scorching summer's day. A few pints of Trench Foot and Froggy's Fate hadn't helped either. He sat on his own in a baled picnic area outside the main fair, sulkily looking around, confirming that he was ready to go home. Then he remembered that, for the time being, his home was the hotel.

'Do you want to be a lifesaver?'

Tancred looked round to see a squire standing next to him. 'Sorry?'

'Our knight has sprained his ankle and can't do the joust. If you were happy to step in, we would be incredibly grateful,' the squire said, reeling Tancred in like a Black Widow spider seducing its next mate.

'Oh, I'd be delighted,' he said.

The squire led the chirpy chattering knight over to the jousting arena. On the way, Tancred told the squire all about his medieval ancestors, but the squire only displayed intense disinterest. When they got to the enclosure, he saw the two jousting tents on either end of it. The one he was closest to was small. The other was much larger. A warning thought tried to doggy-paddle to the surface, but Tancred was too excited to pay it much heed.

As the crowds gathered to watch the spectacle, Tancred was taken into the small tent to meet his steed. He was a bit disappointed to see a Shetland pony. The pony sniffed at him, and then gave that tell-tale narrowing of the eyes. In Tancred's enthusiasm, he'd forgotten horses didn't like him. Indeed, no Punchard had been allowed to get close to a horse since Sir Mordecai Punchard of Bosworth fame. The pony immediately started backing its behind into the corner of the tent, baring its yellow teeth as it did.

By this time, Godfrey was heaving himself up to the podium. He had found Lillian on a hay bale and had dragged her along for moral support.

'What's that awful smell?' Lillian said out of the corner of her mouth.

'Jabba's lunch,' Godfrey slurred, grim-faced. He was beginning to feel light-headed with all the pressure around his girth. The buttons of his shirt were pressed tight and the corset was making alarming noises similar to taut steel cables. Deirdre was hovering menacingly behind them.

At the point where half a dozen squires were fighting to get a knight onto a hysterical Shetland pony, Richard and Joan were standing by the other jousting tent, looking at it with some trepidation. From behind the thin material there came sounds of heavy snorting and a thudding that was sending shockwaves running through the ground.

'What's in there?' Joan whispered.

'A very, very large horse, I hope,' Richard said. He could hear Godfrey's voice booming over the PA system. He sounded a bit strained, and half cut as well. Godfrey announced himself as the 'insistent deputy parliamentary under-secretary of state with responsibilities for rural laws and orders', though, due to his increased slurring, he might as well have been communicating with Jabba the Hutt. The silence that followed was only broken by some isolated clapping from the German family.

'*Psst.*'

Richard and Joan turned around. An old man bent over by years of nagging and infused with home-grown aromas was leaning on a crimson-splashed scythe behind them. This diminutive Grim Reaper looked around furtively, before saying, 'I must be quick. If they see me…' His voice tailed off into a dreadful, swivel-eyed croak. 'Evil witches, the lot of them.' He then thrust a piece of paper into Richard's hand. 'She will help you.'

Richard looked at the phone number written on the inside of a Jammy Dodger wrapper and then looked back up at the Grim Reaper.

'Who do you think we are?' Richard asked.

'You're that police taskforce come down to break up the Granny Cartel.'

'And just how do you know that?' Richard said.

'Everyone knows it. Besides, your mate Sir Lancelot over there is a dead giveaway. He's got police-issue boots on.' Godfrey had announced the jousting and there was an expectant chatter amongst the crowd. Richard balled his fists and cursed. He had known there was something about Tancred that didn't chime. He'd had an inkling about it at the hotel and in the van, but he had been too distracted to properly analyse it. In a way, Richard had to admire Tancred's sheer incompetence. He just prayed they could get through the day without him doing something really stupid.

'Anyway, he's about to get his block knocked off,' the Grim Reaper said. Richard closed his eyes. Tancred's timing was impeccable.

'What do you mean?'

'Have you seen who he's jousting against?' The Grim Reaper didn't wait for a reply and cut back into the crowd. Richard and Joan slowly turned to look at the jousting tent behind them. Just then the sun helpfully came out to show the silhouette of a massive horse. Then they watched in horror as something equally massive rose up onto it. Pippa Blackwood. And she seemed be holding a Highland caber. In unison they turned to look at the other, much smaller tent. The flaps were at that moment flung open to reveal Tancred, sitting on a bucking Shetland pony, with what looked like a curtain pole in his hand.

'Please tell me this isn't happening,' Richard said to Joan.

'It's not happening,' she replied.

'Don't believe you.'

'Worth a try.'

Richard started running. Joan sighed and chased after him. They nearly collided with Jenny and Luke racing up a side path.

'I thought I told you to keep an eye on him?' Richard shouted.

'We looked for him after the cow pie tossing, but he had disappeared,' Luke said.

'See what you mean about the Trench Foot,' Jenny commented and then looked guilty. Richard afforded them a quick withering glare and ran on towards the other jousting tent.

Tancred didn't notice the flaps open on the other jousting tent. He was just busy trying not to get bitten. Hundreds of pairs of eyes were now planted on the David and Goliath scene, a scene which so far had eluded Tancred because of his equine troubles. Everyone was betting on a reversal of Biblical fortunes. What was also noticed with some hilarity was 'David's' warm-up preparations, which were decidedly circuitous and quite tempestuous.

Tancred's technique for not getting a lump bitten out of him was proving reasonably effective. The thin armour had already proved no match for the pony's teeth, so

Tancred had clamped his legs around the livid pony like a boa constrictor and every time the teeth came at him from one direction, he would lean the other, forcing the pony to right itself. The trick was not to lean so far as to upend them both. That was a scenario that Tancred was very keen to avoid. The pony had made it clear that if it had the chance it would open the armour up like a tin can and spread its contents over the field. The upshot was that the crowd were being treated to a strange aperitif of *Excalibur* meets *Bronco Billy* meets *Jaws* meets petting zoo. It wasn't a mix that Tancred was enjoying.

Then, quite abruptly, the pony stopped, as though all thoughts of the horse-hexed lump sitting on it had dissipated. Something of far greater gravity had caught its attention. It had spotted what was digging up bucketloads of divots with its hooves and snorting away like a punctured hovercraft. It had also noticed that the black knight's big brother was pointing something resembling a telegraph pole in its direction. The Shetland had the dubious pleasure of knowing this shire horse quite well.

Through the slit in her helmet, Pippa eyed up her victim with relish and then began to move forward. The lull in activity had also caused Tancred to look up and see what had caught the Shetland's attention. He soon came to the conclusion that the situation hadn't improved. One half of his brain suggested hopping off the pony and running like hell. The other half of his brain informed him that his legs had seized up around the pony. Basically, he was frozen with fear.

It was at this point events conspired to decide the fate

of Tancred, which wasn't the fate that Maude and Pippa had envisioned. As it turned out, it was Godfrey who made the crucial intervention.

Just as Pippa and her shire horse came rumbling down the arena with injurious intent, as Richard and the others looked on in morbid awe, something on the podium went twang. Godfrey's corset finally gave up the ghost and burst through his buttons like an alien sting ray and soared into the air. That's what it seemed like to Godfrey at least. In actual fact, it was more like a pop and flop. The important thing was that it hung at the apex of the pop long enough to catch the attention of one pair of eyes.

Now, this shire horse had always been a curious horse. It would study birds feuding in hedges. It would watch worms getting hot under the collar over a piece of loam. At this crucial moment it noticed a very unusual bird appearing over the podium. It had never seen a bird like it before. That was curious. Then it decided it didn't like curious birds appearing in its peripheral vision and reared up in the opposite direction, almost sending Pippa tumbling to the ground, which the horse would have been pleased about because she was making his back ache.

Up until this point the Shetland pony hadn't come up with an effective plan for not getting sat on or kicked into the crowd. Then, miraculously, a route to safety opened up: straight between the shire horse's legs. Never being one to look a gift horse in the mouth, it skidded onto its side through the gap, with the medieval manikin still firmly attached. It then leaped up and galloped as fast as its stumpy legs could carry it straight through the opposing jousting fence and bolted through the scattering crowd… and kept going. With tears of laughter streaming down her face, Maude watched from the seclusion of a tent, as pony and mount hurtled across the green followed by a string of jesters.

When the pony got to the small pond at the end of Nokney Green, it implemented an emergency stop. Tancred was flung into the air. He bounced straight off an oak tree on the other side and fell on his back into the muddy edge of the pond. He lay there in a daze, looking up at the sun. Then he noticed a tail swish into his aperture of the sky. It was followed by a warm, glittering, golden shower. Once his helmet had drained, the sounds of the fair came back to him. It sounded as though everyone was laughing. Just as consciousness was leaving him, he saw the upside-down head of a jester loom over him.

The jester said, 'Remember the bit about not drawing attention to ourselves?'

TWELVE

A&E in Dorsham Hospital was always busy on the day of Nokney Medieval Fair. About an hour after the beer tents opened, the first wave of feudal specimens suffering from symptoms very similar to those of dysentery started to arrive. It was like the medieval ghost had wafted into A&E with the plague. A sow got loose and injured the proprietor of a sausage stall. A pair of grannies were brought in who had set to with slice and fork after an acrimonious prizegiving.

When a crumpled knight was wheeled into the frenetic emergency department, no one batted an eyelid. While the nurses got to work with can openers, the paramedics explained to the doctor why the wet and smelly knight looked like he had been smacked into an oak tree. This led back to the joust, which inevitably led to discussion of the identity of the other jouster. The doctor remembered when *most* of Blackwood's last victim had come in. Two policemen in a Smart car had come to interview him, but they didn't speak garbled Russian and the man had died soon after. Tancred's armour was peeled open and the doctor looked down at its pungent contents, wondered at what layers of madness still remained. He decided to keep Tancred in for observation for a few days. Richard wasn't about to object.

With Tancred out of action, Richard got down to business. First, he had to arrange for a local garage to pick up the van, as its wheels had curiously gone missing. Richard did find some perverse pleasure when he came to check Tancred out of his hotel. His room was tiny and terrible. His luggage was also missing. The manager said he shouldn't have left it in the hall.

While the van was being sorted, Matthew was given the task of organising new accommodation for the team in Guildbury along with somewhere that could be used as a temporary office. Richard felt it was all a bit pointless. Their cover had been blown even before they had set foot in Dorsham, even before the debacle of the Medieval Fair. The fair which Godfrey had recommended they go to, Richard noted.

By the time evening arrived, the taskforce were all ensconced in the local Travelodge in Guildbury. Matthew had found temporary offices above a Chinese restaurant just out of the town centre. In the meantime, Richard had rented a new van, plus a car for the next day. His intention was to leave the team to transform the offices into an investigation suite, while eating takeaways, giving him time to get a feel for the area. He dialled the number the Grim Reaper had given him, but there was no reply. By the time the team had finished their evening meal at the Beefeater next door, Richard was about ready to turn in. He was heading back to the hotel, when Joan caught up with him.

'So, tomorrow you are intending to do a bit of sightseeing?'

'I'm not sure I'd call it sightseeing. Is it a problem for the others?' Richard replied.

'No, no, it makes sense. See if anything comes to mind, help the old intuition along. Just one thing you might want to consider, though.'

'What?' Richard said.

'Well,' Joan said, and paused to purse her lips. 'We all thought a couple touring in a car isn't as suspicious, that's all.' Richard looked away, fearing the expression in his eyes might betray him.

'I suppose I can see the logic in that. Either Jenny, or you, or, I mean not to say it couldn't be…sorry…Yes, you're right,' Richard finished, feeling a bit lame.

'I drew the short straw.'

Richard stared at her. 'My commiserations. Have you got something to wear that is, I don't know…?'

'Coupley?'

'Appropriate for that image, yes.'

'I'm sure I can dig something out.'

'OK. We'll meet in the foyer at nine.'

Richard nodded. Joan walked off looking pleased with herself. Richard watched her go, and couldn't help smiling to himself, before making his way to his own bedroom.

Richard took a shower and then got under the covers of his bed. He lay there mulling over the rise of the Cartel. It was no wonder so many people had become active supporters of the Cartel. You needed separate sugar licences to transport, store (unless a private citizen), sell, or manufacture any sugar-based products. Inevitability, there was much fudging when it came to products deemed of national importance, especially when it came to the more refined booze. And sweet licences were anything but sweet when it came to cost, resulting in a bag of sugar costing enough to be reserved as a treat for celebrations like Christmas. Indeed, most of the nation's population soon felt like turkeys who had voted for Christmas.

Richard thought of London with its sugar dens and sweet easys, where out of sight people did unspeakable things to marshmallows. It was there that you saw the sickly, sticky underside of society. Yet everyone he knew had dipped their fingers into that underworld from time to time. Himself included.

When it came to all the other criminally sweet organisations scattered around the country, no one was in any doubt that the Cartel was the chief lollipop. It seemed that grey granny matter mattered most, especially Maude Appleby's.

What the taskforce needed was hard proof of the Cartel's illegal activities. So far, the authorities had found no incriminating money trail and no one was prepared to inform on the Cartel. Nor did anyone associated with the Cartel show any signs of increased wealth. So where was all the damned money going, Richard thought, as he waited for sleep. If he had known the truth, he would have been amazed, not to mention impressed.

*

In the morning when Richard walked into the foyer, he couldn't help a lump forming in his throat at the sight of Joan waiting for him. She had a knee-high blue floral dress on beneath a wide-brimmed cream summer hat and large-rimmed sunglasses. Her hair was flowing over her shoulders. Richard felt a sudden guilt and self-conscious: he was wearing a pair of old jeans, a T-shirt and a slightly frayed baseball cap. The only thing that stood comparison was his Ray-Ban sunglasses.

As he walked up to her, she said, 'Shabby chic?'

'Shabby…shabby…more like,' he replied. 'I'm a bit worried we will draw attention to ourselves purely because of the beauty and the beast contrast.' Richard did his best not to blush as he breathed in the scent of her perfume.

'Rubbish, you look great,' Joan responded, looking kindly at him.

It was Joan's turn to be surprised when she came to see the Mini convertible Richard had hired for the day.

'Won't that raise eyebrows on the expenses form?' she asked.

'It's not going on the expense form. Thought I might as well spend it while I still can,' Richard replied. She wasn't sure what he meant, but something about his manner warned her not to ask. She took her hat off, tied her hair back and got in. Richard got in next to her, wishing he had picked another car. Something about it all made him feel vulnerable.

'Where first, boss?'

'You'd better stop calling me that. People will get the wrong idea.' Richard started the car and put it into gear.

'OK, darling.'

The car jolted forward and stalled. 'Mm-hmm, or

maybe just Richard.' They both laughed, awkwardly.

They took the road from Guildbury to Dorsham, dropping down from Newlands Corner with its panoramic views of the Surrey Hills and after a short while turned right and headed into the bucolic lair of the Cartel.

*

Sir Cecil had received a phone call from Mervyn Nipper's private secretary that morning, with some very interesting news. He couldn't imagine Prime Minister Houston was going to be too pleased when he found out.

He sat back in his chair and thought about what he had just learned. What could he make of this opportunity? No, wrong question. What would Maude make of this opportunity? Now that was the question. That thought made him smile as he stretched for the phone.

*

Apart from being nearly run off the road by some spotless four-wheel-drives, Richard and Joan's tour of the countryside was pleasant but not particularly informative. They slowly made their way around the escarpment to Nokney, through winding leafy lanes that tunnelled through multifarious forests, opening up at points to show tree-lined valleys and paddocks. All the villages and hamlets they passed suggested a world where the twenty-first century was by invitation only.

'It's incredibly beautiful around here,' Joan spoke in an

awed murmur, gliding her hand through the warm breeze. 'Who would think we're only thirty miles from London.' Richard looked over to her and allowed himself to enjoy the moment.

'Are you from London?' Joan asked.

'Yes.'

'And is the police force a family thing?' Joan said light-heartedly.

'I don't have any family.' There was a flatness to his reply that suggested it wasn't his favourite subject. They drove on in silence.

Their meandering eventually brought them to Nokney. They parked the car and took a saunter around the village. The lunchtime riot from the small village school could be heard across the green. People milled around the shambles of the fair, slowing gathering in its remaining parts to be stacked in dormancy for another year. The cricket pitch was being manicured by an ancient lawnmower and an equally ancient mower.

They crossed the old Roman road called Stane Street to the village post office, which still boasted an immaculate red telephone box and a wall-mounted, VR-dated post box. A bell tinkled as the door opened to reveal Revd Massey in conversation with Mabel Potts, the postmistress.

'Now, vicar, are you happy for me to go ahead with the commemorative flowers for Fred Marsh?'

'Oh, yes, if you could it would be appreciated,' Revd Massey replied, giving her a wary glance.

'Of course, vicar. It's the second anniversary. Bev will be expecting her husband rightly remembered. Not something I like to think on,' she said.

'Quite, Mabel. Anyway, looking forward–'

'More bits of bone have turned up you know,' she said. Richard glanced up from a notice board and noted the apprehension on the vicar's face.

'Amazing how far bits of him flew.'

'Well, let's not dwell on his demise and just remember the warm, gentle–'

'Poor man, what an end, ripped into pieces of ragged flesh and bone before his very own eyes.'

'Yes, yes, well now to happier events coming up,' Revd Massey stammered, looking even more pallid.

'Just imagine the horror he must have felt,' Mabel said, shaking her head in wonder.

Revd Massey let out an involuntary moan and replied, 'I would prefer not to.'

'It was his own fault. Derek, you know Derek?'

'Yes, the mechanic.'

'He warned Fred about that combine harvester. He said it was a death trap.'

'I seemed to remember the coroner saying as much,' Revd Massey admitted, becoming resigned to the ghoulishness of village gossip.

'The coroner said he was removing a bag of muesli from its path when it slipped into gear and off it went. Derek reckoned he would have outrun it if he had bothered to put on his false leg. Bev said he never liked wearing his false leg, chafed him something awful. You know why he only had one leg?'

'I'm aware that he was a quite accident prone,' Revd

Massey responded, closing his eyes to dreams of his retreat. By now Richard and Joan were standing transfixed, listening to this one-sided conversation.

'Ripped off by a threshing machine, some years back. Anyway, Derek reckons he must have given it a good hop for its money. Wouldn't you with those gnashing jaws slowly gaining on you?'

'I dare say, but he is in Heaven now,' Revd Massey said as he looked up at the ceiling beseechingly.

'Shame he had to go through Hell to get there.'

'Sorry to eavesdrop on your conversation, but why was there a bag of muesli in the field?' Joan asked, sticking her professional nose into the conversation. The look the vicar gave her suggested it was the wrong question to ask. Richard gave Joan a sideways glance.

'Ah, the theory is that the bag of muesli was thrown into the field when there was that terrible accident–'

'Mabel, I really must go,' Revd Massey said as he leaped out the door before Mabel could utter another word.

'Oh,' Mabel said, a bit surprised as the door closed.

'Seems we missed the fair,' Richard said.

Mabel looked a little confused for a moment before she smiled and said, 'Ah, that you did and a good one it was. Put it in your calendar for next year.'

'I heard there was some unexpected horseplay going on this year,' Richard said.

'No different from any other year, I would say,' Mabel replied, now looking guarded. 'Why do you ask?'

Richard decided not to push the subject. 'No reason, just something I heard. We were thinking of visiting Okney this afternoon. What's the best way from here?' Joan was studying what looked like the village library with copies of *Women's Weekly*, a rack of Barbara Cartland novels, and a well-thumbed copy of *Fifty Shades of Grey*.

'Off to see the highlanders are we, with their precious St Morwenna,' she said and sniffed. 'Head in the direction of Dorsham and take the second turning left onto Broomehall Road. Or,' she brightened up, 'you can take the first left down Nokney Road where it is said the gallows used to be and turn right onto Leith Hill Lane. Keep a look out for a derelict property to your right. There's a gruesome story I can tell you about that place.' Mabel looked up into the distance as she recollected. 'Apparently the husband came home one night, axe in hand after chopping firewood, to find…' She looked down as she heard the tinkle of the bell and saw that she was alone in the shop.

Outside the post office Richard sheltered his eyes from the sun as he looked up at the timbered hillside immediately to the north. He picked out Leith Hill Tower standing sentry on the cleared summit. He could almost imagine Sauron's eye blazing above its parapets. The tower sat just above Okney, which was obscured by the trees below the summit. The Cartel's stronghold was their next stop.

'Do you fancy lunch?'

'Do you really have to ask?' Joan said, following his gaze.

When they got back to the car Richard tried the number the Grim Reaper had given him. But again, no reply. This time he left a tentative message, with diminishing hope that the Grim Reaper's phone number would connect him to anything useful. More likely it was Maude playing tricks, but he persisted. Every lead helps, he thought.

When they arrived in Okney they parked up at the edge of the village, by a pond which looked out over the plain through a break in the trees, and started walking towards a pub called the Whortleberry Arms which they had just driven past. It was immediately apparent to both of them that the atmosphere was different in Okney.

As they walked, Joan said, casually and smiling, 'We're being watched.'

Richard nodded. An old woman was sitting on a chair outside her cottage, eyeing them as she stroked a mean-looking Highland Terrier. Two more were loitering across the road on mobility scooters, giving the impression of youths tinkering with their cars. Indeed, the mobility scooters looked souped-up, with thick tyres extending out.

One of the old ladies, Mavis, leaned on her handlebars and said to the other, 'Ah, young love. He could do with a scrub up, though. He's lucky to have a looker like her, if you ask me. Mind you, those bedroom eyes–'

'You know what these young men are like these days, not *cool* to dress up. Not like our day,' Gladys replied. Their mobility scooters moved to track the couple as they passed by with a cursory 'Hello'. The two old ladies nodded and smiled in response.

As they watched the couple move away, the girl linked her arm in his and then turned into him and gave him a fulsome kiss. His fingers splayed, suggesting he wasn't expecting it. The girl then turned and gave them a wink.

'Saucy minx, made him go all embarrassed; look, he's

gone as red as a big toe with gout,' Mavis said.

'Don't stare, Mavis. Poor boy, he's all sixes and sevens now. Still not sure what she sees in a scruff like that, although I must admit there is something about him.'

Mavis angled her head up and sneaked a glance at Gladys, 'Maybe he's got, you know…'

'Lots of money?' Gladys replied, noting that the couple had stopped and were studying the valley behind her, chatting away.

'I was more thinking, you know…'

'No, I don't, and I'm not sure I want to.'

'A large dingle-dangle.'

Gladys gave her a scandalised look. 'Mavis Threadpepper, you're a scarlet woman!'

'Brings back old yearnings, don't it,' Mavis said, somewhat dreamily.

'Ancient, more like, Alfred was never much of a ravisher. More of a bashful worm really. I'll leave it at that.'

'The early bird gets the worm. At least that was the case with Ernest, God rest his soul.'

'Should we call Maude?'

'No. They look harmless enough.'

As Richard and Joan pretended to take in the view, Joan said, 'I hope you didn't mind my improvisation. They were looking at us mighty strangely.'

Richard edged his eyes down to his hand, which Joan had taken in hers and was now gently swaying. 'I was just a little caught off guard.'

'Sorry.'

'No, no, it was quick thinking, officer.'

'You feel me?'

'What!'

'I mean, you understand I had to make it look genuine.' Part of Richard thought it was decidedly genuine. That was why he was desperately trying to concentrate on the deep-sea trawler industry, which was the most ardour-dampening thing he could think of at the time. Joan brought her other hand over to stroke the hand she was holding. The fishing industry was hitting some rough weather.

'Yep.'

'Not that my girlfriend would appreciate it very much,' Joan dropped in. Richard dispensed with the trawlers.

'Only joking,' Joan said, and giggled. 'You need to loosen up a bit, get into the role. They're still watching us, you know.' Richard sensed a maritime disaster was about to befall him. He took a deep breath and bent down to give her a kiss on the cheek, but Joan's lip intercepted his. Faeroes, Dogger, Viking, Rockall…

He surfaced and managed to say, 'Let's get to the pub.'

'Yes, Richard,' Joan replied, leaning into him affectionately. As they walked on, she asked, 'I would love to know what they are talking about.'

'Knitting most likely,' Richard said, still trembling.

Richard and Joan walked into the Whortleberry Arms. Sitting at the bar were a couple of locals who eyed them up as they came in. They mumbled a 'hello' and went back to looking glumly at their noggins. Richard surveyed the surroundings before purchasing two noggins of beer while Joan picked a cubby hole to sit in by the front window. As Richard walked up to her with the drinks and two menus, she put her hand up to fend off any interruption. She was staring intently through the window. Richard sat down and followed her gaze to two old ladies across the street chatting in the sun.

'Maude's called a meeting at the church. Pippa and her Baker's Dozen are going to be there, so something's up,' Joan recited. Richard realised she was lip-reading.

'In about half an hour. I think.' To this Joan added, 'The other one is talking, but I can't see what they are saying.' The first lady was speaking again and Joan interpreted their response. '…find out soon enough. Glad…' Uh, 'Pippa and her band not doing the chilli and karaoke night, here. Maude…too close to home…everything else going on. They are not sorry.' Joan then chuckled. 'Pippa sounds like an ill-tempered wino being dragged along some gravel when she sings. Apparently makes little Gustav howl something rotten. Guess that's a dog.' The conversation briefly moved to the other lady, who must have asked a question, because Joan interpreted the response as, 'The Wallisford Arms. Friday. I think that is where Pippa is going to be next Friday, if I have read it properly.' The old ladies parted company and Joan looked over to Richard, who was appraising her.

'Where did you learn to lip-read?'

'I have a brother who is deaf. He taught me.'

'I'm impressed. Well done,' Richard replied, and he was.

Joan looked down at the menu, crestfallen. 'I know what you are going to say. We can't eat.'

'Sorry. I assume they are talking about the church

we walked past.' Just as they were downing their drinks, Godfrey's name flashed up on Richard's phone. It was the third time that day. And for the third time Richard ignored it.

'Fairtrade?' quizzed Joan.

'Yes.'

'You don't trust him?'

'I don't know, but one thing I'm sure of, is that the Cartel knew we were going to be at the fair, and it was Godfrey's suggestion for us to go.'

'If he's helping them, it's not out of love. He clearly despises them.'

'Right. He also seemed to be scared of them, so maybe they have their hooks in him.' The couple put down their menus, walked out and headed towards the church, where they noticed a number of elderly ladies making their way inside. They also noticed the same, and now very agitated vicar, welcoming them, glancing anxiously around the graveyard. The source of his agitation was clear. What Richard assumed was Pippa's fabled Baker's Dozen were spread out among the tombstones, on guard duty. And they were watching Richard and Joan with great interest. They reminded Richard of geriatric pirates. One hopped onto the flint wall edging the churchyard. Maybe not so geriatric, Richard thought.

'I think we have no choice but to keep going. If they see us hanging around, they'll take more than a casual interest.' Richard said, turning his head away.

'They look a rum lot,' Joan half-joked, keeping her head down as they walked past the church. 'The police report speculates that many of them were recruited off the streets of Eastbourne. Some of the seafront is a no-go area for the police now, especially in the afternoon.'

'Sounds a bit like God's remand centre,' Richard replied. They walked on until they returned to their car. Richard had thought about doubling back to have a closer look, but something was telling him it would be ill advised. Just as they were about to get into the car, he saw another elderly lady wearing sunglasses coming down the road. Very spry she was, Richard thought. He hoped he had that much energy at her age, the thought continued. To avoid staring too much, he turned away and looked out at the view. She stopped when she came level with them. 'It's very clear today,' she said. 'You can see the South Downs on a day like this.'

Richard half turned and nodded before returning to the view. 'It's glorious,' he replied. 'I'm quite envious of you living here.'

'Where do you live?'

'Oh, Surbiton,' Joan added. 'We decided to take a day trip out of the city. We've never been down here before. Bit of a crime not to, what with it being on our doorstep. It's so pretty around here.'

'Yes, I consider myself very privileged,' the old woman said, sizing up the beauty the young lady was. The man seemed a bit on edge. There was something about him she couldn't put her finger on. 'Anyway, I hope you enjoy the rest of your day,' she said as she walked away.

She stopped a bit further on and pulled her sunglasses down her nose as she turned to look back at the couple again. She saw the man stop and turn back to look at her just before he got in the car. The sunglasses and baseball cap had stopped her immediately recognising him, but now she did. Maude pushed her sunglasses up, smirked and continued towards the church.

THIRTEEN

'The electorate's wants and desires are a force only matched by their determination not to pay for those damn wants and desires,' Houston complained.

'It is burden borne by all prime ministers, Prime Minister,' Sir Robert Frenais replied. They were discussing the flourishing public deficit. Sir Robert was a dapper civil servant who looked like he polished his scalp and shoes at the same time every morning. He had long since come to realise that his job amounted to one thing only: damage limitation.

'What do they think we are, wizards?' Houston said.

'I've seen policies from governments in my time that have rather cried out for those kinds of powers,' the cabinet secretary said, examining his cuticles. Houston had learned that Sir Robert's cuticle-gazing was usually a gesture of his disapproval. Houston coughed. Sir Robert looked up and smiled.

'That's as maybe, but the fact is if the electorate put less energy into complaining and more into being productive, the government might actually have more money to spend,' Houston said.

'I agree, Prime Minister. There are too many people

blaming others for their own failings and shortcomings,' Sir Robert replied. Houston opened his mouth to say something, but he stopped and shot Sir Robert a glance.

'Unless there's anything else?' Houston offered.

As Sir Robert rose, he said, 'Only that Mervyn Nipper has organised a walk through the Surrey Hills tomorrow with the Temperance Trotters.'

'What!'

'I rather thought that would be your response. The term "death wish" comes to mind.'

'Why wasn't I told about this?'

'My sources told me that it was a spur of the moment thing, spurred this very morning I believe.'

'Well, I have every intention of un-spurring it,' Houston scoffed. Sir Robert's attention had been drawn to a vase of flowers on the sideboard behind Houston. 'Prime Minister, am I correct in recalling that you are meeting the first minister of Scotland today,' he said as he appraised the flowers.

Houston frowned and said, 'Right after this meeting, as you know.' Houston looked up at the grandfather clock by the door, 'About now, actually, so if there is anything else?'

Sir Robert pointed to the vase of flowers and said, 'Those flowers, Prime Minister.'

Houston glanced round at the flowers. 'Pretty, aren't they? Eleanor picked them from the garden for me, although I have no idea what they're called,' he replied, puzzled by Sir Robert's seemingly unconnected questions and by his face of professional disquiet that Houston knew all too well.

'*Dianthus barbatus*, Prime Minister, better known as Sweet Williams…in England. May I enquire as to where you are meeting the first minister, Prime Minister?'

'Why here? Is that a problem?'

'No problem at all. So long as that vase of flowers is in this room and the first minister is not, or the first minister is in this room and the vase of flowers is not, Prime Minister,' Sir Robert replied.

Houston scrutinised the opposite wall for a second before saying, 'Are you saying the first minister has some dislike or allergy to these flowers?'

'You could describe it as a historical allergy.'

'Is there such a thing?'

'Yes, when it comes to a flower the Scottish call Stinking Billy, named after William Augustus, Duke of Cumberland, the Butcher of Culloden. I would hazard their removal, performed with a certain spring in the step, would be a most prudent action if the prime minister wishes to avoid consequences'.

'I see what you mean,' Houston replied. He stood up and grabbed the flowers out of the vase and was frantically looking around for a place to deposit them when the door burst open. To Houston's horror, two beefy, kilted men with intimidating sporrans stepped in and placed themselves either side of the door. Between them marched the First Bruiser of Scotland, Morag MacGregor. She stood before them with hands on her hips, her ingrained glare bent out of shape to produce a rather unconvincing smile. As usual she was wearing a prim two-piece red suit incongruously matched to thick woollen socks stuffed into her shoes. A hardboiled eye came to rest on the personage of Sir Robert, who took his cue to leave.

'Good morning, First Minister, and good day, Prime Minister,' Sir Robert said and left Houston frozen to the spot with flowers in hand and the rictus of a pained smile on his face. Morag kicked the door shut behind Sir Robert.

It immediately opened again and Florence popped her head round the corner. 'Sorry, Prime Minister, they caught me mid-dunk of my chamomile teabag,' she offered. With Morag's flaring eyes now fastened onto his flower-laden hand, Houston shooed Florence out the room with a contemptuous 'Thank you.'

Outside the room, Sir Robert and Florence heard a female voice roar, 'Stinking Billy!'

*

In their private flat Eleanor Houston dabbed at the small nick on her husband's Adam's apple with antiseptic as she said, 'Fancy her keeping a flick *sgian-dubh* in her sock. You must have been completely traumatised.'

'And she called me a Sassenach dangleberry, so it's safe to say that those damned flowers have put paid to any help she would have given me in becoming clan chief.'

'Oh, darling, I feel so responsible. I thought they looked so pretty and your office so stuffy. Sadly, history was never my strong point.' Eleanor put a small plaster on his laryngeal prominence as the smell of crumpet wafted from the toaster.

'It was an innocent mistake,' he conceded, unaware

that it was anything but. Eleanor favoured warmer climes, which she considered London to be only just on the edge of and had no intention of migrating north to the clan seat in Scotland, which was Houston's intention. So far, her fifth column activity had amounted to some flowers being picked and hunting down an alternative clan chief, which she had fortuitously found in Baltimore. As she packed the first-aid kit away, she casually asked, 'So, Sir Robert told you about the walk?'

'Is nothing secret in this building?' Houston said. He went over to retrieve his crumpet from the toaster and started buttering it aggressively. Eleanor watched him in silence until he had finished and then stole it. 'Now, you aren't going to be difficult about this, are you?' she said as she evaded his lunge for the purloined crumpet.

'And why would you possibly think that?' he replied, putting another crumpet in the toaster.

'No one will know until after the event and he will have a protection team with him. He intends to take a sympathetic journalist with him who will report the demonstration against those responsible for the elicit sugar trade. Both Nipper and I think it would be a great PR exercise. Unfortunately, I can't go because I'm opening a sugar rehabilitation clinic in Slough.' Houston sat down and waited for his crumpet to pop up. 'Do these places have extra-wide doors and glucose-mainlining kits?' he asked.

'Don't be rude. We are trying to help these people, showing them a better path in life.'

'You and Pol Pot?'

'I wish you wouldn't call him that. I know Mervyn can

be a mite extreme in his views at times, but it is all for a good cause.'

'All I care about is getting re-elected and he isn't helping.'

'And I wish you wouldn't speak like that, either. You have to stand firm, and stand by your policies, not scamper for cover when your approval ratings drop.'

'Drop! I've seen slower-moving meteorites.'

'No one said it would be easy to change hearts and minds.' He was about to reply when she raised her finger. 'Are you going to allow the walk?'

'No.'

'Try again,' she said.

'It's too–'

'Ah.'

'It's just–'

'Ah.'

'Will you let me speak.'

Eleanor replied in a voice wooded with dark timbre, 'It better be yes or else you will incur my displeasure.' That meant something nasty would happen if he disobeyed. That could mean anything from weeks of the silent treatment to the plumbing of the bidet being tampered with.

'I guess he will be able to outrun them,' Houston finally said in defeat.

Eleanor smiled and said, 'They will be fine.' She looked at her watch. 'And I must go.'

'And if he has any sense, he will keep a low profile.'

'I'm sure they will be fine,' she repeated as she walked out of the kitchen. Once he was sure she was gone he kicked one of the base boards out from under a kitchen cupboard and searched for a jar of Nutella he had stashed there.

*

Maude smirked as she turned back towards the church while behind her Richard's Mini convertible motored away. As she walked on, her countenance became more serious as she considered what she had planned for the Temperance Trotters. Deirdre wasn't going to like it. Pippa, on the other hand, was going to love it.

When Maude arrived at the church, she saw a line of the more able-bodied grannies descending into the darkness of the crypt. It was going to be a squeeze. The less able-bodied would have to hear Maude's plan second hand. There was a buzz of superannuated electricity in the air and much chatting about what the meeting could possibly be about.

Maude saw the austere figure of Deirdre waiting outside: her confidant and her voice of reason. The problem with reason was that it was generally overrated by reasonable people. And Maude fully intended to be unreasonable. But she needed Deirdre on her side, which meant she had a bit of convincing to do. Maude walked up to her and said, 'Deirdre, I thought we might have a quick word before I speak with the others.'

'What is your Machiavellian mind cooking up this time?' Deirdre replied, as she appraised Maude. She saw the devious look on Maude's face and knew there wouldn't be any reasoning with whatever plan she was hatching: in any case, Maude always seemed to prevail eventually. They walked into the shade of an ancient yew tree, out of earshot of the others.

'I had a call from Sir Cecil. He has received word that Nipper has organised a Temperance Trotter walk through the Surrey Hills tomorrow, to protest against our wicked ways. One of their pet journalists will also be in tow.'

'Oh God. What are you planning?' Deirdre replied, squinting warily.

'Who knows what could befall them in those forests.'

Deirdre pressed her lips together as she weighed up what Maude was implying, before saying, 'Why does the fate of the Ninth Legion come to mind?'

'Actually, that's not far from the truth, except that unlike the Ninth Legion they will most certainly be seen again.' Maude went on to explain what her plan was and then waited patiently while Deirdre mulled her words.

'Do you really want to be entering into such a high-stakes game?' Deirdre contested. As she spoke, she noticed one of the Baker's Dozen perched on a nearby gravestone, stony-faced like a gargoyle.

'Fortune favours the bold. I'm sure Sir Cecil will be able to convince the PM to keep it quiet, which is exactly what we need. All he has to do then is get Tancred's taskforce involved. We use the old fort but make Nokney Village Hall the focus. That way we have a safety net in case things go wrong.' The fort in question was located in the woods and dated back to the Napoleonic era. It was largely unused by the Cartel, but for the odd bit of illicit storage.

'And Pippa will be a good girl, won't you, Pippa?'

'Promise,' replied Pippa, from inside the large yew behind Maude. They both looked up at the pagan relic. Pippa's large head emerged between dense branches.

'Any reason why you are up there?' Deirdre enquired. She became aware that there were now four of the Baker's Dozen perched around them.

'Lookout. Saw you with that Fleming fella, Maude,' Pippa said. The rest of the Baker's Dozen had materialised, not that Deirdre caught sight nor sound of any of them creeping up. She had a premonition of the nasty surprise that awaited the Temperance Trotters. None of them spoke, they rarely did. They just sat, perched, hung or squatted and listened and watched with jewel-bright eyes. Deidre shivered.

'I like him,' Pippa added. Neither Maude nor Deirdre had any doubt what 'like' meant in Pippa's book when it came to men.

Maude gave her a stern look and said, 'Well, you can put that thought straight out of your mind.'

Pippa's face dropped in disappointment.

'Will Houston's wife be with him?' Deirdre asked.

'No, she has commitments elsewhere.'

'Probably for the best,' Deirdre replied.

'We agreed we needed an endgame, and I think this is it. Do I have your support?' Maude asked Deidre, with an expression that was both sanguine and mischievous.

'It's crazy, but it could just be crazy enough to work. So, I guess I'm in. I'm just sad that Richard and the rest of the taskforce have to be involved,' sighed Deidre. 'They're just doing their job.'

'I know, but unfortunately they are integral to the plan,' Maude replied. 'Let's go and break the news to the others, and then we both need to make a few phone calls.'

FOURTEEN

For some infuriating reason that he was at a loss to comprehend, the hospital would not release Tancred until he had convinced a psychiatrist that he was of sound state and mind. This meant he had to endure questions like whether he had received counselling before or whether he had distressing thoughts; or to rate on a scale of one to ten did he…would he…had he…this and that. It didn't take long for Tancred to start doubting his own sanity.

The only answer he sorely regretted was concerning his relationship to his father, who he admitted to being scared of. He shouldn't have mentioned Hannibal Lecter, or the guinea pig incident, which was the last time he had been as scared as he had been at the joust. It had all started at the school fair pet competition when Tancred had shaved his guinea pigs to make them look like baby pigmy hippos. It backfired when the little brutes started hopping. The already suspicious teacher stated that baby pigmy hippos didn't hop and ratted him out to his father. Animals, omitting horses, generally brought out the softer side of his father. The sight of those shaved, sulky guinea pigs was the first time he could remember that sinister, shark-eyed look that his father seemed now so fond of giving him.

Once he had convinced them that his father hadn't beaten him every morning before his kippers, they moved on to a raft of other questions, probing for his inner fruitcake. By the time Tancred was grudgingly signed off by the psychiatrist it was Monday morning. He left the hospital in a foul mood.

Tancred's mood was not improved when he discovered from Rosie and Mark – the two constables who had drawn the short straws on who was going to pick him up – what Richard had accomplished in his absence. That was followed by another argument with the hotel manager about his lost luggage. The manager argued with much sighing and rising of the brow that they couldn't be held responsible for anything left in the corridors. The fact that Tancred hadn't been able get his trunk through the door seemed to have no bearing on the matter. By the time Rosie and Mark were driving the seething jumble of arms and legs that was Tancred to Guildbury, they were both convinced he needed to see a psychiatrist.

As Tancred stewed in the back of the van, a dark cloud of revenge began to settle over his thoughts. Those grannies were at the root of all his humiliations. They had made him a complete laughing stock. They had publicly shamed him. They must have been responsible for sticking him on that deranged pony to face that equestrian troll, which could only have been Pippa Blackwood. His insides twisted at the memory of Pippa bearing down on him and the raucous laughter from the crowd afterwards. He would extract his pound of flesh from them all, and the reckoning would start with the humbling of their repugnant champion.

Those crooked witches wouldn't be laughing then. They would learn to fear his sinister smile and shark-eyed look. But first he needed to go shopping, because he didn't have any clothes worthy of his stature.

The shadows of the day were lengthening by the time Richard and Joan returned to the office. Tancred returned from his shopping spree soon after. As he stepped into the office, he saw Richard and stopped.

Tancred gave Richard his best Hannibal stare. He'd been practising it all day on shop staff, not that it helped him buy any clothes and had caused him to be frogmarched out of one store by a security guard.

Seeing the look on his face, Richard said, 'Tancred, are you feeling all right?'

'Yes, damn it. I want a word with you in private, now,' Tancred demanded.

'Oh, OK,' Richard nodded, following Tancred out of the door, into the chow mein scented corridor.

'Who gave you the authority to move us all over to Guildbury and rent this squalid hovel of an office?'

'Ah, that would be the authority invested in me.'

'What authority?' Tancred snapped.

Richard gave him a guileless look. 'You were incapacitated. I could hardly seek your counsel under the circumstances because it would have been seen as a dereliction of duty.'

Tancred gave him a contemptuous look. 'I was not incapacitated.'

'The hospital said they couldn't discharge you until a psychiatrist had confirmed you were of sound state of mind,' Richard replied. 'See it from my point of view. Imagine how it would look in the police report, taking advice from a sectioned senior officer.'

'I *wasn't* sectioned.'

'But you were being examined by a psychiatrist, weren't you? They must have had their reasons. I wasn't to know where it would lead or if you were to ever leave the hospital. I was just trying to protect you and the reputation of the police force. Surely you understand that?' Richard finished in a reasonable tone. Tancred took a step back mentally and physically.

'It-it was a mistake. The bumbling fools made a mistake. I'm perfectly sane and-and rational,' he stuttered.

That's debatable, Richard thought, before saying, 'Anyway, given the situation, I'm sure you would have done the same things that I did. Dorsham wasn't working as a base for the team to work from. There were too many informants watching us and, worse, sabotaging us.'

Tancred had intended to give Richard a right royal dressing down, but he seemed to have an answer for everything. Seeing Tancred's hesitation, Richard said, 'Maybe it would be best if we kept the psychiatrist out of the police report. Things like that can put a question mark over one's career.'

'Yes, you would know all about that, wouldn't you, Richard. If I were you, I would make sure no one gets to find out about any psychiatrists.' Tancred gave Richard a knowing stare, or at least he thought it was.

'Yes, I do know all about that. And you know I have a vested interest in making sure you succeed. So, work with me. Use me for what your father intended, for your benefit. Surely that is in your best interests.'

'I know what my father said. But I am in control and I will decide how we conduct this operation, and you will do as I say in future, when I say it, or I will persuade my father that jail is the best place for you.'

Richard kept his face neutral, even though he wanted to thump Tancred. 'I've done everything you asked me to and have explained everything I did in your absence. What else could I have done?' Tancred cast around for an accusation he could lay at Richard's feet, but to his frustration he could think of none.

'Then make sure it stays that way,' was all he could think of saying. Then, looking for a new angle of attack, he added, 'I sincerely hope you have some progress to report today.'

Richard leaned on the banister as Tancred paced the landing. 'Yes. Now the office is organised, the team have started to look at how we can build the case against the Granny Cartel. There are a few promising leads we are chasing regarding the grannies' tiff with the Russian mafia, but so far that's all.' Richard didn't hold out much hope of finding anything that hadn't already been investigated. Maude and her crew were too cautious to leave much to pick over. 'Joan and I took the day to explore the area to see if we might come upon anything of interest.'

Tancred quirked the corner of his mouth and lifted his chin accusingly. 'I take it you had a pleasant day touring around with…is that the one that was practising her cricket strokes?'

'Yes.' On you, Richard thought to himself.

'...this Joan, while the others worked away in this,' Tancred sniffed the air, 'stinky office. And what did all this sauntering produce?'

'We discovered that the grannies meet in the church crypt in Okney. We also discovered that Pippa and her Baker's Dozen will be at the Whortleberry Arms in Okney this Friday, for chilli and karaoke apparently,' Richard lied. He had checked out the Wallisford Arms, which was in a village a few miles away from Okney. It was closed for a private party on Friday night, supporting what Joan had lip-read, but he wasn't about to tell Tancred the real name of the pub. Nor was he going to say anything about the note that the Grim Reaper had given him. Only he and Joan knew, and that was the way he wanted it. Tancred would almost certainly tell Godfrey. His suspicions about Godfrey were also something he wished to keep to himself. Let Tancred feed the disinformation and see if it incriminates Godfrey. He saw no benefit in lying about the crypt. He was pretty sure Maude had clocked him, which could potentially filter back to Godfrey anyway.

'That's decent detective work, Richard, not bad,' Tancred said and began to pace again. Richard's surprise was soon replaced with the uncomfortable sensation that something was churning in Tancred's sub-sapient mind.

'That is very good news, because I have decided that this Pippa and her bunch of scrags are our top priority. I want an all-out effort to find the evidence to arrest them, by Friday. With them out of the way, Maude will be easy pickings.'

'The chance of finding compelling evidence by Friday is pretty slim,' Richard pointed out. 'And we don't have the resources to apprehend them all in one fell swoop. Slow and steady wins the race.'

Tancred wasn't listening. 'You will just have to make do with what we have,' he replied. He descended back into his own thoughts for a while. 'I'm sure there must be a way,' he murmured. Richard wasn't sure who he was talking to. It certainly didn't seem to be him.

Tancred's face then lit up as though he had just experienced a Eureka moment. He brought his attention back to Richard and seemed as though he was about to say something when he stopped with a furtive look on his face. In Richard's opinion, a furtive look on Tancred's face was a distinct health risk. Before he could work out the reason for the look, Tancred declared, 'Just do as I command and tell the others to concentrate on Pippa and her Baker's Dozen.' Tancred walked back into the office without waiting for a reply. Richard followed him in, thinking how reckless evolution could be. At least he could console himself with the thought that there was no way they were going to find the evidence to nab Pippa and her gang by Friday. Time brought the hope that he could still find a way to influence Tancred.

Richard was blasted out of his passive-aggressive thoughts when Matthew came bounding up to him. 'I've just spoken with New Scotland Yard. They said that a member of the Russian Mafia has contacted them...saying that they have information that might help us put Pippa behind bars.' Matthew's beaming face moved between

Richard and Tancred. A look of triumph came across Tancred's face.

'The gods are indeed looking down on us,' Tancred bellowed with gleeful pompousness. Richard rather felt the looks were coming from the other direction.

'But…why…now?' Richard urged, scratching his chin. The news felt too convenient.

'Apparently, they heard the government was now serious about bringing down the Granny Cartel. There is a catch, though,' Matthew paused. 'They won't cooperate until Pippa has been detained. It seems they are terrified of her getting wind of anything while she is still at liberty.'

'As I said, we need to call in some help if we intend to bring Pippa and her gang in,' Richard said to Tancred, searching his face for missing links.

'And as I said, we will use what we have got,' Tancred responded. Tancred had a historical problem with help. At least help imposed on him. As far as he was concerned, it was almost never helpful. In fact, it was generally quite abusive and apt to claim all the credit. This was his time to shine and no one was going to muck it up.

'We need help,' Richard said flatly.

'Oh no we don't.'

'Oh. Yes. We. Do.'

'That's my final word.'

'It's not my final word,' Richard blurted. Matthew was standing in front of them looking like he was watching a tennis match. The others in the hinterland were doing the same, other than Joan, who had her hand over her mouth, looking suspiciously like she was giggling. 'Do you think they are going to come quietly, saying 'OK, we're bang to rights, please cuff my liver-spotted wrists'?

'Don't worry about how we apprehend Pippa and her scrawny thugs,' Tancred retorted. 'I have a cunning plan.'

Richard felt the gathering drops of excretion beginning to pat down on him at the sound of the words 'cunning plan'. It brought up all manner of terrors. 'What cunning plan?' he moaned.

Tancred gave him a particularly draughty stare, 'You just do your job and keep your nose out of mine. I will tell you when the time is right.' Richard heard 'Greensleeves' coming from Tancred's pocket. Tancred pulled out his mobile phone and turned dismissively away from Richard.

Richard gazed at Tancred in despair. A sickening realisation came to him that the debacle of the Medieval Fair had been a mere prelude. Not only did Tancred not have a Scooby-Doo what he was doing, he seemed intent on some hare-brained scheme which he had no intention of sharing. Richard had to remind himself that he wasn't exactly being open and frank either. But at least he had good reasons behind what he was doing. Tancred had probably never seen reason because it had seen him first and slinked off before it could be abused. He badly wanted to tell Tancred to go screw himself and leave him to it. But apart from it guaranteeing him a psychotic, and possibly overly amorous, cellmate, he had to think of the welfare of the others.

Richard's shoulders dropped and he began to shake his head. He predicted that Tancred was talking to Godfrey and, as expected, he was updating him on everything

Richard had just told him, along with his intention to raid the pub, minus any mention of his cunning plan. Richard walked over to a chair by the window and sat down.

If only he had held his temper, he wouldn't be in this mess in the first place.

FIFTEEN

Despite the early ascent of mist over the southern hills and the warm, humidified scent of the air predicting a balmy passage through the day, the assembled group of ramblers had come clad as erstwhile participants of the Duke of Edinburgh's award. Rolled-up anoraks roosted on top of their day sacks and water bottles protruded out of side pockets. Maps, compasses and reading glasses swung from their sweaty necks. Waterproof walking boots were also seen as a sensible precaution against the dry, dusty paths turning into streaming quagmires, given the meteorologists' typically cagey predictions for the capricious English weather. This was de rigueur for the Temperance Trotters; those Middle England freedom fighters who campaigned against all things tainted by cane or beet. The most extroverted of these champions of mineralised spring water and herbal teas had chosen bandanas over cloth hats and, unsurprisingly given the number of artificial knees, walking poles were also a common accessory.

Mervyn Nipper mustered his fervent band of eight women and ten men in front of the aptly named Temperance Hotel in West Street, Dorsham; a fitting venue for them to gather their strength, even though the hotel had long since fallen into intemperance. Across the road crouched the ancient beams of the closed-up King's Arms which seemed to leer at them through its leaded windows.

Nipper was wearing his usual leg-hugging running shorts and tight-fitting T-shirt. He liked to travel light, so his rucksack and other possessions had been palmed off on to the four portly members of his protective duty, who looked none too pleased about the prospect of a protracted hike through the countryside. Nipper made a mental note to broadside whoever was responsible in Specialist Operations for assigning protection. He had two female and two male police officers. And all of them had a BMI that as a measure of centigrade would have made a very hot day.

'This isn't my normal protective duty,' Nipper said to his lieutenant with an angry furrow of his eyebrows. 'They're a scandal to the force. Look at them!' Richard Dickey, Nipper's Trotter lieutenant, looked at the police officers with equal affront.

'It's a disgrace. They should be bounced out of the force,' Dickey replied.

'Apparently they were all that was available at such short notice,' Nipper retorted. 'Fear not my little Trotter (Dickey was just over five foot four inches), someone will be getting a drop in their pay grade for this. I can promise you that.'

Dickey harrumphed: 'Good thing too.'

Nipper turned to the gathering and in a raised voice announced, 'Now, ladies and gentlemen, let's show these grannies that we mean business. Our path is through the hills beyond.' Nipper stopped to check the map. 'And, er, past an old fort, to finish up at, at… Leith Hill.' He turned his animated face to Nick, the invited journalist who looked as though he was on a safari photo shoot. 'I think we should unfurl our banners and have a picture of all of us in front of the hotel.'

'Excuse me, sir, but is that such a good idea?' said Chris, one of the protection duty officers, as he appraised the growing crowd that was watching them.

Nipper gave him a withering look and said unpleasantly, 'Why ever not?'

'Well, it might be a bit, you know, provocative, being in the middle of Dorsham as we are.'

'Rubbish. We are here to show the way, not cower in the face of their corruption.' The group began to unfold their banners and line up in front of the Temperance Hotel. Passers-by looked at the flapping banners in horrified awe. 'End Sugar Debauchery Now!' read one. 'Lips That Touch Sugar Shall Not Touch Ours!' declared another. Anyone in the growing crowd of glowering locals could have assured them that there was no chance of that happening. The journalist seemed unaware of the seething tide rising up behind him as he framed his shots, at least until a flapjack smacked into the back of his head. He quickly finished his shots. 'Maybe best we get going,' he said, looking around nervously at the circle of angry faces surrounding them as he packed his bag. The Temperance Trotters seemed in agreement and quickly rolled up their banners and made ready to go.

'Onward, fellow Trotters, and let's show this cardigan-clad cartel that their days are numbered,' Nipper said defiantly and led off with the protection detail lumbering on behind. Chris' partner, Doug, turned to Chris and said as he snatched a miniature bottle of Southern Comfort from mid-air, 'I have a very bad feeling about this.' He considered the shrunken spirit bottle in his hand and then dropped it into his pocket.

'Me too,' said Gail and Rosalind in unison, the two police officers trudging behind them. Tucked away in a side alley were Frank and George, sitting in their Smart car, watching the group move away under an increasing hail of confectionery.

'There's nowt stranger than folk,' Frank muttered. 'Where'd you reckon they're off to?'

'My guess, Leith Hill,' George replied.

'Good luck to them,' Frank chortled.

'Aye, you're right there. It reminds me a bit of the lost army of Cambyses.'

'Of who?' Frank asked.

'The fifty thousand strong army of the Persian King Cambyses II, that disappeared in the Egyptian desert around 524 BC.'

'I'm not sure that really fits, what with all that sand and no trees,' Frank replied.

'Oh, all right, the Ninth Legion. Happy now? Anyway, God help them if Lady Blackwood has her way. That's all I can say,' George said.

The Temperance Trotters made their way to the village of Westcott and stopped on the other side of the village before making the ascent up to Leith Hill. Flasks were opened and mixed seeds and nuts were shared out as the weary protection duty traipsed up only to slump down wheezing on a fallen tree.

'It's all uphill from here,' Nipper said to them with a sadistic edge. They sullenly looked up at him and, in a show of professional pride, dragged themselves up from the tree.

'Don't worry about us, sir,' said Rosalind, none too convincingly. The rest of the Temperance Trotters were in a gentle debating fervour, covering subjects such as the iniquity of pension providers and the preponderance of polyester in twin sets, conversing amicably as only those who are the keepers of truth can do.

'Right, onwards and upwards. We're mighty, we're crazy! And we're never, ever lazy!' Nipper shouted, remembering his schooldays chant from St Finian's public school. And so off they all ventured, into the enfolding woods. It was a good wide track, with few obstacles to worry those with titanium knees and replaced hips. They chanted as they strode along the track, the sun dappling the mote-purled way ahead. The sappy smell of pine was in the air. Assorted wildlife observed their passing, thankful that the noises that accompanied them were also passing.

About half a mile on, the pines had given way to the boughs of oak and beech. The sunken track was lined with trees whose roots snaked down the banks. It was here that the group came to the sign that read 'Path Closed'. There was a detour sign pointing to a small path off to the right. After a flurry of maps, compasses, water bottles and the odd surreptitious look at a GPS, the group eventually decided the detour was still good for their destination. They set off down the single file path through the increasingly dense undergrowth, chanting as they did, blithely unaware that it wasn't just the wildlife that was watching them now.

As the sounds of the group faded into the forest, the flora along the path they had just walked along began to stir with fairy-tale menace. Bushes began to rise up and strange forest beings started to gently abseil down from the verdant canopy. Through the heavy camouflage, sinewy oak and olive-coloured limbs could be seen. Hard wrinkly faces looked down the track with remorseless intent. And then, in their midst, something akin to a shrubbery began to slowly ascend from the forest floor like a verdant apocalypse. Inside the foliage dwelt a monstrous apparition reminiscent of Rambo. Pippa's animalistic gaze pointed in the direction of the dwindling sounds of their unsuspecting prey. She grinned. She was thinking about the hunt, and fantasising about the celebratory 'cuddle' she so desired with Mervyn Nipper, although she knew Maude would chastise her for even thinking it. But the yearning was powerful, nonetheless.

Up ahead, the Temperance Trotters stopped. It took a few seconds for them to realise why. The forest had turned deathly quiet. A dark cloud covered the sun and sent them into an ominous half-light. In the silence Rosalind whispered, 'I see a bad moon a-rising.'

Chris grinned and whispered back, 'Something wicked this way comes.'

The smile was wiped off his face when the unholy peace was shattered by the sound of blood-curdling howls assailing them from all sides. The forest had not heard it's like in many a century. It was the howl of a wolf pack, with one long, bellowing, bladder-slackening, titanium-knocking ululation rising above the rest. Doug saw a rabbit on its hind legs looking at him with fearful eyes. It performed what he could have sworn was the sign of the cross before it scampered off.

As the howls tailed off, a stunned silence enveloped the group. In the interlude of peace that followed, Gail timidly asked, 'What was that?'

SIXTEEN

A few hours later, Rupert Littlefoot and his twelve-year-old son Malcolm were out for a walk in the same woods. Both of them followed the family tradition of tripping over a lot. Rupert had spent his formative years watching the ground closing in on his face or finding his father spread-eagled somewhere in the house. Rupert's father had met his untimely end as a speed bump on a pelican crossing. It could be said that the Littlefoot lineage was something of a blot on evolution's copybook.

It was no surprise then that Rupert was worried about his son's aspirations to go into forestry. Being a statistician, Rupert had calculated how many times he could fall over in his life before the big trip came along. He had calculated that he could live to sixty-three if he was careful. He had also calculated that Malcolm was unlikely to reach thirty if he went into forestry. But his son was adamant about his career choice. Rupert sincerely hoped that in time this dangerous aspiration would be knocked out of him. Meanwhile, Rupert would have to face the perils of these nature trails.

They had both tripped over a few times already that day. Now they came stumbling to a stop before a low depression. They gazed around in confusion at the scene before them. The ground was covered with rucksacks, water bottles, anoraks and the odd Ordnance Survey map. The items were strung out, suggesting that they had been hastily discarded. Rupert wrinkled his crooked nose. He had the distinct impression that the owners of these items were being chased. As they slowly descended into the depression, they found a rough ring of walking poles. Many had been snapped. By them were some torn banners. Rupert had the uneasy feeling that he was looking at the scene of a last stand. He anxiously circled around, fearing assailants with larger feet, or possibly four feet.

'What does "Debauchery now!" mean, Dad?'

'Never you mind, Son,' Rupert replied, picking over a few items on the ground: a truncheon, a notebook and a squashed hardboiled egg with a boot print on it. As he moved on, he came across a pile of wallets. There was cash still in them. He began to check for identification and his eyes widened when he came to one in particular. He quickly got out his mobile phone as he heard his son trip over behind him. Rupert had no reception, so he began to tentatively climb up the depression until he had a proper signal. Then he phoned the police. After his civic duty was complete, Rupert looked down the steep bank. 'Oh dear,' he said to himself as he tried to pick his way down. This was followed a few seconds later by 'Oh no.'

As Rupert cart-wheeled down the bank he thought he caught an upside-down glimpse of a wizened face illuminated under a bush. It, or rather he, rushed past too quickly for him to be sure and by the time he hit the base of the bank he was more than happy to believe it had been a trick of the light.

Under the bush in question, one of the Baker's Dozen called Agnes whispered into a mobile phone, 'The police have been called.' Only a solitary wood pigeon noticed Agnes rustling up the undergrowth to the rim of the depression before disappearing into the forest. A few miles away, Maude ended the call and dialled another number. In Whitehall, Sir Cecil answered the call.

*

The home secretary, Sir Cecil Mandeville-Blythe, entered the prime minister's private office to find Houston pacing around in a state of high agitation. He was pleased to see that Sir Archibald had also been summoned. That would make his job easier. The Metropolitan police commissioner looked up and said gruffly, 'Home Secretary,' followed by a nod. Before Sir Cecil could reply, Houston yelled, 'You won't believe what Nipper has gone and done now.'

'Been caught dipping his fingers into some Eton Mess?' Sir Cecil ventured as he sat down. After all, Houston had gone to Eton.

Houston ignored the quip. 'He's only gotten himself kidnapped in the Surrey Hills, along with that bunch of Temperance twits. I knew I should have put my foot down about this walk,' Houston muttered as he dropped into his chair.

'I'm lost for words.' Sir Cecil assumed the look of one who was really lost for words.

'We have already received a ransom demand from the Cartel. Basically, if we don't leave the Cartel alone, the hostages will be returned fat and spotty. Our representative must be sitting on the bench to the left of the war memorial in Dorsham at 11 a.m. tomorrow morning.'

Sir Archibald stirred and said, 'Nasty business, all this. Being force-fed all those empty calories day in day out. It will take its toll. The risk of malnutrition, not to mention cavities…and they actually had the cheek to drop the ransom letter by carrier pigeon onto the doorstep of No.10.'

'Yes, the cheek of it. The pigeon managed to escape with a bit of fancy footwork and was last seen flying straight for St James's Park.'

'Clearly a pre-planned move.'

'The letter is being examined as we speak, along with the bird droppings on the envelope.'

'Foul business, all of this,' Sir Archibald growled. Quite how the Temperance Trotters had got themselves kidnapped by a bunch of grannies was beyond him. And the protection duty would be lucky to find jobs as night-watchmen once he'd finished with them.

'This time the grannies have gone too far,' Houston hopped out of his chair and slammed his fist down onto his desk. 'This time they are going to face the full force of the law.'

'And rightly so,' rumbled Sir Archibald. 'Go in hard. You can't negotiate with kidnappers, especially elderly ones. Bad precedent: makes the government look weak, an easy target. Could backfire horribly.'

'I agree.'

'A slippery slope, I say.'

'I know that.'

'Every Tom, Dick and Harry will be having a go next.'

'Yes, yes,' Houston replied irritably.

'Tail wagging the dog, I would say.'

'I think you've made your point, Sir Archibald,' Houston said firmly. In the following silence Sir Cecil simply said, 'Hmmm.'

Houston's eyes sidled over to Sir Cecil. 'Is that all you've got to say?'

'Ah, yes, well, obviously the hostages must be found at any cost, Prime Minister,' Sir Cecil hesitated, 'that goes without saying, regardless of the damage it could do to your political career.'

'Pass that by me again?'

'I said that they must be found at all cost.'

'No, no, the little bit after that.'

'That goes without saying?'

'No, after that.'

'Oh, regardless of the damage it could do to your political career.'

Sir Cecil's words caused the hair on the back of Houston's neck to rise. 'B-But I would have thought the opposite was the case for a hostage rescue, assuming it was successful, at least,' he said.

Sir Cecil shifted in his chair and arched his fingers. 'Yes, in normal circumstances, Prime Minister. But because it is the Granny Cartel, it has left you in a decidedly awkward position.'

Houston lowered himself into his chair: 'How awkward?'

'Look at it this way. You know they have widespread popular support...'

'You don't have to remind me of that.'

'...whereas the Temperance Trotters, if you pardon me, don't. And then there is Mervyn Nipper.' Sir Cecil stopped to let his words ferment.

'I'm beginning to see what you mean,' Houston said into the silence. Nipper was hardly the most popular politician. There were even rumours that the National Union of Teachers had a contract out on him for his time as education secretary.

Sir Cecil took a deep breath and let out a slow, pained exhalation. 'It grieves me to say it, but one has to look at where the sympathies of the public lie. So maybe when I say at all costs, one such cost may be in entering into negotiations with the kidnappers, rather than using overt force which in turn could be used against you politically. Think of all those Twitter tyrants and Facebook fascists whipping up an online lynching mob. And who's to say that that mob won't decide to take to rioting in the streets?'

Houston's eyes were drawn down to the bronze statue of Margaret Thatcher swinging a brick-like handbag over her head on his desk. 'No SCO19 or the SAS, then?'

'The press would have a field day once they discovered you sent armed, highly trained combatants up against stick-wielding grannies.'

'Prime Minister, you can't negotiate with kidnappers,' Sir Archibald persisted, as Sir Cecil was hoping he would.

'You can when your intention is only to buy time. It has occurred to me that we already have a covert operation going on in Surrey. Run by the cream of Hendon, we were told. So, doesn't it make sense to use them to locate and free the hostages, while we buy them time. A more measured response,' Sir Cecil said, looking pointedly at Sir Archibald, who returned the challenging look, while silently cursing Sir Cecil. Sir Archibald had already considered this idea, and had quickly discounted it. Having Tancred even connected, let alone nominally in charge of something as critical as a hostage rescue, was too risky. Now the cream of Hendon was on the table, not SCO19 or the SAS, which had been his hope.

The prime minister sat back and mulled the idea, before saying, 'Yes, I like your reasoning. Any objections, Sir Archibald?'

Sir Archibald could think of one excellent objection, but he was hardly in a position to voice it. He did have Richard Fleming to keep Tancred in check. And if they could release the hostages *and* bring the Cartel down…he would just have to trust that Fleming would come through. Tancred's second certainly had plenty of motivation. 'I believe they can,' he replied, trying not to sound too tentative.

'Then I believe we have a plan. Now we need somebody to represent us?'

'I would consider using Godfrey Fairtrade as our negotiator. After all, he has a diplomatic background and is perfectly placed,' said Sir Cecil.

'I thought you considered him a bumbling fool?'

'Mervyn said he was a bumbling fool. I merely agreed,

which is entirely different.' Houston wasn't sure how, but he let it go.

'If you believe he's the best person for the job?'

'Yes, I do. As you know, I'm away meeting my European counterparts for the next few days. Would you like me to cancel my trip?'

'No. It will raise too many questions.' Houston turned to Sir Archibald: 'You have the go ahead to brief the taskforce.' He picked up the phone. 'Florence, get me Godfrey Fairtrade.'

The rest is up to Maude, thought Sir Cecil.

*

Richard pushed the remains of his seafood pancake around his plate as he half-listened to the conversation around him.

'It's not a power station?' Thomas said.

'No, you berk, it's Guildbury Cathedral,' Muhammad replied.

'I thought it was a funny place to put a power station.'

'I've never really believed in God myself,' said Matthew.

'Nor do I, but I believe in religion,' Alwin replied. Richard frowned and glanced at him.

'How can you believe in religion and not God?' Mark said.

'Simple. People *need* to believe. When the world goes to Hell in a handcart do you really want to be surrounded by a bunch of atheists? God, no. All they are going to do is tell you the truth, if they haven't already topped themselves first, that is.'

'Being surrounded by a bunch of dead atheists? Useful sign for a budding prophet.'

'Isn't atheism a godless religion?'

'I think Tancred's trying to chat up the waitress,' Jenny said. They all looked across the restaurant towards the reception desk where Tancred was standing, talking and laughing loudly at a reluctant-looking waitress.

'Yep, he is definitely trying to chat her up,' Matthew said.

'What's he doing now?' Mark said.

'I think he's showing her some of his martial art skills,' Emmeline said.

'No martial art I know of,' Joan responded.

'Kung-twit,' Jenny said. Richard opened his mouth to say something, but let it go and went back to pushing his food about. A mobile phone began to ring. He had heard that awful 'Greensleeves' jingle before…he looked up just as Tancred answered his phone. He watched as Tancred seemed to cower from the words coming out of his phone, along with lots of pointless nodding. By the look of his clipped replies, Tancred was being dictated to by whoever had called him. Richard concluded it must be his father. What he didn't expect was for Tancred to then smile once the call ended. That smile told him that something unpleasant was about to come his way.

Indeed, a few moments later Tancred motioned for Richard to come over. He pulled himself up with a groan and left the others in a heated debate about godless religions. He glanced back and his eyes met Joan's. She gave him a warm smile and returned her attention to the others.

Tancred led Richard to the car park, then looked around to make sure that they were alone before he spoke: 'We have been given a golden opportunity to prove our worth.'

'Opportunity?' One man's opportunity is another man's curse, Richard thought.

'Yes, an opportunity, for the perceptive among us. I have just come off the phone to my…to the Met commissioner. Earlier today, a group of Temperance Trotters led by Mervyn Nipper were kidnapped by the Granny Cartel while they were walking in the Surrey Hills and–'

'Whatever possessed them to go walking in the Surrey Hills!'

'Who cares. What matters is that we have been tasked with finding and rescuing them.'

'You've got to be kidding me. We are *not* a specialist hostage rescue team and we don't have the resources or manpower.'

A flash of tundra appeared in Tancred's eyes. 'Do you know why you will never rise to the top?'

'Maybe because I'm not full of–'

'Because you don't have the breeding. The British Empire was built by people, such as my ancestors, men who had a can-do philosophy. I should imagine yours were just skulking around looking for people to mug at the time.'

'I thought that was what the British Empire did,' Richard retorted. Before Tancred had a chance to respond, Richard intervened, 'And why would Maude kidnap the Temperance Trotters anyway? Why would she do something so…provocative?'

'I don't care.'

'You should.'

'In sport, you play your own game, not the opposition's.'

'This is not a sport.'

'But it is a game, and one you can't afford to lose. Tomorrow, I'm off to London and when I return, I expect to taste victory, understood? I'll leave you to tell the others.'

'Does this mean we are not raiding the pub?'

'It most certainly does not. That's the reason I'm going to London,' Tancred said and walked off before Richard could ask what he was planning. He placed his hands over his face and slowly drew them down, groaning.

At least there was one silver lining to the gathering clouds. Tancred was away tomorrow, which meant that he didn't have to make any excuses about where he was going. The woman the Grim Reaper had said would help them had finally returned his call. She was vague and cranky and wouldn't give her name over the phone. Richard could have imagined her being dunked into a pond in previous times, given her gravelly voice which was clearly owned by someone of advancing years. She invited Richard to make a house call the next day, although Richard wasn't really sure what to expect.

Richard was about to go back into the hotel when Chief Inspector Barrington called to confirm what Tancred had said. Barrington sounded pained when he conveyed a message from Sir Archibald, reminding him what would happen if Richard were to fail.

SEVENTEEN

The next morning, Richard sent Matthew and Jenny off to check out the site of the arboreal abductions to see if they could pick up any clues there. Alwin and Rosie were tasked with watching what happened to Godfrey at the war memorial. The rest were to look for potential locations where the Cartel might be holding the hostages. Richard knew that what they really needed was a bit of old-fashioned luck.

He asked for one volunteer from those six remaining officers to come with him to see the Grim Reaper's nameless informant. Five pairs of eyes looked away; one hand went up: Joan's. Richard wasn't sure what to make of that. He couldn't help feeling happy at the thought of being alone with Joan, even if it was tinged by thoughts of his own uncertain future. He pushed his feelings aside. He had a job to do. What he missed were the surreptitious smiles directed at Joan by the others when the meeting broke up.

Richard drove a circuitous route out of Guildbury to make sure they weren't being followed. This time, Joan was dressed in blue jeans and her old Exeter University jumper, which now clung to her rather wonderfully. On the journey their talk was confined to the case and Richard kept his eyes glued to the road, which then gave way to a rough track that travelled deeper and deeper into the Tardis that was the Surrey Hills. The track eventually came to an end next to a makeshift sign that read 'Galletting Hill'.

'Apparently, it's a little way up there,' Richard ushered, pointing to a steep path up ahead.

'I bet couriers love this place,' Joan replied. It had been raining on and off for most of the morning. Now the sun was shining down through a blue lens surrounded by swollen cumulus, its rays sparkling off every puddle and drop. As they moved under the trees it was as good as raining again. They stopped when they came to an oak gate gouged with the words 'Samhain Cottage'. Samhain Cottage was standing, or rather was slumped, behind it.

'It reminds me of something out of a fairy tale. One where children get eaten,' Joan mused.

'It is a bit creepy,' Richard agreed. The cottage was a chronological hodgepodge made up of sandstone, ancient bricks and gnarled timber; all crouched under an undulating tiled roof. Two small, dirty net-curtained windows stared back at them – between them there was a heavy oak door. The front garden was an herbaceous riot interspersed with deformed gnomish ornaments and wind chimes. They all made it look like their creator had been a tortured soul. In the middle was a well.

They opened the gate. Joan stopped at the well and peered down. 'Ding-dong bell,' echoed her voice into the dripping blackness. Richard tapped her shoulder and she looked up to see the door of the cottage silently swing open. At that moment the clouds closed in on the sun and they heard the rain charging up the hill behind them.

'I don't mind getting wet,' Joan said.

Richard lowered his brow and said, 'Oh no, you don't.' Joan gave him a mock scowl. They walked up to the door and dark beyond. 'Hello?' Richard said into the air. A voice immediately croaked back, 'Hello. Come in. I don't bite.'

As Richard edged into the door, he sensed some movement above him and twitched his head back just as a ginger limb swished past to scratch the ancient oak frame of the door.

'Don't mind 'im, e's 'armless,' said the muffled voice. Richard looked at the scratch left on the door frame. A large ginger tabby cat leaped down and appraised them carnivorously before wandering off into the shadows.

'Shut that door. Damp's a curse on me poor ol' bones.' Joan stepped in first and Richard reluctantly closed the door. The air in the cottage had an oppressive muskiness to it.

'This's who me friend sent me then,' said the voice from the shadows, as their eyes slowly became accustomed to the pale light in the room.

'I'm assuming you are referring to…the …'

'The Grim Reaper?'

'Aha. He said you might be able to help us?' Richard said. He heard a soft rattling laugh come from the corner. It didn't seem to have anything to do with humour.

'You wants to knows about Appleby.' It was a statement.

'Yes.'

'I forget myself. Let me get summat to drink.' Richard

saw the shape rise. Light flooded into the room as a door was opened at the back. Framed in the door was a small, squat old woman swaddled in an amorphous mass of drab and frayed clothes. Rather incongruously, she was wearing a pink woollen beret with a bright-pink pom-pom attached. When the elderly woman passed out of view, Joan turned to Richard and pulled a face. He just shrugged. While they waited for the old lady to return, they cast their attention around the room. It seemed that whoever the tortured sculptor was had also been an avid amateur taxidermist; specialising in the grotesque: the walls were covered with the disfigured heads of dead animals. Richard's eyes settled on the face of a rather surprised-looking Jack Russell. Meanwhile Joan had become transfixed by something else hanging on the wall.

'Richard… *Richard!*' He turned around and followed her line of sight. They both moved closer to the plaque and studied it in fascination.

'I really don't want to say what it looks like to me,' Joan whispered. 'Can you read what it says?'

There was a cough behind them. They turned around to see the old crone holding a tray. 'It says: "The moustache of General Custer". Don't know the names of the original owners of them four scalps surrounding it.' Richard and Joan both looked at her in blank horror.

'Me great-grandfather bought it off this Indian souvenir stall near that Little Bighorn River, a little while after the battle.' She put the tray down and pointed to a painting of a distant ancestor on the wall: 'Grab a seat.'

'How long have you lived here?' Richard asked, as they sat.

'Time enough to know where all the bodies are buried,' she replied with a soft cackle. Richard had the feeling that some of them had been used to stuff the sofa, and his nose was also quite supportive of the theory.

'Stuffed 'em all meself, of course.' A crooked finger was pressed into service as a tour guide. 'Self-taught, I be.'

'It's a very impressive collection,' Joan said in the kind of tone doctors use on patients in asylums.

'What you want to know about the old witch?' the old hag said, without preamble. Richard thought that was a bit rich. Richard was about to speak when she offered the words, 'Guess I ought to say why I'm 'elping yer first.'

'It would be useful to know, yes,' Richard replied. She picked up a bottle from the tray and filled up two sherry glasses. 'This is me own homemade wine; me very best. I calls it Noble Rot.' She proffered the two glasses expectantly. 'What's it made of?' Joan asked warily.

'Fungus.'

Richard didn't blink before replying. 'Unfortunately, we can't drink while on duty. I forgot my manners. I'm Detective Inspector Richard Fleming and this is Police Constable Joan Bailey.' The old lady looked a little perplexed as she put the glasses back down. Joan wondered if she was experiencing déjà vu.

'Call me Ishmael,' she said. 'I know. Me parents were a bit odd. Anyways,' she sighed, 'Maude. We went to school together, not that I 'ad any caring for 'er even then. She always thought 'erself was better than the rest. A right stuck-up bag o' frills, prancing around with 'er entourage of drawling suitors and 'angers on; she were always the popular one.' Her conversation then lurched in a different direction: 'My speciality is what yer might call game pies. That is, anything that is game enough to get close to me.' Ishmael flashed a wicked grin before concluding, 'Point is, used to have me own stall at that Medieval Fair down Nokney. That'll be until Maude got me barred.'

'Why?' Richard said.

Ishmael's tone was defensive in reply. 'It were an unfortunate set o' circumstances, I'd say.'

'Being?'

'Dog walkers should take better care of their animals. Find a dog on its own, well, in me book that's just a pampered stray. Good eatin' on a nice plump stray.' Richard's eyes moved over to the Jack Russell on the wall.

'A collar might be a giveaway,' Joan said.

'Eyesight's not so good these days.' Ishmael looked Joan up and down, squinting her eyes one at a time.

'How did Maude get involved?' Richard asked.

'One of me pies. Broke a tooth on one o' them new-fangled whatchamacallits for tracking pets. Didn't take the old bag long to put two and two together.' She harrumphed and said, 'Yer learn by your mistakes.'

'I see,' Richard said.

'Took it all personal.'

'Being a dog lover,' Joan added.

'Partly, I guess. Mainly 'cause it turned out to be 'er own missing dog.'

'Ahh. I guess that would do it.' Despite himself, Richard had to ask. 'And that dog?' nodding towards the surprised-looking Jack Russell.

'Ah, Bingo. I mean, that were his name. He were mine, until things got a bit tight one winter. Me best friend and gave me ten thousand calories in his passing, and a handsome rug to boot.' Ishmael tapped her foot on a small dog-shaped pelt under her feet. It brought a whole new meaning to Pedigree Chum, Richard thought.

'OK, I think I have ascertained your motivation for helping us. What I really want to know is if the Granny Cartel has any secret facilities around here?'

'What yer mean? One they could be 'olding those people in?'

Richard blinked and cautiously asked, 'What people?'

'The ones they nabbed yesterday.'

'You...know...about...that?'

'I've lived in these woods all my life. Not much I don't know about what's goes on,' she preened. 'The trees talk to me.' Then she drew her lips down and admitted, 'OK, it were more by chance. I were walking the trails yesterday when I caught sight o' that bunch o' wizened thugs and, yer know, the *other* one. They were pushing a load of bandy legs into a big old panel van.'

Richard sighed and said, 'Did you not think to call the police?'

'When that lot is involved yer *don't* call the police, least not the local 'uns at any rate.'

'Don't suppose you have any idea where they were taking them?'

'I'd lay money on 'em being under Nokney Village 'all.'

'Under?'

'Yep, under. Few years back Maude 'ad it excavated. It's

bigger underground than it is above ground now. Uses it for smuggling, you see.'

'Would you be prepared to make a statement about that?'

'Bugger that.'

'OK,' Richard could tell he'd be flogging a dead horse to push that idea any further. He followed up: 'Any other potential sites?'

'Can't discount it, but none that could 'old that lot, I reckon.'

Richard changed tack. 'What do you know about this Baker's Dozen and Pippa Blackwood?' A floorboard creaked from somewhere in the house. And again.

Her face darkened. 'Don't underestimate any of 'em.' Ishmael stopped as though she feared that the very forest would betray her for being a rat. She lifted her chin up, in a gesture of defiance and said, 'I'm sure yer know what you're doing,' but there was clear warning in her eyes.

Richard felt that their presence was no longer welcome. 'We should be going. Thank you very much for talking to us, you have been most helpful.' Ishmael looked away and nodded as they got up. Then she turned her wrinkled face to him and motioned for him to sit back down. Her eyes seemed to penetrate right into his soul. She stood and drew a stool up next to him, then sat and looked into his bemused face.

'I 'ave a sixth sense, yer know. Somethin' of an expert in matters mystical, I be. As was me mum and 'er mum and so on. Give me your 'ands.'

'Look, I don't–'

'Don't be a silly...' Ishmael cut in, firmly pulling his hands forward.

By this time Joan had retreated towards the front door, and was now sporting a crooked smile. Ishmael ignored her and screwed her face up in concentration. Richard looked over to Joan and grimaced. 'Don't look at 'er...look...at...me.'

Richard dutifully turned back to Ishmael with a demeanour of mild sufferance. For the next few seconds, Richard watched a range of emotions scud across Ishmael's face. One moment her face was full of dread, the next she was smiling. Eventually she released his hands and said rather morosely, 'Oh well,' and after a pause briskly added, 'Best yer get going now. I 'ave some chores to face.'

Richard looked at her in puzzlement for a second and then wiped his hands on his knees, got up and walked towards the front door, still looking rather baffled. 'Again, thank you for your...help,' he repeated. Then he stopped, turned back and said, 'Aren't you meant to tell me what you saw?'

Ishmael raised her eyebrows and said, 'So, you're interested in me mumbo-jumbo.'

'Humour me,' Richard replied.

Again, Ishmael seemed to weigh up what to say, before she replied, 'All I'll tell yer is this. When you're looking at death, roll to the right. Remember, to the right,' and then with a smirk, she added, 'Of course, I may be speaking claptrap.'

Richard paused, unsure how to respond. 'I will bear...that...in mind,' Richard replied, gradually turning to Joan who was surreptitiously motioning with her eyes to the outside world. When they got to the gate Joan said, 'What in God's name was that all about?'

'I have no idea,' Richard responded, looking back at the cottage as the front door silently swung shut. 'But I have this urge to put some miles between me and this place.'

'Do you believe her? Joan said as they walked briskly down the hill.

'I believe that her animosity towards Maude is real,' Richard said. 'Nokney Village Hall, I'm not so sure about. Something didn't feel right.'

'You think she was playing us?'

Richard hesitated before replying. 'Possibly.' His brow furrowed.

'What are you thinking?'

'I think someone else might have been in the house.'

'The creaking floorboard. I heard it too.'

'If we're right, someone was listening.'

Back inside the cottage, Ishmael spoke out loud, 'You can come out now.' The door behind her opened and a figure darkened the frame. 'What was the point of that little bit of improvisation?' Deirdre asked as she moved to a front window and peered out.

Ishmael scowled and said, 'It were just a bit of fun. Stop fretting, I did what yer wanted.'

'In future, keep to the script. We don't want any of your mischief-making,' Deirdre said. 'Just remember what Pippa will do to you if she finds out that you have been putting her beloved four-legged friends in your pot.' Deirdre turned and looked up at Bingo.

'I 'ave a pretty good idea,' was the surly reply.
'So, was it claptrap?' Deirdre asked, looking quizzical.
Ishmael sneered. 'Maybe. Maybe not.'

EIGHTEEN

Godfrey was woken by the hoover, accompanied by Lillian's singing. He recalled the term 'misery whip' being used to refer to a two-man cross-cut saw. At that moment it felt like a misery whip was being dragged through his brains. Lillian and his last stashed bottle of cognac from the night before were on one end and the memory of his conversation with the prime minister was on the other. His eyes crept over to the alarm clock. Eight-thirty. An ethanol fist punched into his temple as he rose up and he gradually moved his legs to the floor. There he sat, hunched on the end of the bed for a while, contemplating his furry frog slippers, wondering what on earth he was going to do.

The prime minister had said he was perfectly placed to be his negotiator. He didn't realise how right he was. Godfrey had nearly come clean about the blackmail. After all, the carpets in the corridors of power squelched with the political ordure that had been brushed under the metaphorical weave over the years. Only his fear of Maude's vengeance had stopped him.

Godfrey had been harassed by that Wotheringspot woman's incessant calls asking for updates. That buffoon, Tancred Punchard, had proven easy to extract information from. Richard Fleming, on the other hand, had been very cagey the few times he had bothered to answer his call. That worried him because it was clear who was the brains behind the taskforce.

He managed to shower, and then debated doing his new exercise routine, which consisted of kicking his old Lady Trim corset around the room and violently jumping on it. But he decided his head wasn't up to it. After the humiliation of the Medieval Fair, he had refused to use it anymore. As a result, Lillian hadn't been happy and his untrussed paunch had raised some eyebrows in parliament. How had his life turned so bleak so quickly? His mother had once said there was a harsh poetry to life. He hadn't thought it particularly appropriate at the time: it had been his wedding day.

At 10 a.m. Godfrey slipped out of the house, with his ethanol sparring partner thumping away at his head, and drove to Dorsham. By eleven o'clock he was sitting on a wet bench by Dorsham war memorial, crouched under an umbrella in the pouring rain. Apart from a few umbrellas on legs battling up and down the street, the pavements were deserted. He enviously watched a man and woman in the Waitrose supermarket opposite, enjoying a coffee in the dry – not that he would be foolish enough to drink coffee in an enclosed space surrounded by his constituents.

Anyone new to Dorsham who had stopped to look at the war memorial may have found their eye drawn to a blue door to the left of it. If it had read 'Toilet' on the front then no one would have given it a second glance, unless you happened to be desperate for the toilet. The door said nothing. It was just there, like some idiosyncratic municipal broom cupboard. Because of his time in the Dorsham Historical Society, Godfrey knew better. The door led to a labyrinth of tunnels that stretched across Dorsham. Given his position, there had seemed little benefit in pointing this out to the police.

After about five minutes he heard the door crack open behind him. This was followed by a 'Psst'. He turned to see a bony finger beckoning him from a crack in the door. He got up and stepped over to the door, whereupon a hand came out and dragged him in, before the door slammed shut.

Across the street Alwin cursed while Rosie grabbed a Waitrose shop assistant and said, 'Where does that door lead?' pointing to the blue door across the street.

The shop assistant looked at it and said, 'Dorsham caves. Dorsham is riddled with them.'

'Where do they come up?' Alwin asked.

'Dunno, everywhere, I think.'

'Thanks,' Rosie said and started towards the exit, but Alwin added, 'Waste of time. Let's just call the boss.'

In the beam of a lantern, Godfrey found himself standing next to a small lady wearing a parka and a quilted skirt. Over her head she wore a stocking and over that there was balanced a pair of large horn-rimmed glasses with a bit of sticky tape to hold them on. She was clutching the type of handbag that could swallow the contents of a small house.

'Well, don't just stand there,' she said, pointing down the flight of stone stairs. Godfrey began to descend the sandstone steps. Once they were at the foot of the stairs she said, 'Give me your phone.'

'Why?'

'Just do it,' she snarled. Godfrey gave her his phone. She dropped it on the floor and stamped on it.

'What did you do that for!'

'It's what they do in the films.'

'This isn't a film.'

'Shut it and stand still.' The woman proceeded to frisk Godfrey. She turned him around and pushed him against the rock. He felt a hand race up his leg and come to an eye-watering stop at his groin. 'Er, sorry.' She turned him back and after a few more cursory checks pronounced, 'You're clean.' Then she pulled a black fabric out of her handbag. 'Put this on.' Godfrey looked at the makeshift hood, a local bookstore's branded tote bag. 'It's all I had,' the woman muttered. He did as he was told and was guided the rest of the way in darkness, using his umbrella as a blind person's cane. After a short while they stopped. He heard a clunk followed by the heavy grinding sound of stone against stone. They moved a few feet and stopped. He heard the grinding sound again, this time ending in a crunchy thud. He wondered if it was the type of sound a pharaoh's burial retainers might have heard, above the wailing.

'Where are we?'

'Never you mind.'

Godfrey couldn't say how long they walked for. He knew the path went downhill for a while before it levelled off. He could also tell that the only light was coming from what he assumed was a mobile phone torch. Eventually they stopped and he heard the grinding sound again. His guide then said, 'There are some steps now.' He was led up the steps and suddenly there were other voices around him and the sound of a slot machine.

'Hello, Dory, like the stocking.'

'Keep your trap shut, Henry.'

'Oh, sorry, didn't realise you were on duty.'

Godfrey heard another voice say, 'Another noggin of best, James.'

Godfrey was shuffled out into what passed for daylight and bundled into a waiting car. After a short journey the car stopped and he was helped out. Dory pulled the tote bag off Godfrey's head and said, 'In there, they're waiting,' as she pointed to a building across the road. She then got into a car with a sign saying 'Dorsham Taxis'. He watched the taxi drive off as he unfurled his umbrella. He knew where he was.

There was one area in Dorsham that most residents of Dorsham dreaded becoming inhabitants of. He was standing in the middle of it. Entities congregate in certain areas for mutual interest. Technological companies cluster and financial institutions that huddle. Godfrey was standing in a cluster of like-minded concerns, a sort of public/private partnership all in the service of the frayed end of the mortal coil. Directly behind Godfrey were the cemetery and the crematorium under its own localised smog. On the other side of the road were a funeral parlour and the morgue to the left and a doctor's surgery and pharmacy to the right. Balancing the scales in the middle was an old people's home called Last Days Centre. It was considered to be the epicentre of the whole enterprise, although in winter the epicentre was more tilted towards the morgue.

Godfrey scampered across the busy road, thinking that old people's homes were like cats, in that you shouldn't keep one close to a busy road. He stopped and looked at the funeral parlour. The sign above read 'Wish, Bone and Ash'. Under that it read 'Dorsham Branch'. Under that was the company slogan: 'No one lays them down cheaper'. There were various offers pasted to the windows in front of some aesthetically placed coffins. 'Buy one get one free', '30-day free trial' and 'Reconditioned caskets available at knock-down prices'.

Godfrey walked into the Last Days Centre, making a note not to die anywhere near Dorsham. As he opened the door, the stale smell of boiled cabbage hit him. At least he thought it was cabbage. He could hear daytime television – *Cash in the Attic*, he guessed – thundering out of a room directly ahead. No one was at the reception desk. He noticed a whiteboard on the wall behind the empty reception desk. It had a list of rooms running down one column next to another column listing the occupant, followed by the room's estimated date of availability. His eyes moved across to a poster from a children's theatre company, advertising a play they were going to perform in the home called, 'From Here to Infirmity'.

Godfrey heard a whooshing sound behind him. He turned around to see an old woman standing by a pillar. She was wearing a paramilitary uniform, hobnail boots and a bandana above a vaguely homicidal face and was spinning a nunchuck with enough fluidity to give Bruce Lee's bones the fear. He had a suspicion that she wasn't an inmate and really hoped she wasn't a staff member. She flicked one of the sticks under her armpit and nodded down the corridor. 'Door at the end.'

Godfrey gave a nervous nod and edged his way past her down the corridor. He opened the door to find a common room smelling of yesteryear. There were two types of occupants. The first type was either wandering around, sleeping or in conversation, generally with themselves. The second type had a remarkable similarity to the entity in the corridor. They were all slouched over the armchairs with relaxed menace. At the end, in front of a bay window, sat Maude and the grizzly bear that went by the name of Blackwood. Her face was hidden behind a magazine called *Jane's Defence Weekly*.

'Godfrey. Please pull up a pew,' Maude said. A booted foot pushed a chair into the middle of the room. Godfrey sat down.

'I'll be brief,' Maude announced. 'You are here on the behalf of the government to offer a deal: something along the lines of "If you curtail your criminal activities, we in turn will leave you alone". Is that right?'

'Uh, pretty much.'

'Am I also right in my firm belief that your real purpose is actually to buy time while certain parties try to locate and free the hostages?' Maude continued. Godfrey looked down.

'Hmmm?'

Godfrey nodded.

'In that case I'm going to make another assumption.

Such forces as the SAS and SCO19 have been discounted for the fear it could result in a public relations disaster, which only leaves the taskforce holed up in Guildbury. I'm assuming they have been tasked with retrieving the hostages. Is that true? Bear in mind that if you lie to me, Pippa is going to cuddle you.'

'Please lie,' Pippa said from behind the magazine. Godfrey didn't want a cuddle, so he nodded again.

'I want you to go back to that miserable worm that we call our prime minister and tell him that the hostages are being held under Nokney Village Hall. You will say that you came by this information through a local police informant that you trust explicitly. You will convince him. If you don't, I will arrange a weekend break for you and Pippa. Somewhere romantic and secluded, I think. Trust me, it will be a scream.'

'It'll be a scream all right,' Pippa added helpfully from behind the magazine.

'You don't have to remind me of my circumstances. I'll do as you ask.'

'Yes, you will. Now, off you trot.'

A lot of tomfoolery for a short message, Godfrey thought. It was clear Maude was laying some sort of trap for the police. He got up and left without another word being spoken. Next, he was going to stand in front of the prime minister of his country and lie to his face. That thought wasn't mixing well with his hangover.

When he was gone, Maude picked up her phone and dialled Deirdre. 'Did Richard bite?'

'Hard to say with him. He brought the girl, Joan, along,'

Deirdre replied. 'Tancred had gone up to London.'

'Becoming a bit of an item, those two,' Maude replied and felt a pang of guilt. 'OK. From now on we mustn't let any of them out of our sight, just to be on the safe side,' Maude said.

'And you're sure you can rely on Godfrey,' Deirdre questioned.

'I've got the measure of Godfrey. He'll do as I demand.' There was no satisfaction in Maude's voice. Truth be told, she felt a bit of a cad.

★

Richard was locking up the office for the night when his phone rang. He looked at the caller and rolled his eyes.

'Tancred,' Richard said by way of hello. Richard hung on the banister as a smug Tancred said, 'Do you know why I am so excited?'

'Too many E numbers?'

'Oh no, you won't get a rise out of me.'

'Glad to hear it.'

'Can you guess what I discovered today?' The line went silent as Tancred waited for Richard to guess. Richard was exhausted and in no mood for games. Alwin and Rosie had lost Godfrey down a hole in the ground, the rest of the team hadn't been able to make any headway and Ishmael had thrown up more questions than answers.

'That your real parents were crack-heads from London,' Richard nearly said. Instead, he exhaled and said, 'Sorry, I'm no good at guessing games.'

Tancred sniffed. 'We have received a firm tip-off on where the hostages are being held.'

Richard straightened up. 'Oh, where?'

'Under Nokney Village Hall, it seems,' Tancred said. The corner of Richard's mouth turned up. As a police officer he had a healthy suspicion of coincidences. 'And just where exactly has this information come from?'

'The information came from Godfrey Fairtrade. Fortunate for us he has an informant in the local police force who's discovered where they are being held.' Richard slid his hand over his hair. *Maude, have you just overplayed your hand?*

'We will need to speak to this informant,' Richard said.

'We can't. They want to remain anonymous because they fear reprisals, but I'm confident that the information is sound,' Tancred went on. Richard could almost see the haughty rise of his inbred chin.

'It just seems a coincidence,' he replied as he went down the stairs to the landing window.

'What coincidence?' Tancred replied with irritation.

'Because that's exactly what the old woman told me earlier today,' Richard replied.

'Well, that just goes to prove…' Tancred stopped. 'Wait. *What* old woman?'

'The one I told you about after the Medieval Fair. Remember me telling you about the Grim Reaper giving me her number, saying she could help us. Don't you remember?'

'No, I most certainly do not!'

'Ah, that's the problem with concussion, plays havoc

with the old short-term memory. Anyway,' Richard carried on airily, 'I saw her today and she said the same thing.' Richard looked out through the landing window, across the street, to an old VW camper with its curtains closed. He had clocked it earlier in the afternoon: the occupants had given themselves away through the tell-tale movement of the curtains.

'Are you sure you told me?' Tancred asked.

'I'm absolutely certain I did,' Richard said. 'Are you still intent on raiding the pub?'

'What? Of course I am. My trip up to London has proved extremely fruitful. Take the fight to the enemy, that's what I say. With Pippa and her band in jail, Maude will be at our mercy, and if things go to plan, I might even let you keep your liberty, assuming you prove your worth.' Richard presented his middle finger to the phone. 'It would help if I knew what that plan was,' he said.

'You'll just have to wait and see,' Tancred replied.

'You're not planning to do anything…illegal…are you?'

'Absolutely not,' Tancred said and quickly followed it up with, 'Anyway, I'm having dinner with some old school chums tonight. I'll be back sometime tomorrow.' The line went dead. Richard put his frustrations about Tancred to one side and thought about what Maude was up to. His instincts were telling him that Maude was trying to lead them into a trap. The big question was why. To humiliate the government seemed the obvious answer, but if so, she was risking a lot just for a publicity stunt. Maybe she had become overconfident, and that had made her rash. But when Richard thought back to his chance meeting with

Maude in Okney, his instincts told him something else.

In the campervan across the street a Cartel member called Grace watched Richard leave the office with a rheumy eye through the curtains. She made a call from her mobile. When it was answered, Grace declared, 'Target on the move, repeat, target on the move.'

The mobile phone squeaked back, 'I heard you the first time.'

'Can I go now? I'm desperate for a pee.'

NINETEEN

The shaft of waning light from the small cut in the wall shone down on Nipper's upturned face, disembodied and haunted. Every now and then his eyes would dance around the ramparts of their sockets, searching out the darkness from within and without.

It was still raining outside: the heavy clouds were pressing their load into the ground in unrelenting waves. Rivulets flowed down the walls and disappeared into the shadows, but most of the cell remained dry. He had no idea where the others were and gave them no thought. He was too preoccupied with wondering what was going through his jailer's mind. Nipper had read the police reports and this giant fitted the dimensions. He knew precisely what threat she posed. It only took one petrifying smile through that gimp mask to convince him that her intentions towards him were dishonourable. He had shunned the food and drink he had been given, for fear of what it might have been laced with. He would rather starve than be chased around the cell whilst standing to attention.

He simply had to find a way to escape; but he had no idea how to do that. The thick walls of the cell and the heavy iron door only cultivated despair. He sat for a while with his thoughts chasing around and around as if they were stockcars on an increasingly wreckage-strewn track. The light dwindled, the rain poured and the rivulets burbled away into the dark. Then his mind came to a crashing halt on one thought. It was a thought borne out of desperation. Where was the water going?

Nipper had been given a small candle, a half empty box of damp matches and a bar of soap with a large bottle of Evian for washing and drinking. These items, along with an old tin plate he had found, currently represented all his worldly possessions. After a few frantic attempts with the matches, one caught and a slim flame rose into a small aureole of light, which he transferred to the candle. He moved the light around the walls until he found a trickle and followed its murky path. The trickle merged with other tributaries at the beginning of their long journey to the underworld or the sea. He tracked the flow to a pile of rubble, where a portion of the inner wall had succumbed to the passage of time. There was no pooling. He felt a pitiful flicker of hope, put the candle to the side and began to pull the rubble away.

Half an hour later he was squatting, filthy and exhausted. In one respect he was elated with what he had found. He was also horrified by the prospect. On the floor in front of him was an open grate. It had taken every maniacal drop of his strength to prise it open. He had the torn muscles to prove it. He drew himself closer to the black square in the ground. As he brought the candle near, the flame bent towards the void. He dropped a stone and heard a shallow splash a short distance below. He had half expected it to be full of water. Whatever the drain's original purpose, at least it wasn't collecting runoff. The flame also told him there was an opening somewhere, but was it large enough for a man to crawl through? Would the opening be barred? Would he be crawling into his grave? Would Mervyn Nipper, a minister of the British government, end his days like some doomed prehistoric miner wedged in a seam? The memory of those frenzied eyes peering out from that gimp mask gave him the motivation to find out.

It was dark now and the rain seemed to have subsided. He shuffled up to the void. The drain had the pungent bouquet of a compost heap with a pinch of animal excrement thrown in. He grabbed his tin plate and bar of soap and shoved them into his Lycra shorts. Then he tried to ease himself down into the hole, hoping that he might be able to touch the bottom with his feet, but his exhausted arms gave out and he fell. There was a wet thud followed by a yelp, and then silence. Then one four letter word came floating up from the void that neatly described his situation.

In the hole, Nipper looked up at the vague glow of the candle. The walls felt slimy. Even if he could find purchase, he doubted he had the strength to pull himself out. Put simply, if the drain was too small for him to wiggle through, the next person he was going to see was his jailer looking down at him. He began to fumble around, without any real hope. However, to his amazement, he found two large openings which seemed just about large enough to accommodate his slight sugar-starved frame.

As he was considering his options, the candle went out and he found himself in dank darkness. A few moments went by in silence before a few more fruity expletives came filtering out into the shadowy cell. He spent the next half an hour bucking up the courage to finally crawl into the drain. And so began his hellish journey to freedom. Metre by gruelling metre, using the tin plate as a spade, he began to burrow through the drain, telling himself that the outlet could only be a short distance away.

It took him until dawn to crawl the length of that stinking drain. In pitch black he dug through partial cave-ins, pulling or gnawing away roots in his path, fought through spiders and ants and was forced into a desperate fight to the death with a mole. But all the while through the sanity-shredding claustrophobia that faint breeze of freedom egged him on. By the time he eventually emerged half-crazed from the bracken-covered drain – scratched and bruised and with a nasty bite on his nose from the mole – the sun was cresting the horizon. It was soon smothered by a dark cloud, giving notice that the rain was about to return. Mervyn Nipper had escaped. No sooner than had he drunk in the clear air; he heard the distant bellow of his jailer. He hoped he would've had more time to flee before being found missing.

When Pippa found the exit to the drain all that was there was a grubby handkerchief, a bar of recently lathered soap next to a soapy puddle and a worn and dented tin plate. Nipper had crawled to freedom through fifty metres of foulness that few people could even imagine. She had to admit she was quite impressed. The problem was, Maude wouldn't be.

Pippa reluctantly made the call.

TWENTY

The elation of escaping had left Nipper as soon as he had heard the first sounds of his pursuers, who seemed to be getting closer by the second. He scrambled through the undergrowth in mounting panic, which because of the muddy ground made him look more like an unbalanced ice skater.

He lost his footing and skidded down a bank on his backside, until his buttocks were snagged by an old line of barbed wire. The result was remarkably similar to a fighter jet landing on an aircraft carrier, which proved to be a highly disagreeable method of deceleration. He had just managed to prise the last barb out of his buttocks when he heard the heavy bark of a dog that was clearly tracking him. He scrambled up and started running again.

Nipper stopped for breath at the top of a wooded hill. His spirit lifted when he looked down to see signs of habitation through the trees. He could make out a lake and what seemed to be a small hamlet to one side. He turned to see two of his pursuers coming into view at the base of the hill behind him. One was his jailer; the other was the dog. Even from that distance Nipper could see that it was a fearsome creature. He charged down the hill as fast as his tired legs could carry him toward the lake.

Nipper reached the lake, only to find that it was longer than he anticipated. A stream flowed into the lake on his left, on the other side of which was the hamlet. To his right a road ran across the end of the lake. There was no cover between the two ends and he knew that his pursuers would be cresting the hill at any moment. They would spot him for sure. His despair soon turned to terror at what punitive measures he might face for trying to escape. The last time he had been so scared was when his mother had caught him with a chopping knife, re-enacting the French Revolution on her vintage doll collection. He lurched one way and then the other before coming to the numb conclusion that he was wasting energy. His wretched eyes settled on the reeds that fringed the lake. Then an idea came to him.

Pippa came to the top of the hill and scanned the valley below. With the scent of the quarry in his nostrils, Burt barrelled down the slope. Pippa quickly followed, nostrils flared, sensing they were closing in. She was enjoying the chase, despite the harsh dressing down she knew she would get from Maude for him escaping in the first place.

Pippa caught up with Burt at the pond. The dog was milling around in confusion and that worried Pippa. For a moment she feared that Nipper had waved down a passing car. But she hadn't seen or heard any cars. No, he was still around, but where? She squatted down at the water's edge to try and pick up the trail. It seemed to go in both directions as though Nipper had tried one way and then the other.

As Pippa considered the situation, she plucked a topped

reed from the water's edge and spun around to study for movement on the hill behind. Surely Burt would have picked it up if Nipper had double-backed. Behind her some bubbles broke the surface of the pond where she had plucked the reed. Burt looked at them and cocked his head. He then watched as another reed descended into the water to emerge again a few seconds later missing its top. A jet of water squirted out of the top. Burt frowned and whined and started to pad around by the bank. Pippa turned around to see what had caught his attention just as a rabbit on the opposing hill broke cover and caught Burt's eye. Pippa followed his gaze and said, 'Up there?'

Burt thought about it for a second and came to the conclusion that if the boss wanted to go off chasing rabbits instead that was all right by him. He panted his approval.

'Go, Burt,' Pippa yelled. Burt took off around the pond, followed by Pippa.

A few minutes later, Nipper's head emerged out of the water to eye level. He circled round like a periscope and then rose cautiously to shoulder height. He saw Pippa rounding the pond, heading for the opposite hill. Despite the numbness of the cold water, he began to breaststroke across the pond towards the hamlet, while keeping a close eye on Pippa. If he could just get to a phone…

Pippa had disappeared from view by the time he reached the opposite bank. Nipper made his way to the first property, which was a honey-stoned cottage. He dragged himself over the garden wall and up to a back window and peered into a kitchen. A clock on the wall was edging towards five forty-five. Then he saw a cordless phone on the work surface in the corner. He didn't waste any time thinking about what he should do. He just picked up a large pebble and lobbed it through the kitchen window. He waited for a minute or two to see if had woken anyone. Satisfied that he hadn't, he lifted the latch and just about managed to drag himself in over a sink to flop down onto the floor. Once inside he took a few deep breaths and then scrambled over to the phone, wincing at his lacerated buttocks as he pulled himself up.

He was just about to dial emergency services when he realised it would be Surrey Police responding. To his frustration, he could only recall his home and office numbers. Paul, his private secretary, had just gone on holiday, so he called his diary secretary instead. Nipper was forced to listen to his diary secretary's excruciatingly slow presentation of the options. 'Come on, come on,' he groaned.

Beep.

'It's Nipper. We've been kidnapped, me and the Temperance Trotters, but I-I escaped sometime around dawn. I don't know what's happened to the others. I'm in the woods. It's all woods, all around. They were keeping me in some form of bunker. I'm by a lake. There is a hamlet at one end. There is a road at the–' After many years in politics, Nipper had picked up a second sense for people sneaking up behind him. Instinctively, he pirouetted to one side a split second before something whirred past his head and shattered the phone. He was now staring into the face of his assailant: an old man in a dressing gown with a moustache that reminded Nipper of a thatched bullhorn.

'Ha! Think you can break into my house, do you?' yelled the hoary householder as he lifted up his stick like a samurai sword.

'I can explain,' Nipper pleaded. Thirty seconds later, he toppled out of the front door, helped along by a well-aimed kick. In the interim he had suffered blows to his head and solar plexus, and had his nose tenderised by an electric whisk before receiving a swift kick in the nuts.

'I didn't fight for my country only to be burgled by vermin like you,' the old veteran shouted as Nipper limped off down the lane.

A few hundred yards down the road he met a car coming in the other direction. A stunned elderly woman looked at him through the windscreen as he fell upon her bonnet. He realised what he must look like, so he was relieved when she opened her door, popped open an umbrella and got out. 'Heavens…are you OK?' she asked.

'Please help me. I'm being chased,' Nipper said, trying to find his breath.

'Chased?'

'Kidnapped, I was kidnapped,' Nipper moaned.

'You were kidnapped?' The woman repeated. Nipper rather wished she would stop repeating everything he just said.

'Just get me away from here,' he barked.

'Get you away from here?'

'Christ, woman, are you a parrot?'

'A parrot? No need to be rude.' There was a pause and Nipper took the hint.

'Sorry.'

'I should say so. Going around being rude to people won't get you anywhere in life.' Nipper couldn't say that he had noticed. 'Besides, how do I know you are not some dangerous fugitive?' She said as she edged back into the car. 'You could be a crazed psychopath or a sex fiend for all I know.'

'A sex fiend…no, no… I'm a government minister,' Nipper said, frowning and waving his hands.

'That's not much better.'

'Please, I'm begging you.'

'Why didn't you try to get help from someone in the hamlet up the road?' she called from the open door.

'I did try, but they thought I was a burglar,' he replied, looked around for any sign of his pursuers.

'And why did they think that?'

'I broke in to use the phone. I was desperate. But this moustached maniac appeared and attacked me with a stick, and an electric whisk.'

'An electric whisk did that to your nose?'

'What? No, a mole did. It's a long story.'

'A mole did that to your nose?'

Nipper groaned. 'Please, they could be here any second.'

'You still haven't told me who kidnapped you.'

'The Granny Cartel,' he replied.

'Oh dear, I've heard of them,' she replied with mild concern. 'Are you sure?'

'Yes! Although they were all wearing gimp masks.'

'What's a gimp mask?'

'It doesn't matter,' he said in the most even tone that he could muster.

'Where did this moustached maniac live?'

'What? The first house you come to on the left.' Nipper was getting frantic with impatience and considered rushing her, but she looked too sharp-eyed to risk it.

'That's not my brother. I've just driven down from London to visit him,' before she added, 'I like to beat the traffic.'

'Are you going to help me or not?'

She took in the surrounding forests and then turned to him and frowned. 'On one condition.'

'What?'

'You have to get in the boot.'

'The boot!'

'I don't want to be seen with you, not if it's that Granny Cartel, and I don't entirely trust you either, what with all these electric whisks, mole fights and gimp masks.'

'But... OK, OK, I'll get in the damn boot!' Nipper muttered.

'And I don't appreciate that language.'

'Sorry, sorry.'

She released the boot catch next to the steering wheel and waited for Nipper to crawl in before she came around to close the lid. It occurred to him at that moment that she hadn't actually asked him who he was, why he had been kidnapped, or discussed where she was going to take him.

After a pause he felt the car move off and then turn around. As it travelled on, he began to feel a huge wave of relief and fatigue. He was going to make the Granny Cartel pay dearly for what they had done. Despite his cramped surroundings, he felt his eyes beginning to close. But they were jolted open when he felt the car lurching, as though it was going across some uneven ground. Then it stopped. He heard a car door open. Then he heard the splashing sound of heavy feet approaching, followed by some hushed words. Nipper felt a sickness grow in the pit of his stomach. He suddenly knew that he had been betrayed.

Outside, Pippa said, 'Lucky he landed on your bonnet.'

'Except that now he has seen my face,' Deirdre replied.

TWENTY-ONE

'I smashed it,' Major Reginald Atkins said in an emphatic voice.

'Yes, but was he talking to anyone before you smashed it?' Deirdre asked again in a loud voice. She was standing in the kitchen of Nipper's elderly assailant.

'What did you say?'

'I said, was he talking to anyone?' Deirdre shouted.

'Not that I could hear. Filthy swine bruised my shin, but I got him a good one in the goolies.'

Deirdre sighed, put her hand on the old gentleman's knee. 'If anyone asks, you never saw me,' and followed it up with a coquettish smile.

'The dirty beast bruised my shin not my knee. Hurts like billy-o.'

'Never mind,' she exhaled. Once Deirdre was outside the house, she called her nephew, apologised for the early hour, and said what she needed. When Andrew called her back, Deirdre was in her car, heading for Okney. He confirmed that a short call had been made and where to. Deirdre asked for the call logs be erased from the telephone network. Andrew Harrington, the director general of MI5, was happy to oblige.

★

As Pippa had predicted, Maude wasn't impressed.

'What dimensions of horrors persuaded him to drag himself through that hole, I do not wish to contemplate.'

'I didn't do anything.'

'If I find out that you've been up to no good, there will be Hell to pay.'

Pippa kept her eyes planted on her size twelves as she said, 'I haven't.'

'You *did* something.'

When Pippa didn't reply, Maude placed herself between Pippa's shovels and her eyes and looked up. 'DIDN'T YOU.'

Pippa cowered away from Maude like an abused circus bear. 'Maybe the odd smile,' was the sheepish reply. Maude jabbed her finger at Pippa as though it could spit venom.

'I knew it! What were you thinking? Haven't I told you before about smiling at defenceless men.'

'Sorry.'

'Did you show your teeth?'

'May have.'

'That would have done it. Let's just pray that this hasn't compromised the fort. Deirdre said he looked in a frightful state. Got himself into an altercation with a mole. And you know how ill-tempered they can get.'

Pippa nodded.

'Nasty. Tenacious little brutes. God knows how he managed to prise it off without losing his nose.' Pippa held up her pinkie finger as an explanation, which Maude chose to ignore. 'The problem now is that he has seen Deirdre's face.'

'Maybe, maybe not,' Pippa said. Maude was just about to start an angry tirade about Deirdre and houses of cards, when she saw that Pippa was smiling. 'Pippa, what are you plotting?'

When Pippa had explained her idea, Maude had to admit that she was quite taken with it. It was not without risk, but it could play well into her plans.

'And they will do this for you?'

'Yep.' Pippa knew that some men found it intoxicating being with a passionate woman who possessed the strength of a silverback gorilla. It was one of these moonstruck masochists that Pippa was referring to. 'Owes me his life as well.'

'Maybe you are more than just a pretty face?' Maude said. Pippa beamed, showing a mouth full of archaeological mysteries. 'Metaphorically speaking,' Maude muttered.

'OK, make it happen.'

'Thanks, Maude.'

'Hmmm.'

★

Five minutes later, Godfrey was listening to the phone in a trance of horror.

'He could have completely contradicted what I said.' Godfrey was keeping his voice down, despite the door of his office being closed. He was fairly sure that whatever Nipper described, it wasn't going to be Nokney Village Hall.

'Not completely. He was being kept separately to the others so he wouldn't be able to say anything about them,' Maude replied, knowing that would be of little comfort.

'They will smell a rat,' he moaned.

'Pull yourself together. Just find out what Nipper may have said and then get back to me. They'll expect you to make contact with your informant.' Maude paused. 'Just stick to your guns and–'

'And get blown out of the water. I could go to prison.'

'You will do as I say.' The cold edge in her voice caused Godfrey to turn pale.

'I will do as you ask,' Godfrey affirmed.

'The moment you hear anything, you tell me. And, Godfrey, just remember, if I go down so will you.' Maude put the phone down and cursed the fact that Sir Cecil was abroad.

Godfrey slowly put the phone back into its holster and lowered his head onto his desk. He was just wondering how long the news of Nipper's escape could officially take to reach him when the phone rang again. He looked at it from the corner of his eye with his forehead still planted on the desk. After a deep breath he rose and picked up the phone to hear the other half of the tag team from Hell.

'Godfrey speaking…good morning, Sir Archibald. There has…he has…he did…are you absolutely sure…I see…I will immediately.' Godfrey slowly put the phone down. His hand hovered over it as he tried to decide whether to call Maude. Instead, he drew his hand away and went to put his jacket on.

★

'It's Nipper. We've been kidnapped, me and the Temperance Trotters, but I-I escaped sometime around dawn. I don't know what's happened to the others. I'm in the woods. It's all woods, all around. They were keeping me in some form of bunker. I'm by a lake. There is a hamlet at one end. There is a road at the–'

'This message was left on his diary secretary's answer machine. The existence of the recording is being kept a close secret. Only us, Sir Archibald, the PM and a few government staff know of its existence. The voice has been confirmed as Nipper's and we are working on the assumption that he has been recaptured,' Richard concluded.

'What time was the call made?' Matthew responded.

'About ten to six this morning,'

'Has anyone tried to track the call?'

'I don't know yet. See if you can.'

'Where's Tancred?' Jenny said. Richard shrugged. 'I don't know. I'm waiting for him to call me back.' Sir Archibald had also been very keen to discover where his son was. Richard had told him that Tancred hadn't returned from London and wasn't picking up his calls. He was again reminded by Sir Archibald of his position, as if Richard needed reminding. Richard had wanted to raise some questions about Tancred's planned raid on the pub, but Sir Archibald hadn't given him the chance, being more interested in chasing his son down.

Privately cursing that lost opportunity, Richard clapped

his hands together and smiled. 'Right, if we can find this pond it might lead us to where Nipper was being held. So, let's get to it.'

Matthew soon discovered that there was no trace of the call on the network. By lunchtime, Richard and his team had narrowed their search down to a mill pond deep in the Surrey Hills next to a hamlet called Friday Street. They then broadened their search out from there, based on an estimated limit of how far Nipper could have travelled. Half an hour later, Richard was looking down at the symbol of a disused fort on an Ordnance Survey map spread before him.

'Let's find out what it is and who owns it,' Richard commanded. Muhammad ascertained that it was a Napoleonic-era fort but its ownership proved to be tied up like a Gordian knot of offshore shell companies. Richard decided that a disused fort in the middle of Cartel country, with so much secrecy attached to its ownership, was very likely Cartel owned. His gut was telling him that they had found what they were looking for. He also wondered what else the fort might be hiding, apart from captives.

'Jenny, Rosie, I want you get down to the local army surplus store and get some camouflage clothing. Then I want you to go and recce this fort. I want to know if it is capable of holding the hostages. Look for any signs that suggest they are being kept there. And, for God's sake, don't be seen.'

Richard had managed to work out an inconspicuous way to leave the office using the fire escape and a few valley gutters of neighbouring buildings that led to a short sturdy drainpipe they all were all capable of using as an improvised ladder down to some large bins. Going up was a little more hassle, but achievable. He told everyone to use the route in future when leaving and entering the office because he was certain they were now being watched from the front. It would make sense for Maude to be tracking their every move. Richard then walked into Tancred's office, closed the door and picked up the phone. When he came out Joan approached and enquired, 'Shouldn't we check out Nokney Village Hall as well, just to be sure?'

'No, I have a much better idea,' Richard replied as he headed briskly for the fire escape leaving Joan in his wake, 'If Tancred gets back before me tell him…tell him I'll be back.'

'OK, Arnie,' said Joan, saluting. 'Wild guess, you're off to see Ishmael?'

'Yes, but there is someone else I need to see first, and I need to see them on my own,' he said. With a smile and a wink, he left.

*

It had been Sir Archibald's psychotic smile that had persuaded Godfrey that the Sword of Damocles was on its downward swing. The smile had been accompanied by an insistence that Sir Archibald wanted to see Godfrey's informant at the earliest opportunity. Godfrey had left Sir Archibald's office in a state of panic. He called to make his excuses to his secretary and took the train home. By the time he got to Ewell, he had hatched a plan, albeit a lousy one. He stopped off at a grotty backstreet travel agent and bought two tickets to Valencia and reserved a room in a hotel in the centre for a couple of weeks, which he later regretted. The flight was leaving Saturday lunchtime. They were the earliest tickets he could get because of industrial action by air traffic controllers. He had been tempted to get an earlier flight to Tajikistan. He had friends in Dushanbe and Tajikistan had no extradition treaty with Britain. But he knew that Lillian would never set foot on a plane bound for Tajikistan.

In his frenzied state Godfrey had conceived the idea of going to Spain and then disappearing. If all those crooks could do it, so could they. He would tell Lillian they were going on a weekend break and once they were there, he would tell her everything, minus the bit about the girl from Wolverhampton. He would convince her that their lives were in danger, that they had no choice but to flee. They would reinvent themselves. With changed appearances and identities, they could start over again. They would liquidate their assets and live off the proceeds in the sun and he would grow a moustache to change his appearance. Quite how he was going to do all of this he wasn't sure, but if there was a will there must be a way. In fact, part of him was quite excited by the prospect.

He got home to find the house empty. He tried to remember what Lillian was doing today. It didn't matter, she was out and that was good. Two days to keep the wolves at bay. It felt like an eternity. He placed the tickets on the kitchen work surface and stood there deciding whether or not to phone Maude, and which would buy him more time: telling her about Nipper's message or not?

'Hello, Godfrey,' a man's voice said behind him. He whirled around to see Richard sitting at the kitchen table.

'How did you get in?'

'I'm a police officer. I know how to break into a house.' Richard stood up and walked over to him.

'You can't just break into my house.' Godfrey was aware that he was shaking. He tried to draw the tickets behind him, but Richard stayed his hand and took the tickets. He looked at them and then at Godfrey with a knowing smile. Ever since the Medieval Fair Richard had suspected Godfrey's relationship with the Cartel. Now he just needed Godfrey to admit it. Godfrey looked washed-out and scared and was planning to leave the country in the middle of the hostage negotiations.

'We are going on a–'

'In the middle of a hostage negotiation? No, you're running. You're running because you are terrified. Maude is blackmailing you, isn't she?' Godfrey crumbled. Richard gently took him by the arm and sat him down.

'I am not here for you, Godfrey. I won't stop you leaving the country as long as you do a few things for me. This is between you and me. Do you understand?' Godfrey's eyes wandered up from the table-top and he nodded meekly.

'How did you know I was here?' Godfrey said.

'Your secretary told me you had left for home. Does Maude know that Nipper left a message?' Godfrey shook his head. 'She knows he tried, but not that he succeeded. I haven't told her, but someone else might have. She has friends in high places.'

'Maude told you to say that the hostages were being held at Nokney Village Hall.' Godfrey nodded.

'Do you know where they are really being held?'

Godfrey shook his head.

Richard considered things for a moment before carrying on. He picked up the cordless phone and placed it in Godfrey's hand. 'I want you to phone Maude and say that you asked Sir Archibald if there had been any developments and he said no. If Nipper had managed to leave a message, given your situation, he would have told you. I also want you to tell her that the taskforce intends to raid Nokney Village Hall first thing Saturday morning.' Godfrey stared out of the patio doors into his garden.

Richard sat down next to him. 'Godfrey, do the right thing.' Godfrey's eyes dropped to the phone and, after a long pause, he exhaled and began to dial Maude's number. When she picked up, Godfrey said precisely what Richard had told him to say, adding only that the taskforce was still operating on its own.

Richard heard Maude's muffled response of 'Good,' before the line went dead.

'Thank you,' Richard said when Godfrey put the phone down. 'By the way, if Tancred calls and asks about pubs, tell him it was the Wallisford Arms you thought we were raiding, not the Whortleberry Arms. Got it?'

'If you wish,' Godfrey replied without inquiring why.

'What does she have over you?' Richard said. His tone was gentle, but Godfrey still gave him a wary look. He ran his hand over his mouth and then came clean: 'That skunk Clive Katnipp, MP for Runnymede and Weybridge, set me up in Wolverhampton. Maude was blackmailing me with the pictures and threatened me with the affections of her pet troll.'

'Blackwood?'

'What was God thinking?'

In Richard's experience, paradoxically, you couldn't always tell if a person was lying, but you could usually tell when a person was telling the truth. He could tell that Godfrey was telling the truth.

'Good luck, Godfrey,' he said and stood up to leave.

'You asked me if I knew where they were being held.' Godfrey looked up at Richard. 'I don't, but I have a hunch. There's an old Napoleonic fort in the woods. I know because I'm part of the Dorsham History Society. We never managed to get permission to see it. Could never find out who owned it or whom to ask. Nipper mentioned a lake and a hamlet. That sounds like Friday Street to me, which is not far from the fort. If that is any help.'

Richard nodded at Godfrey with appreciation and left as silently as he had arrived.

Forty-five minutes later, Ishmael opened her front door to find Richard standing there.

'Ishmael, you lied to me.'

A look of alarm flashed across her face. 'I done no such thing,' she replied defiantly. Richard pushed past her into her fusty front room.

'You know, while coming over here, I was thinking what would have persuaded you to help someone you obviously disliked so much. Then it occurred to me. Old Pippa, she does love her dogs and if she was to find out about your culinary preferences, I couldn't begin to imagine what she might do.'

Ishmael stood before Richard like a pillar of salt, betraying no emotion, which in itself told him all he needed to know. Richard's face hardened. 'Give me a reason not to tell her, Ishmael.'

Ishmael's head dropped. 'Why don't people just leave me alone?' Ishmael said and went over to plonk herself into her chair. A plume of dust and hair ejected upwards. 'OK, maybes they not under Nokney Village 'all.' She gave Richard a sideways glance. 'Don't mean I knows where they are.' Richard felt his phone vibrate in his pocket. He glanced at it to see that Tancred had resurfaced. He ignored the call and said, 'Oh, yes you do.'

'Don't.'

'Don't try my patience, Ishmael. I'll take you to Guildbury police station for questioning, if necessary. And I'm sure you don't want that?'

'All right, all right. I may 'ave a...yer know, a 'spicion.'

'That's better. I just need confirmation. Note the word confirmation.'

Ishmael scowled at him. 'Come for me she will, if she finds out.'

'She will not find out from me. I promise.' Richard placed his hand on his heart.

'There be an old Napoleonic fort at the end of a ravine called 'eifer's Deep, not far from the 'amlet of Friday Street.'

'That's all I needed to know,' Richard said.

★

Richard crept back into the office through the fire exit and surveyed the interior from behind an old filing cabinet with a coffee machine on top. He spied Tancred stalking up and down in his office, working up a lather on the carpet. Richard caught the attention of Muhammad and motioned for him to come over.

'He's not a happy bunny, boss,' Muhammad said out of the corner of his mouth, making the last two words sound like one.

'Don't worry about that. I need twenty-four-hour surveillance on the fort. I'm convinced that is where the hostages are being held. I have spoken to Jenny and Rosie. They need to be relieved, so can you arrange a rota with the others, myself included. I want two others to go to Nokney. I want them to be seen checking out the hall, but not to make it too obvious. Tell them to leave by the front door.'

'OK, boss.' Muhammad nodded and went to speak to the others. Richard emerged and walked towards the office while Tancred had his back to him and opened the door just as Tancred turned.

'You dirty rat,' Tancred said by way of hello. Richard looked down at his clothes and up again at Tancred. 'Bit harsh.'

'You squealed to my father about me being up in London.'

'Ah, your father managed to track you down then.'

'Judas.'

'Oh, come on, Tancred, what was I supposed to say.'

Tancred glared at him in impotent rage, but Richard remained impassive. 'Where've you been?' Tancred snapped.

Richard glanced at the others, who were surreptitiously watching them through the glass partition while pretending to work. 'I went to check out Nokney Village Hall. I guarantee you that the hostages are not being held there. There is nothing under that hall other than hard ground.' Richard had no idea if that was true, but he wasn't about to complicate matters.

Tancred regarded him with wary sullenness. He lifted his chin towards Richard and said, 'So where then? This fort you are suddenly so interested in?'

'I have spoken to Jenny and Rosie, who are–'

'I know where they are.'

'They have confirmed that the grannies are guarding it. They have also seen food being taken into the fort.' Richard made a mental note to tell Jenny and Rosie to back up his story.

'Fairtrade's source is a stooge, then. My father thinks so.'

'Maybe. I have arranged twenty-four-hour surveillance on the fort. They are there Tancred. I am absolutely certain.' Tancred sat down. He always found it difficult thinking on his feet.

'Are we really going to waste time and resources raiding this pub first?'

'Not this again,' Tancred growled.

'Are you intending to do anything illegal?'

Tancred looked fit to scream. 'I have already told you no. Blackwood is to be caught and arrested. She put a serving police officer, *me*, in hospital, where I was forced to talk about hopping hippos. She humiliated me at that ghastly fair. I was peed on by a Shetland pony! No one treats a Punchard like that and expects to get away with it. This subject is closed.' Richard stared at Tancred in amazement, wondering what the hopping hippos was all about, as Tancred tapped his fingers on the desk in suppressed rage. 'We will raid the fort, but only after the pub. And, Richard, you better be right.' He left the threat hanging as Richard left the office without a word. He had his own plans to make.

TWENTY-TWO

Gladys and Mavis sat on their off-road mobility scooters and watched the row of Highland Terriers going through a training session with Pippa and Burt on the common land by the church.

'How does she do it, Mavis?'

'She's a dog whisperer, that's what she is,' Mavis replied. They heard Pippa bellow, 'Comp*nee* Atten...*shun!*' All the dogs lined up and stood to attention, apart from one which seized the opportunity to sniff the line of bums. A barked order from Burt made it scurry back into line.

'I can't see a lot of whispering going on,' Gladys said.

'Doris says her Bella has gotten really big for her boots. Pushing her paws around like a truculent teenager, she says,' Mavis said. 'Keeps running off to hang out with the big dogs on the Fraser Farm. And Mildred says her little Gustav has been...what they call it when you're cast out?'

'Ostrichised?'

'That's it. I think? He's been ostrichised from the pack just because he's a little Pekinese.' They both watched as all the Terriers started limping around. The handful of the Baker's Dozen who weren't guarding the fort at Heifer's Deep were on the lookout in the trees. Gladys and Mavis headed for the church and descended the ramp into the crypt and lined up with the others.

A few minutes later, Maude sauntered down the crypt steps. The row of grannies stood, or sat up, to attention. Maude walked down the line, inspecting their distressed clothes and abused faces. When she had finished, she said to them all, 'Girls, you've done me proud.' She gave the order to fall out and walked up to Deirdre. It was Friday afternoon and the first fat drops of rain were beginning to fall. A storm was coming and, according to the handsome weatherman on the BBC, it was going to be a real humdinger.

'Now, we've got to take it all off and put it all back on again tomorrow at Nokney Village Hall,' Gladys moaned.

'Practice makes perfect,' Mavis replied.

Maude pretended not to hear the grumbles. 'They look marvellous, Deirdre. You've all done a fantastic job. Are the uniforms ready?'

'They are,' Deirdre said, but Maude could tell that something was on her mind.

'Out with it.'

'Do you think it is wise to allow Pippa and the Baker's Dozen to go out tonight?' she asked.

'It's not ideal, I know, but I don't want to dent their morale. The taskforce is being watched and we know they intend to raid the Whortleberry Arms tonight. And that's where they will stay, once we have immobilised their van. I will ensure that it will be the early hours before any breakdown truck gets to them. Tomorrow they will be tired and Tancred will have been humiliated again and desperate for some success at Nokney Village Hall. In the event of something untoward happening, Pippa and the Baker's Dozen will be alerted. They have been given strict orders not to drink too much. That's the deal.'

'I don't like being so reliant on Godfrey's word,' said Deirdre.

'I know, but, so far, he's been right. He's said they're on their own and our police informants have heard nothing to suggest otherwise. We know where they are and where they are going and will know the moment they move. Sir Cecil will be back soon. If anything is amiss, we will soon find out. Until then, let's not be too paranoid.'

Deirdre had learned to trust her instincts in her previous life with MI5, and now her instincts were telling her something didn't feel right.

Maude and Deirdre heard a commotion outside and quickly made their way up the crypt steps. Outside, they found the Revd Massey lying on the grass, having fainted at the sight of the grannies Maude had just reviewed.

'That's going to be an interesting conversation,' Deirdre commented dryly.

*

Tancred was studying a copy of the plans for the Whortleberry Arms in Okney when some activity in the main office caused him to look up. A line of soggy strangers was climbing in through the fire escape. For a moment he just stared at them, wondering if his eyes were playing tricks. Once he was confident that his eyes weren't deceiving him, he hopped out of his chair and charged into the main office.

'Would someone mind telling me what the devil's going on?'

Seven men (six of which were Polish bricklayers) and four women were lined up in front of him. 'Hired decoys,' Richard said. Tancred waited for a more in-depth analysis of the situation, but Richard seemed more interested in sizing up the new arrivals.

'Decoys?'

Richard thanked Alwin, who had been responsible for finding the body doubles, then walked over to Tancred. In a low voice he said, 'If you care to look outside you will see a camper van parked across the street that has been watching us for the last few days.'

Tancred had been oblivious to such a vehicle.

'Further down the street,' Richard continued, 'is an old Mini and an Austin Metro that I assume are intent on following us wherever we might go. We would prefer it if they didn't. So Alwin is going to take these good people in our van and head to another pub, dragging our groupies along with them. Meanwhile we are going to leave via the fire escape and use two other vans which I have rented to take us to our destination.'

'You mean to the–'

'Yes,' Richard intercepted before Tancred could say any more. Tancred went over to the window and peered between the blind. He pulled back from the window and sniffed. 'Why wasn't I consulted about this?'

'Maybe we should talk in private,' Richard said as he

motioned Tancred to follow him into his office. One of the Polish bricklayers leaned over to one of his mates while still looking at Tancred and said something in Polish, which roughly translated meant: 'Who's this joker?' Tancred was still sizing up the new arrivals with distaste when he realised that he had left the plan of the pub on his laptop and bounded after Richard. Richard was looking at the plan when he came in.

'You've got the wrong pub, Tancred. Pippa and her troupe are at the Wallisford Arms tonight.'

There was a small intermission while Richard's words percolated into Tancred's skull. When it finally registered, Tancred planted his hands on the desk and said, 'Hold on a minute, you said–'

'I said usually they go to the Whortleberry Arms, but because of our presence they had changed the venue. I explained all this to you on–'

'Oh no, oh no you don't. I know exactly what you said.'

'You can phone Fairtrade if you don't believe me. Ask him what pub you told him we were raiding.'

'I will!' And he did. And Godfrey dutifully said what Richard had told him to say. Tancred ended the call looking a bit frantic. Richard watched him in silence with that passive look that Tancred was learning to hate.

'Are they still having chilli and karaoke?' Tancred asked, with an air of nonchalance that Richard would have found comical in different circumstances.

'I don't know. Does this affect your plans?'

Tancred looked vexed by the question. 'Of course not, and if you don't mind, I have things to do.' Richard left without bothering to ask what Tancred was up to. He had half hoped that Tancred might put his need for revenge on Pippa to one side. But it seemed that the cunning chilli and karaoke plan was still operational. Richard had a hunch what it was.

At seven o'clock, Maude's spies saw the police taskforce make their way to their van through the pouring rain. The van left with the Austin Metro and Mini following in its wake. As the van travelled along, it went past more watchful eyes and accrued a bunched line of dim headlights behind it. As expected, the van drove to the Whortleberry Arms in Okney, followed by Maude's motorised corps, and parked up a little way from the pub. And there it waited and waited. They just sat there with their windows steamed up, in the crepuscular light of the storm. No one in the van noticed a small figure creeping up and pushing a couple of potatoes down the exhaust pipe with a walking stick.

While Maude's spies were focused on the wrong van, the rest of the taskforce set off for the Wallisford Arms, minus Emmeline, who had been tasked with keeping an eye on the fort. Tancred had spent what time he had available finding out as much as possible about the pub. He tried not to show his anxiety to the others, but his plan's success was now completely in the hands of fate, and Polish bricklayers, it seemed.

Richard had positioned himself across from Tancred so that he could keep an eye on him. First, he needed to catch Tancred in whatever stupid act he was about to commit. Richard would then have some harsh words to say (or whisper, depending on circumstance). Tancred would then be taken back, by the ear if necessary, to the waiting vans. Pippa would be left to her drinks, while Maude's eyes were eyeing up the wrong van. What better time to raid the fort?

Once they had parked the vans on a rough track a hundred yards down from the pub, Richard asked, 'Are you going to tell us what the plan is now?'

Tancred zipped up his long Barbour coat. 'The plan is for you to wait until I tell you otherwise,' he replied with characteristic pique and stepped out of the van. As he melted into the deluge, Richard said, 'I'm going to follow him. Joan, can you check in with Emmeline and see if she has anything to report at the fort. And get everyone to check their tasers.' Joan put her hand on Richard's and said, 'Be careful.' Richard returned the thought with a warm smile and a deep gaze into Joan's eyes.

When Richard arrived at the pub, he chanced a look into one of the windows and saw that everyone was dressed up as Mexican bandits. Pippa was on the stage, belting out her version of 'Los Compañeros' in a voice that reminded him of Tom Waits with laryngitis:

> *You see them in old Dorsham,*
> *Playing cards, drinking tea…*
> *And they're polishing chrome fenders*
> *On their little old Rover cars…*

The Baker's Dozen were hooting and shouting. A fusillade of party poppers went off. When the door to the pub was suddenly flung open, Richard was forced to hide behind a large planter as two of the Baker's Dozen came out onto the porch and lit some rollups. He realised he couldn't move without being seen and quietly cursed his luck.

Meanwhile, a very pleased Tancred was staring from the pouring darkness at a large pot of chilli con carne through a window at the back of the pub. Next to it was a pot of rice and next to that the rotund landlord was picking his nose. The landlord flicked his excavations away, only for it to land in the chilli. Tancred curled his top lip and wrinkled his nose, creating a fine impression of a disgusted donkey. The landlord proceeded to scoop out his nasal offering with a spoon and after a moment of indecision opened the window and casually flicked it out. The chilli-coated globular lump hit Tancred straight between the eyes as he ducked down. The window closed and the landlord went back into the pub.

Once Tancred had finished washing his face in a puddle, he saw that the kitchen was clear, slipped in and tiptoed up to the pot of chilli. Then he produced a bag of powder from his pocket and proceeded to stir it into the stew, while grinning at the simplicity of his plan. Richard could whine all he liked, Tancred thought, until he discovered that the drug was completely untraceable and wore off within an hour. That would wipe the smile off his face. Tancred relished the thought of seeing Pippa's face looking out from a cell, knowing that she had been foolish enough to tangle with a Punchard. And just in case she didn't realise it, he would tell her. Maybe he would laugh extravagantly in her face just to rub it in. Or maybe he would give her his own Hannibal Lecter stare.

As he stirred, Tancred listened to 'Los Compañeros' being butchered in the bar:

Once we were bold compañeros,
Bun running in the Surrey Hills,
On the beaches from Eastbourne to Bognor,
We were fighting for a sweeter day.

Tancred was just questioning the validity of the lyrics when he heard the landlord returning. He darted into the pantry behind him and drew the door close. The landlord came back in muttering about the infernal racket in his otherwise deserted pub. He gave his chilli a stir and tasted it, before pursing his lips in approval. Tancred, brandishing a large tin of Marrowfat peas, watched in horror through a crack in the door as the landlord then filled a bowl with chilli and began to eat it.

'Hey, Andy, where's our grub?' boomed a voice from the bar.

'Cut your hollering, Pippa. It'll be out soon.' Tancred watched as the landlord busied himself with plates and cutlery, eating a spoonful of chilli in between. He then took the plates and cutlery into the bar. Tancred made a dash for the back door. Unfortunately, he slipped on a wet tile and fell flat on his face. Just as he was picking himself up, he heard what sounded like a rolling pin thwacking against a meaty palm. He looked up to find the landlord standing over him with said rolling pin in his hand. The landlord was just about to enquire as to Tancred's present circumstance when his brow knitted together and he staggered, then dropped to his knees and fell forward onto Tancred.

About the same time, the two of the Baker's Dozen trapping Richard turned and went back into the pub.

Richard ran to the back. When he got to the kitchen door, he peeked in. The kitchen was empty. He withdrew when he saw one of the Baker's Dozen enter the kitchen.

'Andy?' The pint-sized bandido looked around the kitchen. Andy was nowhere to be seen. Her nose drew her to the chilli. 'Well,' she muttered, 'seems as though it's self-service.' 'Scarlet,' she yelled as she picked up the pot, 'help me with this chilli.'

Scarlet came in and looked around. 'Where's Andy?'

'I dunno, in the bog probably. Grab the rice, will you?' Jessabelle replied.

Jessabelle and Scarlet took the food into the bar. By now Pippa had been replaced by three of the Baker's Dozen croaking out a garrotted version of 'La Bamba'.

Richard peered into the kitchen again, wondering where Tancred had got to. His question was answered when he saw him emerge from the pantry and scurry towards the kitchen door. Richard grabbed him on his way out.

He was just about to interrogate him when his attention was drawn to a shoe just visible from the open pantry door. Richard marched into the kitchen towards the pantry, where he found the landlord prostrate on the floor. The gods of havoc looked down on Richard and added a crack of thunder just for effect. Richard walked back out to Tancred, grabbed him by the lapels and planted him against the wall. Tancred looked into a face distorted with rage.

'What have you done?' Richard demanded.

'I really don't know what–' Richard smacked him into the wall.

'Try again.'

'I didn't expect him to eat–'

'Please tell me you haven't done what I think you have done,' he said, thumping Tancred against the wall again.

'Too late now,' Tancred said and smirked. Richard pulled his fist back to hit him, but with a titanic effort he managed to stop himself.

As Tancred pulled himself from his grip he snarled, 'You have the impertinence to threaten me with your fists. You will pay for that, mark my words.'

'What have you given them?' Richard hissed. Tancred flourished the empty packet and Richard grabbed it from him. 'I have been assured it's completely untraceable and will wear off within the hour. So it will be their word against ours.' He gave a clipped laugh and looked disdainfully at Richard, 'You see, we Punchards are bred to win.'

'Where did you get this from?' Richard said in a deadpan voice. Whoever had given Tancred the drug had also helpfully stuck its name on the packet.

'I got it from an old school chum who works in the pharmacy department at UCL.'

Richard stared at the white label on the packet. He wiped his hands down his cheeks.

'Oh. Good friends, are they?' Richard carried on in the same dead tone, which was beginning to unnerve Tancred.

'Uh, yes. Well, actually, there was a bit of animosity at school after the roasting, but old boys–'

'Do you know what gamma-hydroxybutyric acid is also called, Tancred?'

'No,' said Tancred, apprehension creeping into his voice.

'G or Gina or Liquid E, amongst other things. And it is most definitely traceable, Tancred,' Richard said with a manic edge to his voice as he crushed the empty packet in his fist. 'Detectable for up to twelve hours and is dangerous in high doses, *especially* if mixed with alcohol.' Richard shoved the packet back into Tancred's hand. 'You idiot! You have just given a bunch of old women one of the most common date rape drugs on the market.'

'That swine.'

There was another clap of thunder and as it waned Richard realised the pub had gone quiet. He went through the kitchen and peeped into the bar. Then he stepped into the bar and looked around in dismay. The Baker's Dozen were flopped over various stools, tables and the bar top. Pippa was sitting on a bench seat with her chin resting on her chest. A large plate of chilli had been consumed and wiped clean. Tancred appeared next to him.

'My God. How much did you give them?'

Richard pulled out his walkie-talkie. 'You'd better get over here, now. Over.'

★

It was seven-thirty before Sir Cecil eventually managed to step off his plane. His flight had first been delayed by the storm and then redirected from Heathrow to RAF Northolt because of the air traffic controllers' strike. The summit with his European counterparts had been gruelling and he hadn't had time to keep abreast of events in the Surrey Hills. Once he was in his ministerial car, he used the secure line to call Godfrey for an update but he wasn't picking up. He tried the Met Commissioner, Sir Archibald, instead, and learned of Nipper's escape and the message he had left. Sir Cecil immediately called Maude on a burner phone.

*

Tancred faced a half circle of six angry faces outside the pub in the pouring rain.

'What are we going to do?' Rosie said.

'Rosie, phone Guildbury police station and tell them that we are bringing thirteen elderly women into custody,' declared Richard, thinking on his feet. 'Tell them to have a doctor waiting for us when we get there.' Jenny, Luke and Muhammad came out of the pub and walked up to the others. Jenny said, 'We've checked them all and they seem OK. They must be tough old birds.'

Richard pointed his finger at Tancred. 'And when we get to the station you will explain why we are bringing in thirteen comatose women into custody.'

'What are we going to do about the landlord?' Jenny asked.

'We certainly can't leave him here. I'll take him to hospital when we get to Guildbury,' Richard said, thinking what mess it had all become. 'We'll make sure the pub is secure before we go.' He turned and gave Tancred a cold stare. 'If this goes south, I hope you have a bad lawyer.' Thunder broke over their heads again as the rain grew heavier.

'What am I going to say at the station?' Tancred whined.

'How should I know? Just make sure they are locked up,' Richard snarled.

'Shouldn't we take them all to the hospital as a precaution?' Joan said.

Richard rolled his head around and grimaced as he rubbed his forehead. 'Yes, yes, I know, but we need them somewhere more secure than hospital and they all seem all right. We need them secure while we try to release the hostages. We have to put the safety of the hostages first, which is a lot more precarious now.' Richard prayed he was right about their sleeping beauties.

'I've spoken to the duty sergeant,' Rosie interjected, wiping rain from her face, wishing they could all talk in the dry pub, but Richard seemed oblivious to the weather. 'He wanted to know why we need a doctor.'

'You'd better phone him and explain,' Richard told Tancred. It was then that he noticed Tancred was shaking like a leaf and gaping up into the dark in terror. Tancred began to back away; his eyes fixed on something behind them and then turned and started to run. As one they all turned around. A bolt of lightning forked down behind the pub, incinerating a rabbit in a burrow and illuminating the snarling figure of Pippa standing right behind them.

Before anyone could react, both Rosie and Muhammad were flying on diverging trajectories through the air. Pippa lurched unsteadily forward as the others retreated before her. 'Tasers!' Richard shouted as he fumbled for his own. Jenny was the first to hit her. Pippa stiffened but on she still came, felling Mark, Thomas and Luke with one single swing of her arm. Joan and Richard fired, closely followed by Matthew.

Electricity began to arch around Pippa as her eyes went up and down like a confused slot machine while her jowls began to flap around her chattering teeth. Her hair was reaching for the sky. Unfortunately, so was the rest of her. To their combined horror she swung an arm down to grab the taser wires and proceeded to reel all four of them in. The tasers had done nothing, apart from seemingly giving Pippa a surge of power.

Through clenched teeth Joan howled, 'Boss, maybe some running might be in order.'

'What happens if you poke a grizzly bear and run for it?' Richard chewed back.

'Wild guess, nothing good.'

'Get the picture.'

'But bears can run up to thirty miles per hour.'

'They'd run a darn site faster if she was chasing them.'

At that moment Pippa got within striking distance and with an upward flick of her hand knocked Richard clean off his feet. His head hit the ground hard, and the world began to spin a sickening dance. He tried to focus, but his whole mind was a blur. He pulled himself up on his elbows, head lolling from side to side. Two Pippa-like shapes were now standing over him like Frankenstein's twin creations. He saw two dark figures leap on the monsters' backs and vaguely heard a woman scream, 'Get off him, you bitch!' The monsters pawed at them and swung around in a drunken frenzy until they eventually flung their attacker aside. Richard was gripped by a shuddersome realisation as he watched the monsters take hold of two pub benches and lifted them high into the night, ready to crash them down on Richard's head. Ishmael's words came back to him and with a titanic effort he rolled to the right, just before consciousness left him.

★

Maude had never been one for panicking, but Sir Cecil's phone call had left her as close as she had ever been. Her nerves were further frayed when she couldn't raise anyone at the pub. She dialled Deirdre.

'Are they still just sitting in the van?'

'Yes they are,' Deirdre confirmed, confirming what Maude feared. 'This doesn't feel right. I think we have been duped.' Suddenly, the penny dropped. 'The van's a decoy,' Maude said. There was silence down the line.

'Maude, are you there?'

'Yes,' Maude said.

'We've got to tell–'

'I can't raise them, Deirdre,' Maude said in a quiet voice.

'Hell's teeth. I'm driving over to the Wallisford Arms. I'll call you as soon as I know something.' Deirdre hung up.

Maude sat down and began to think.

★

Richard heard a distant voice call his name. As his senses returned, he felt something soft first touch his neck and then stroke his face. He opened his eyes and felt like he was looking up into a shower. A shadow passed over him and the shadow resolved into what he thought was the most beautiful face, despite it being etched with anxiety. Richard tried to rise up.

'Easy does it,' Joan said. 'You had me worried there.' Richard heard a groan to his left. He turned his head to see Pippa's face inches away from him. Jenny and Matthew were on top of her, busily applying a variety of restraints.

'How do you feel?'

'I'm about to find out,' Richard said, and, against her protestations, began to sit up. Both his jaw and the back of his head were throbbing. He noticed the shattered remains of the pub bench on the other side of Pippa. He felt nauseous and it obviously showed because Joan gently pressed him back down.

'Take it easy for a second,' Joan said. She paused, and then added, 'Lucky you rolled right when you did, else Pippa or the bench would have landed on you. It seems Ishmael was right.'

'If you say so. How long was I out for?'

'Just a few minutes.'

Richard was dreading the answer to his next question. 'How are the others?'

'Rosie and Mark have suspected fractures and Luke looks as though he has cracked some ribs, but they are all holding up. It looks as though Thomas has got a more serious break to his arm and Muhammad badly sprained his ankle when he landed. The rest of us just have cuts and bruises. It could have been a lot worse.'

Richard slowly exhaled and swore. 'You can thank Jenny for saving your life.' Jenny looked over and stuck her thumb up. Joan smiled at her as she said, 'The landlord had left a spade out by the fence. Jenny found a good use for it.'

'I vaguely remember someone jumping on her back and screaming,' Richard said. He heard Jenny murmur, 'And some.' Joan looked embarrassed. 'That would have been me,' she said, averting her eyes.

'Has anyone seen our wise and courageous leader?' Richard croaked. Joan looked behind Richard and said, 'Yep.' With a wince he craned his head back to see Tancred standing behind him, looking at them with a sullen face. 'Nice of you to join us,' he snarled and turned back to Joan.

'Help me up. We have some sleeping beauties and walking wounded to transport.'

TWENTY-THREE

Once Richard had found his feet and looked like he was able to remain standing, Joan said, 'We can't go on, not without help. I think we've all had enough. Pippa and her band will be out of jail before we know it and no one is keen to become a sleeping policeman in the woods.' Thunder could still be heard prowling in the distance through the steady drum of the rain.

'I agree. Can you load Pippa and the Baker's Dozen into the vans? I'll have a quiet word with Tancred.' Richard looked around, but he was nowhere to be seen.

Richard found Tancred at the back of the pub pouring the remains of the chilli con carne into the undergrowth. Richard found himself wondering if any of the furry local forest dwellers would eat it. Some hours later the landlord would return to find the answer littered around the garden.

'Just how are you going to explain how these thirteen women came to be drugged,' Richard said to Tancred's back. Tancred looked around briefly and went back to finish cleaning the pot out.

'Come here to gloat?'

'Because of the fight with Pippa, we now have five injured police officers. You have to ask your father for help.'

'That's my decision to make, not yours.'

'None of us are prepared to raid the fort otherwise.'

'You must be loving this.'

'Did you hear what I just said?'

'I will not be held to ransom. I'll have them drummed out of the force and you flung in prison.'

Richard took a step forward and checked himself. 'Pull your head out of your arse and listen to me. We have to rescue the hostages and we have to do it fast. It won't take Maude's solicitors long to realise that the arrests were illegal. But we have to make sure they can't spring them until tomorrow morning because none of us want to be in the woods when they are released. Those are your two jobs. Remember, this is your mess.'

'They'll do as they're told,' was Tancred's stubborn reply as he headed towards the kitchen. Richard grabbed him by the arm and growled, 'If you don't, it's over and I won't make any bones about what happened here.' Tancred pulled his arm away from Richard's grip and regarded him with unalloyed venom.

'I'm not bluffing, Tancred, and nor are the others.' Richard walked off without waiting for a reply, moving to within a foot of where Deirdre happened to be hiding in the sodden undergrowth. Furious, Tancred saw a dissolving mound of chilli con carne on the ground and gave it a vicious kick. He stamped around muttering and cursing for a while, before stopping short, as if gripped by some ingenious idea. Deirdre watched this transformation and watched him begin to sneer. Tancred spoke to the darkness that Richard had dissolved into, 'Damn you and damn my father. You want back-up. I'll give you the *crème de la crème*. You'll see!' He laughed at the thought of his next ingenious plan.

Tancred retreated back into the pub kitchen, leaving the coast clear for Deirdre to get back to her car which was parked down the lane. She knew that what Tancred did next might well decide the fate of the Cartel. The sensible thing would be for him to call his father. But Tancred was a narcissistic fantasist who was petrified of his father. *And when men are desperate*, thought Deidre, *they do stupid things*.

Richard found the others heaving Pippa onto the back of a van. 'Talk about heavy bones,' Matthew said. It was all the more disconcerting having Pippa glaring at them, a couple of bar towels wedged in her mouth to muffle the growl.

'Once we've squeezed this lump in, we are good to go,' Jenny said, adding, 'Thomas is in a lot of pain, boss.'

'We'll have to swing over to the hospital first, then,' Richard replied.

'Better keep that one under our hat, what with the state of this lot,' said Matthew, motioning to their sleeping charges.

Joan chipped in, 'Alwin called. Someone stuck a spud up the exhaust. The breakdown truck is apparently going to take hours, so now he's surrounded by some very disgruntled decoys.'

'If they are still stuck when we drop this lot off, we'll go and get them. There's not much else we can do. Anyone find the keys for the pub?' Matthew dangled a pair of keys in front of Richard.

Richard took the keys and was about to head back to lock the pub when his attention was drawn to a car parked down the lane. It hadn't been there before. The phones they had collected had been ringing and no one had been answering. Maude would know something was wrong by now. He therefore assumed it was one of Maude's spies watching them. It occurred to him that the actual justification for arrest relied on the Russia mafia knowing Pippa was in jail. He wanted to scream.

Richard found Tancred standing at the bar with a noggin of whisky in his hand. He tilted his glass when Richard came up to him and said, 'Purely medicinal.'

'I assume you paid for that?'

Tancred theatrically swung his tumbler up, spilling whisky onto his hand. 'We must all pay our debts. Mustn't we?'

Richard was in no mood for Tancred's casual threats. 'Put the damn drink down and get up. We're going.'

'The vans are finally loaded, I take it.'

Richard stared at him for a moment before he walked to the front door and waited for him to move so that he could lock up. Tancred turned towards the optics and downed his whisky as he stared at Richard through the mirror behind the bar. Then he pushed himself away from the bar and strolled out of the pub. There was an insolent confidence about him that gave Richard pause for thought, but he had more pressing matters to worry about.

When Richard got back to the van Joan said, 'Emmeline just called.' Richard's face dropped. 'Don't worry. She just phoned in to see how things were going. I think she's quite pleased now that she was stuck under a sodden rhododendron bush watching the fort. She wanted to know if she's going to be relieved any time soon.'

'I'll call her when we get to the station.' He looked back at the car parked down the lane. 'Let's get out of here.'

Deirdre watched the vans leave. She had already called Maude and told her what she had seen and heard.

★

The bark of a fox outside broke through the weary tick of the grandfather clock in the hall. It was approaching the wee hours and Maude felt she finally had a good idea what had happened. The van in Okney had indeed been a decoy. What Deirdre had seen and heard had convinced them both that Pippa and the Baker's Dozen had been drugged by Tancred and it was clear that Richard and the team were none too happy about it. Maude's lawyers were now laying siege to Guildbury police station but the duty sergeant, who was not on the Cartel's books, was running plenty of interference to prevent them from springing Pippa and the others too quickly. Maude's lawyers were nevertheless confident they would be out first thing in the morning.

'We have to buy time,' Maude said to Deirdre.

'We have no one to defend the fort and I think moving the hostages is too risky at present, regardless of what Tancred is planning.'

'Agreed. What do your instincts tell you about what Tancred is up to?'

'My hunch is that he will not go to his father for help.

That leaves me scratching my head about where he will go. It's not as though he has any sway in the police. I'm a little stumped.'

Maude pulled herself up, went to the window and stared up at the moonlight beaming through the broken clouds. 'Tancred will be thinking the fort is undefended too.' She turned her face to Deirdre. 'Given Tancred's record, there's a decent chance that whatever he's planning will be the last straw for Richard and the others.'

'Who knows. It's possible, but we certainly can't rely on that happening. One way or another we are going to be facing something.' Deirdre paused and then ventured, 'There's a lot in the local community that would come to our aid.'

'I want other people's involvement kept to a minimum. It's our fight and we are going to fight it and if we fail, it should be us who pays the price, not well-meaning people.' Maude moved her face back into the moonlight. 'If we can just hold out until Pippa and the others are released, then we may still be able to follow our original plan. Just modified for the fort.'

Maude began to smile a wicked smile, made all the more sinister through the dimmed rays of a clouded moon.

'What are you hatching?'

'Something to make Pippa proud.'

*

Richard had no idea what Tancred had said to the duty sergeant at Guildbury Police Station, nor did he care.

Whatever it had been, it was working because Maude's lawyers were being kept at bay, at least for the time being. Matthew had drawn the soggy short straw for the night shift at the fort. He left Tancred to sort out their resource issues while Joan drove Richard to hospital. She had insisted that he was checked out. Apart from cuts and bruises, he had a mild concussion, which he shrugged off. It was eleven o'clock by the time he got back to the station, where he found Tancred waiting.

'I have arranged for the extra manpower,' Tancred said loudly, puffing out his chest. 'They will be with us before dawn breaks.'

'They can't get here earlier?'

'No.'

Richard was too tired to argue. He paced over to the station's grubby vending machine and bought a cup of tea. 'And extra manpower means what exactly?'

'It will be enough. That's all you need to know. Now that I've done what you have asked, I expect you and the others to go to the fort before first light to secure the area. I'll follow on once the new additions to the taskforce have arrived.'

Richard took a sip of his tea and looked Tancred up and down. He was buzzing, which worried Richard. 'I think we'll all wait for the others to arrive.'

'Do you think I'm lying to you?'

'I don't know, are you?'

Tancred attempted a smile. 'Have it your way.' Tancred turned and walked off. He hadn't lied, but he hadn't been completely truthful either. He certainly hadn't contacted his father. That prospect still filled him with dread. He felt he had to redeem himself before his father got to find out about the pub. Luckily, he had come up with an audacious solution and felt quite proud of his lateral thinking. After all, they were only coming up against some wizened old bags, and once the hostages were released no one would care about what he had done at the pub, least of all his father. All that mattered was the victory, by whatever means. History would shine down on the Punchard name, there would be songs about his deeds against the evil Cartel crones, and no one, least of all Richard, was going to stand in his way. Destiny was calling and he would be there to greet it with open arms.

★

It was midnight by the time the Granny Cartel had fully assembled at the church of St Morwenna in Okney. As it was a full meeting of all forty-eight elderly members of the Cartel, the crypt was too small to accommodate all of them. An uneasy babble suffused the packed hall as everyone took their places. Once her audience had been reduced to rustles and murmurs, Maude walked up to the pulpit and let the silence hold for a few moments as she surveyed the room. 'Tonight, as some of you may know, Pippa and the Baker's Dozen were arrested by the police. And we have good reason to believe it was done illegally.' Maude waved down the furore this news caused. 'Our lawyers are confident that they will be released by tomorrow morning, but we think the police taskforce will take advantage of their absence to attack the fort before first light in an attempt to release the hostages. And when they come, we are going to be waiting for them.'

A buzz went through the hall again. Maude again lifted her hand for silence. She splayed her arms towards her audience. 'How can we stop them I hear you say.' As one, the hall replied, 'Yes.'

Maude began to nod her head. 'What we are going to do is this…'

Her speech was punctuated with many intakes of breath and whisperings of disquiet. When she finished, the mood in the hall wasn't especially optimistic. But Maude knew how to turn a crowd. 'Sisters, why are we here?' A subdued murmur went through the hall. 'We are here to fight against injustice,' she said emphatically, before raising her voice: 'We are here to fight for our way of life.' Maude glared around at her congregation. 'And we shall prevail.'

As her voice washed over them, a few lone voices shouted: 'Hear, hear' in support. 'We may be old, but we have the hearts of lions. And together we will make a mighty roar.' The audience were now warming to her words. Cries of 'Yeah' could be heard around the church. Someone shouted, 'Let's kick some butt.' Another shouted 'Cupcakes for ever!' More joined in as the excitement rose. Maude then went for the jugular.

'We shall fight to the end. We shall fight with growing confidence and growing strength in the air. We shall defend our way of life, whatever the cost. We shall fight in the beech woods, we shall fight on the cricket grounds, we shall fight in the fields and in the streets. We shall fight in the hills. We shall never surrender!' Maude's voice rose in a blitzkrieg of passion. Tears were now streaming down her cheeks. Ever since she was a small child Maude had been able to cry on cue. The effect was incendiary to the emotionally charged church.

In a voice cracked with emotion she said, 'And, in time, they will again say that never was so much owed by so many, to so few.' The hall erupted in whoops and cries. Maude wasn't the only one crying now.

'When they attack tomorrow, we will be waiting. Tomorrow our objective will be reached. Tomorrow the chains of oppression will be smashed. Do you believe me, Sisters?' Maude cried out towards all below her with arms stretched high and tears rolling down her face. The church erupted in cheers. Fists were punched into the air. Backs were slapped. Hankies were thrown and lost. Deirdre was sure there were a few knickers amongst them. There was a lot of hugging going on, with muffins and flapjacks held aloft.

'Then let's get baking, because time is short!' Maude cried out again above the ferment. *That should do it*. She caught Deirdre appraising her.

'What?'

'I can't believe you went full Churchill,' Deirdre responded.

Maude shrugged. 'It worked, didn't it?'

TWENTY-FOUR

Saturday morning seeped into existence with only a few of God's most puzzling creations aware of its existence. Those who weren't still dribbling on their pillows went about their business as if bound by a vow of silence. The exceptions to this rule could be found in abundance in the clink of Guildbury police station. At least that was what every nerve end of the duty sergeant was telling him. Anyone would have thought they had cornered the market on rabid early morning risers.

By now, most of the shell-shocked flatfoots on the nightshift possessed a fine dusting brought on by the constant pounding of two meaty anvils against one cell door. Recently added to this were the pornographic utterances from the other cells of her compatriots. The thin blue line waited for the end of their shift, anxious to be out of harm's way before those jail doors opened. Those on Maude's payroll also played their part, preying on their colleague's fears, whispering that hollow martyrdom awaited the ones on the wrong side of that line.

Despite resolute and repeated assurances from the Metropolitan inspector with the blond mop that the nation's very security was at stake, that Metropolitan

Commissioner Sir Archibald Punchard himself would step in to give reason for the incarceration, no calming call from above had been forthcoming.

Regardless of the obvious dubiousness of the arrests, the duty sergeant had stood firm against the pressure on him from all sides. This was mainly down to Pippa's lack of understanding of human nature. Threatening to make breakfast of your jailer's organ was not much of a door swinger, especially when it was abundantly clear that she meant it. It was now about survival, as he bitterly admitted to himself. All night he had fended off Maude's legal serpents as they writhed and sunk their twisting fangs into his resolve, but the end of shift was drawing near. Quiet, desperate calls to his now-terrified wife meant that the car was packed, the children loaded and her alarmed sister in Newcastle informed of their impending arrival. The pounding continued as the baying broke over him. His thoughts turned to that inspector with the blond mop of hair. He spat on the floor.

*

The spit landed on the floor at the same time as old hands in the Surrey Hills laboured to complete Maude's defences at the fort. Sore eyes and old hands tended ovens, baking from midnight till near dawn. Others tended sore fingers from darning. Cartel sympathisers were watching the hotel the taskforce was staying at, ready to give warning. One farmer had been happily pressganged into the cause, working under arc lamps to do the Cartel's bidding while a vintage fire engine had been lent by a villager sympathetic to the cause. Old bones creaked with iron resolve.

*

Richard, Joan, Emmeline, Alwin and Jenny emerged into the pre-dawn of their hotel car park. Matthew was still watching the fort and the others were still nursing their injuries. The five police officers stretched away the exertions of the previous night as they loitered. Richard's absent gaze passed over the trees until he happened upon a couple of wood pigeons on a branch above looking down at him with passive orbs and the odd bit of cooing. He pulled his eyes away from the mesmerising orbs and phoned Matthew.

'How are you doing?' Richard enquired.

There was a pause before Matthew responded in a flat voice, 'Oh, I'm fine. A bit cold, but at least it's not raining.'

'I appreciate you sitting out there. I assume there has been no movement at the fort?' Richard's voice radiated out from the speaker of Matthew's phone.

'No, apart from a few sentries I've seen no sign of life,' Matthew replied, his eyes fixed on the scarred creature immediately before him.

'I guess Maude's hoping Pippa and her lot will get sprung before we get there.'

'I guess so, boss,' Matthew said, slowly moving his foot back from the drawling jaws. 'I guess so.'

'Well, hopefully we will be there soon, so long as Tancred gets his arse into gear.'

'Yes, hopefully. See you soon.'

A rather haggard-looking Maude bent down from the shooting stick she was sitting on and said, 'Well done.' She drew Burt away adding, 'and sorry. This gives me no pleasure whatsoever, young man.' Matthew grunted in response.

'Before I gag you again, have a cupcake.' Maude stuffed a red velvet into Matthew's mouth. As a police officer Matthew was sworn to uphold the law, but the cupcake did taste delicious.

Richard frowned as he held the phone away from his ear. Something about Matthew's voice troubled him. Then again, he thought, he was bound to be a bit subdued after spending a night under a shrub.

By 6 a.m. Richard was pacing around the car park in high agitation. Repeated calls to Tancred had been met with repeated assurances that reinforcements were on their way, and that he would be down shortly.

'Boss, it's getting mighty close to the witching hour,' Alwin said.

'At this rate Pippa might get to Heifer's Deep before us,' Joan added.

Emmeline sneezed and said, 'He assured us that they would be here an hour ago.'

'I'm well aware of what he said. I've had enough of this,' Richard declared and was just about to go in and drag Tancred from his room when Tancred walked out of the hotel. He sauntered up to the others and looked at the remains of his beleaguered and broken taskforce with a dismissive air. 'They're here.'

'Great, Maude will never see them coming,' Richard retorted. Tancred responded with a smug smile and pointed to the entrance, 'There.' At that moment two late model Range Rovers and an Aston Martin pulled into the car park. The cars parked up and twelve young men jumped out, dressed in polo shirts, salmon shirts, with a couple of blazers thrown over shoulders and leaned on the bonnets with a casual arrogance. One hulking man towered above the rest. The team stared at the new arrivals in disbelief. Mouths literally dropped. Richard lifted a finger up and slowly pointed it at the assemblage before pressing his lips together and turning his finger towards Tancred.

In a slow, deliberate voice Richard said, 'Who…are… *they*?'

'Keen as mustard, they are,' was Tancred chirpy reply.

'Shall we have another stab at *who* they are?'

'You asked for extra manpower and this is it,' Tancred replied, plumping up his chest.

'I must be dreaming.'

'Keen as mustard, they are.'

'Yes, I got that bit. Would you mind telling me, without any reference to condiments, just who the hell they are?' Richard said.

'Don't you take that tone…' Tancred stopped when he saw the look on Richard's face. 'They are all members of the YPC, who have patriotically lent their time to assist us.'

Richard's right eye started to twitch. 'As in…the Young Progressive Conservatives?'

'You are looking at the future leaders of our country. And they don't mind getting their hands dirty, I can tell you. A fine body of men, wouldn't you say? I pulled a few connections in the party. It's not what you know, but who you know.' Tancred slipped Emmeline a wink, which she returned with a disgusted look. Tancred began to move towards the group, but Richard stepped in front of him. 'Tancred, could I have a quiet word?' he said, placing his arm heavily on Tancred's shoulder. Tancred tried to shrug it off but Richard's fingers dug into his collarbone. Tancred had the distinct impression that Richard's fingers were itching to creep over to his windpipe.

Once Tancred had been manoeuvred away from the others, Richard began in a menacingly conversational tone, 'I take it, my narcissistic friend, that you didn't speak to your father.'

Tancred managed to free himself of Richard's grip. 'I don't need my father to fight my battles.'

The day, and indeed history, could easily have taken a different course had Joan not stepped between Richard and Tancred at that moment. She placed her hand on Richard's chest and shook her head. He looked into her cautionary eyes and the red mist began to dissipate.

'Everything OK, old boy?' They turned to see one of Tancred's new arrivals standing behind them. The others were standing to the side watching them closely.

'How the devil are you, Barty?' Tancred asked, ignoring Richard and Joan. He slapped palms with Barty. 'Right for a fight, Tankers,' Barty said as he greeted Tancred. 'I went to boarding school with his brother, Seb. Both of our families came over on the boat together,' Tancred added to the speechless officers.

'What boat is he talking about?' Jenny said out of the corner of her mouth to Emmeline.

'Doesn't he mean yacht?' inserted Alwin.

'I don't know, but they're giving refugees a bad name,' Emmeline muttered back and sneezed.

'And this strapping lad...' Tancred said, waving his hand at the statuesque giant, '...is Rodney Montagu, BUCS inter-universities MMA heavyweight champion,' Tancred winked at Richard, 'just in case Blackwood joins in the fun.'

Richard looked up at Rodney and said, 'She'll kill him.'

'Well, let's just see what happens when she comes up against a trained fighter,' Tancred said.

Richard spoke at Rodney, 'Have you ever imagined what it must be like for a fly in the grip of a sadistic five year old?'

Rodney thought it was probably a rhetorical question, but he answered it anyway. 'No,' he said, unsurprisingly.

'You'll find out once Blackwood gets hold of you.'

'He's just trying to frighten you,' Tancred chimed in.

'For once we are in agreement. Rodney, she'll rip your arms off and beat your head in with the soggy ends.'

Richard sat down on his haunches and cupped his head in his hands. He sat swaying for a few moments before he finally rose to a standing position, drawing his hands across his face; something he felt he was doing all too often. He smiled at Tancred's new recruits, nodded and smoothed out the crumples in his jacket as he did so. When his eyes eventually settled on Tancred he said, 'So here we are, Wyatt Earp and his posse.'

'Yee-hah,' Jenny whooped, earning a withering look from Tancred. He was about to defend himself when Richard butted in. 'But this is not the Wild South East and this is not going to happen. Tell this bunch of inbred half-wits to get back in their Chelsea tractors and go home.'

'Now look here–' Barty began to say.

'Shut it!' Richard exclaimed.

'They will do no such thing,' Tancred replied, the green wood of his resolve quickly hardening into iron purpose. 'Quit if you want, but we have no intention of running from a fight.'

Richard's anger got the better of him. 'What, like you did last night, when you ran away from Pippa rather than standing your ground like the rest of us. You're pretty courageous when you're not the one having to do the fighting.' Richard moved his face right up to Tancred's. 'They're only here because you didn't have the balls to call Daddy. If we send this lot over to the fort, Maude will just add more hostages to her collection. It's over, Tancred, and so are you. And I'm going to make so damn sure of it.'

Tancred's jaw dropped, seemingly in preparation to catch his eyes which, at that moment, were perilously close to popping out of their sockets. Such an affront in front of his equals was a humiliation that a man of such standing couldn't endure. He could almost hear the hushed voices in the London clubs, dissecting his honour, an autopsy of his worth and, by extension, the worth of his lineage.

As his rage took hold, he did a strange tight-fisted little jig. Eventually he managed to utter, 'How-How dare you! If it wasn't for an accident of birth, you would barely have held down a job as a janitor. Even then you'd probably have found a way to screw that up.' Richard knew he was going too far, but a whole week with Tancred would have pushed Mother Teresa to the edge of homicide. Tancred drew his chin up, and his eyes narrowed to machine gun slits. So here it was: pistols at dawn. Joan was actively trying to get between the two of them again. Tancred took aim and fired.

'Now you can see what I have to work with. This boorish thug has been undermining me from day one. You all saw a glimpse of his aggression and it is not the first time, I can tell you.' Tancred turned back to Richard, warming to the attack. 'Tell them why you are here, Richard. Tell them how you beat a prisoner half to death in custody. My father saved you from prison and this is the thanks he gets. Maybe betrayal is a family trait. Of course, no one will ever know, will they? Yes, I know all about you. Even your own junkie mother didn't want you and dumped you on the state to bring up. I bet she couldn't wait to get rid of the little beast that dropped from her legs.'

Alwin, Jenny and Emmeline all piled in to help Joan hold Richard back. Joan shouted over her shoulder to Tancred, 'I think it's safe to say you're on your own.' Tancred turned away and waved the others back to their cars. He then turned back and declare, 'I am the one in charge and be in no doubt that I will make you all pay for this disobedience.' He was met with stony silence, apart from Jenny, who simply told him to sod off.

Joan looked back at Richard and saw a deep pain in his eyes. He pulled himself free and walked off. She caught up with him at the edge of the car park.

'I'm so angry.'

'If I can rise above it, so can you.'

'Not with him, with me.' Richard looked down. Joan desperately wanted to hug him and tell him he was wrong to blame himself for losing his temper. He pulled his phone out of his pocket and dialled Matthew. Matthew did not pick up. Richard tried again and this time Matthew answered.

'Matthew, there has been a change of plan. Tancred has outdone himself. He thought it would be a good idea to bring his chums along, made himself his very own posse.'

'Posse?' Matthew replied tentatively.

'You heard me. We're having no part in it. I want you to get back here.' There was a pause. 'How many?'

'A dozen, not that it matters.'

'Oh.' There was another pause. 'Not policemen, then?'

'No, just a bunch of upper…no, not policemen, just a bunch of his mates.'

'I see, typical. Here I am all night under this bush with only squirrels for company and nothing to show for it. At least I missed the dust-up at the pub last night.'

Richard froze. He had to think quickly.

'Yes. You were lucky there. We'll see you soon,' he managed to say. Richard ended the call and squeezed his eyes shut.

'What's the matter?' Joan asked.

'They've got Matthew.'

'How do you know?'

'Why else would he say he was at the fort last night and not at the pub? He was trying to tell me something was wrong.'

'Oh God, what are we going to do?'

'The only thing we can. We're going to rescue him.'

Maude and Deirdre had been standing over Matthew, listening to the conversation. They put the gag back over his mouth and drew Burt away.

'Do you know, I could kiss Tancred,' Deirdre murmured.

'How could we ever have doubted him. How foolish we were,' Maude responded with a chuckle.

'Once more unto the breach, dear friends.'

'If Tancred is King Henry, Henry is going to be having a very bad day.'

TWENTY-FIVE

Since the dawn of time, people had come to Newlands Corner to stand on the crest of the ridge overlooking Albury Downs, saying profound things like, 'That's nice,' or 'Isn't it pretty,' or 'Oh crap, I can see a Roman legion down there.' The view of the Surrey Hills that Saturday morning from Newlands Corner was certainly worthy of admiration in the vaporous morning light. But as the group of YPCs crested the ridge, Tancred was filled with a vague foreboding. This apprehension hid something in his heart that his pride could not admit, namely that he missed having Richard by his side. He sat in pensive isolation as the conversation around him went from foxes to pheasant beating to vintage yachts.

His mood wasn't helped when the duty sergeant at Guildbury police station left one last message on his phone at the end of his shift at 7 a.m. to say that Pippa and her pint-sized devils would soon be released. The duty sergeant subtly interlaced this with the suggestion that Tancred was without a father as well as being a staple food of flies.

Tancred's crew of merry men turned off the main road to be swallowed up in the mist.

★

Calamity may have been averted if Sir Archibald had not been about his early morning perambulations around the environs of Wolfestone Manor. It was a time he regarded as sacrosanct and certainly not to be sullied by the chimes of a mobile phone. This indulgence would come at a heavy price. The repeated calls from Richard went unanswered. Meanwhile, Alwin had been busy mobilising the technological capabilities the police had to offer to track down the position of Matthew's phone. His success at finding its rough location was tempered when Jenny came with news from Guildbury police station that Pippa and her gang were soon to be released. Richard prayed that Matthew and his phone were still close, because it was no day for an extended search of the woods.

★

Tancred's convoy drove down the lane towards Heifer's Deep beneath the twisted limbs of trees that threatened to stretch down and pluck them from the land. Tancred's apprehension had by now infected the others in the car. They all looked out into the mist with a growing unease. When they came to the end of the lane, they were surprised to find a vintage fire engine already parked there.

'Seems a strange place for such a vehicle?' said Peter Alnwick, heir to Alnwick pork products.

'It does kinda beg the question,' replied Bartholomew Hudnall, AKA Barty, third son of Sir Rodney Hudnall.

His father owned, amongst other things, a stud farm in Newmarket and had also made a fair income over the years manipulating EU farming subsidies through what was called 'slipper farming'. There was something else concerning Barty.

'Tankers, I think I have spotted an error in our plan,' he said to Tancred, who at that moment was pondering what dark significance an old fire appliance might have when found abandoned in the woods.

'Which is?' Tancred replied absently.

'Well, when we spring these good folks from the grip of their withered persecutors, I think we may have a transport problem.'

'Huh?' Then the penny dropped. Tancred redirected his eyes to their cars.

'Unless we take, how would you say, a rather swarmed approach to our transport,' Barty added, looking at their cars.

'Could I possibly sidle into the conversation here?' This was Lawre Hargreaves, only son of John Hargreaves. Lawre's family were a shining example of upward social mobility within society. His own grandfather had changed his name from Dumitrescu to Hargreaves when he had escaped Romania and the Nazi hunters after the Second World War. From those dirt-poor beginnings after the war, Lawre's father had inherited the shady family business, which the National Crime Agency now had a thick file on. Despite the rumours, he had ample funds to buy a well-heeled reputation. Lawre's nickname was Cuckoo at public school, not that anyone felt it polite to say it to his face.

'Sidle away,' said Barty.

'Well, if my father ever found out I had nicked his prized Aston and then allowed it to be treated like an Indian locomotive, he might be displeased.'

Barty paused. 'How displeased?'

'Enough for me to put all the blame on you.'

'I've decided it's a terrible idea using our own cars. Anything to say, Tankers?'

'What, apart from blast?' Tancred spat with some chagrin at the oversight. 'The hubbub in the car park blinded me to this obvious fact.' Tancred summoned all his Punchard cunning to the problem at hand. It wasn't long before a big red solution presented itself. 'Does anyone here know how to hot-wire a vintage fire engine?'

This was the perfect opportunity for the towering form of Rodney Montagu to step into the fray. Despite Rodney's size and penchant for violence inside the ring, he was a pretty docile sort out of it. His father was a bishop who didn't much care for his son's recreational habits or the company that he kept, seeing them for the viperous bunch of backstabbers that they were.

'No,' Rodney said. He was also a man of few words.

'I do,' Lawre offered, which surprised no one.

'Problem solved,' Tancred said. 'They can all scrabble on that.'

'Should make quite a sight,' Barty said with a chuckle.

'Certainly will,' Peter Alnwick replied. 'But I see another problem on the horizon, namely a certain lack of offensive capability.'

'Father usually keeps a sawn-off twelve-bore in the boot of the Aston,' Lawre said. For once Tancred saw sense.

'And you can keep it in the boot. We're battling little old ladies, not bloodthirsty criminals.' The general sentiment of the group was that Tancred had been a touch indelicate. This was expressed by all eyes swivelling in any direction but towards Tancred and Lawre.

'Sticks.'

'What?'

'Sticks,' Rodney repeated, motioning towards the foggy expanse.

'Of course,' Barty said. 'Rodney, your mind is a rapier,' Barty said. '*Swallows and Amazons* it is!'

A few minutes later they were all brandishing the necessary lumber and ready for a day of liberation. But Barty always had a good sense for another's mental atmosphere and it was plain to him that Tancred was suffering from some internal squalls. He stepped into Tancred's space and for the second time that day Tancred found a hand on his shoulder drawing him away. When they reached the sizeable boot of Barty's Range Rover he said, 'Tankers, I fear something ails you.'

'I must admit to feeling a little in the rough regarding this, er, operation. I'm wondering if my enthusiasm for justice has blinded me to the potential risks embodied in the person of Maude Appleby.'

'Ah, you fear this old rag's reception for unwanted visitors.'

'A nail well smacked. I fear that success may spurn our embrace.' Barty's company often had this effect on Tancred's language.

Barty patted Tancred on his shoulder. He was a man

who rarely loitered with doubt and he had no intention of courting it now. Like Tancred, Barty felt himself anointed by destiny to a future in high office and now saw before him a pressing need to show his natural leadership.

'Tankers, let me ask you why I became head boy of our hallowed Belmarsh College,' Barty said, knowing that Tancred's own demonstration of executive prowess hadn't amounted to anything more than being milk monitor throughout his school years. Tancred's head bowed in unspoken shame. Barty gave him another paternal pat on the shoulder, feeling that the point was made and needed no further rubbing.

'This is the task before us and we will not flinch from the perils therein.' Another pat on the shoulder. 'So, let's get to it and give credit to our family names, undisturbed by any ridiculous thoughts of failure. There is something I wish to show you.' Barty opened the boot of his Range Rover, pulled out a staff and planted it into the ground. Tancred looked at the top of the staff in awe.

'Is it...?'

'It is, indeed, Tancred, in the flesh so to speak. It will be our standard and if you serve it well...' Barty left the potent of what he was saying for Tancred to interpret. Before Tancred was the hallowed mascot of the YPC. It was the legendary and rather desiccated pig's head of the Blatherton Club, a club more shrouded in mystery and meaning than even the Illuminati. Tancred's fingers reached up to touch the head, but he withdrew them when he remembered the details of the initiation ceremony, which brought a whole new meaning to the term hogging.

'I will not let you down,' Tancred whispered, aroused by the mere thought of becoming a member. Barty smiled, knowing that the chances of that were slim at best. But Tancred, newly constituted by Barty's stirring words, could feel his ancestors smiling down from their heavenly pews. His cleft chin swelled and his pale-blue eyes glistened as he said, 'My destiny calls and it will not find me wanting.'

'Quite. We shall put this moment of weakness behind us.' Barty took the staff and the others reverently lined up behind it. Barty thrust his arm forward, in a way that reminded Lawre of his grandfather in his more impassioned moments before his grandmother could stop him, and yelled, 'Forward!' As soon as these impassioned liberators were out of sight a few bushes rustled towards their cars. Soon the sound of hissing was drifting through the mist.

★

'Park the van down there,' Richard said to Alwin, pointing to a rough track forking off to the left of the lane. 'We should be able to come in behind the fort from here.' Once Alwin had parked up he checked in to see if Matthew's phone had changed location. 'It hasn't moved,' he confirmed.

Richard preferred real maps to phone apps, so had brought along an Ordnance Survey map of the area. Richard laid the map on the van's bonnet and they all gathered round. 'Alwin and Jenny will take this direction while Joan and Emmeline move along here. I will go along–'

'But that will leave you on your own,' Joan said.

'We can cover–'

'No.'

'No?'

'No one should be on their own, including you, boss,' Emmeline said.

'But—'

'I'll go with you this way, the other three can go together, that way,' Joan said, as she directed her finger over the map. Richard looked at the others and saw that they were all in agreement.

'All right,' Richard conceded. 'Let's get going. Hopefully Tancred's twits will prove a useful diversion.'

★

Barty, now fully in charge of Tancred's liberators, was leading the band towards Heifer's Deep and the fort, down a wide well-churned forest path. The group came to an abrupt halt when someone at the back said, 'Hold it.'

Everyone turned around to discover it was one of the Portendorfer brothers. Nathan and Terence were identical twins. One of them said, 'Someone has tried to hide these tyre tracks, and recently, looking at these cut branches.' The other twin was pointing at the evidence. They started to pull away the cut branches to reveal a track leading to a clearing. An old digger and a large trailer full of soil had been parked up in the open space.

'That soil looks freshly dug to me,' Lawre pointed out.

'I can't see any hole anywhere,' Tancred replied. A number of them started looking around for a hole the size of a small swimming pool.

Barty pulled a Kit Kat from his pocket and munched it meditatively. This seemed the cue for everyone else to pull some confectionery out of their pockets, which vexed Tancred greatly, not because it was probable contraband, but because he didn't have any.

'Strange. Why would anyone want to hide an old digger and a large trailer full of soil? Barty said. It was at this point that Rodney felt it incumbent on himself to give voice to his thoughts.

'Dunno.'

'Nor me, so let's get back to the main track.' Barty motioned them back, some still looking around for holes.

As they moved down the track, the banks on either side rose up until only Rodney could see above them. The mist was still thick on the ground although the gathering light from above suggested it would soon disperse. Before long Barty noticed a sound that stood in conflict with the natural surroundings. 'Did anyone hear that?' They all froze and listened hard for noises coming out of the mist.

'I can't hear a thing,' Tancred finally said. Apart from some cooing from the branches above, the forest was silent. Barty shrugged and signalled for the band to move forward. A moment later, Barty signalled the group to stop again. This time they all caught the faint whirring sound percolating out from the mist. The sound stopped and the forest was again reduced to silence.

'I do believe we are being followed, but by what I know not,' Barty whispered. Rodney braced himself for only he knew the portent of the sound. The bracing bit wasn't so much to do with the sound, as with the number of words it would require to explain it.

'It's a mobility scooter,' Rodney said.

'Say again?'

'Made by Wilber, Jackson and Wilber, the type 45 Robber Baron class of all terrain mobility vehicles.' The others looked at him in bemusement. 'My parents forced me to have a Saturday job working in a mobility scooter shop. I'd know the whir of that powerful motor anywhere.'

Barty stopped frowning at Rodney and turned to Tancred. 'So, the natives know we are here. So be it. Much good it will do them,' Barty said and gave Tancred a wink. This elicited a haughty sneer at the bushes from Tancred. Inside, though, he was getting a familiar feeling: that his position of authority had once again been usurped.

In a raised voice, Barty shouted, 'We know you are in there!' The misty forest was silent.

'Resistance is futile!' Tancred added. Somewhere from within the leafy mist the sound of somebody blowing a raspberry could be heard. This was followed by a high-pitched whir, as though something was accelerating away.

'Charming,' Barty retorted. He gave the signal to proceed. The group moved forward with Barty parading the pig's head before them.

The squat fort sat at the base of the depression that was Heifer's Deep, with its steep sides covered in trees and shrubs. When Barty came to the mouth of Heifer's Deep, he stopped and was immediately pitched forward by the thick knot of liberators behind him, nearly sending the pig's head to the ground. Once Barty had collected his dignity he said, 'I do believe we have arrived.' They all looked at the hazy outline of the fort, which was sunk into the base of the far bank.

'What now?' said a bored Terence Portendorfer. Nathan Portendorfer, meanwhile, was wondering why the vehicle tracks that had accompanied them along the trail had come to an abrupt stop. They had given way to a suspiciously untouched carpet of forest litter leading into Heifer's Deep. He was just about to point this out when Barty replied, 'I think a full-frontal assault is the best course of action. Do you concur, Tankers?'

'As wolves amongst the flock we will bear down on these whiskered crones and send them all scurrying back to the hovels from which they came,' Tancred proclaimed.

'Oh, well,' said Tankers.

Nathan began to say, 'Just one thing–'

'Yeah, let's kick some withered butts.'

'If I could just point–'

'Like taking candy from a geriatric,' said Nigel Coxcomb, another member of the band.

'I really should–'

'The time for words is over. Line up in attack formation!' Barty commanded.

'But don't you think it looks a bit suspicious,' Nathan persisted, waving at the way ahead.

'Nathan, zip it,' Barty said before Nathan could say any more. They all dutifully lined up. Tancred jostled to be by Barty's right-hand side, determined to assert his status within the pack. Barty raised his stick up and looked down the line. 'Remember, shock and awe.' He paused and then shouted, 'Charge!'

The line surged forward into Heifer's Deep, with much yelling and yodelling. They ran at full pelt towards the looming fort, with battle lust coursing through their veins.

They all hit the camouflaged trench at the same time. One moment they were running, the next they were floundering around a trench filled with slushy silage. A moment later, two off-road mobility scooters leaped out from some bushes in front of them and sped past hauling a scramble net of old belongings over them. No sooner had these passed, then another two scooters came from behind them hauling a second scramble net over them.

Grannies materialised on the banks like a Germanic horde, whooping and crying. On the flat roof of the fort Maude strode into view flanked by Deirdre and her superannuated warriors. In the stinking, sinking melee below, Tancred looked up into her implacable face and shook his fist in fury. Almost immediately, the liberators had become captives.

TWENTY-SIX

Matthew heard the roar and tried to gauge what was going on. He was gagged and tied to a birch tree with only one guard to keep an eye on him. His guard, Gloria, was looking anxiously in the direction of the ruckus and didn't see anyone come up behind her and drop a canvas bag over her head.

'Don't make a peep,' Alwin said, close to her ear. The canvas bag nodded. Matthew found Emmeline and Jenny by his side, quickly undoing his woollen restraints.

'Am I glad to see you guys,' Matthew said to them as his gag was removed. As he walked over to Gloria to retrieve his phone, he said, 'What's happening over there?'

'I don't know, but we need to get out of here. Blackwood has been released and we're really keen not to bump into her again.'

Alwin called Richard while the others tied up Gloria: 'Richard, we have Matthew.'

'Great, now get back to the van. We'll meet you there.' Richard ended the call and said to Joan, 'They've got him back.' He looked in the direction of the ruckus. Joan followed his stare, sensing what Richard had in mind.

'Leave it.'

'I can't.'

'They made their own bed. It's not your problem.'

'I'm just going to take a look.'

Joan groaned. 'And just what do you think you can do?'

'I don't know until I look. I need you to go back to the van.'

'Forget it. We go together or not at all.'

'Joan–'

'It's not going to happen.' Richard could see there was no point in arguing.

'No heroics,' she added.

'No heroics.' Richard agreed.

★

Gladys and Mavis were part of one of the heavy artillery platoons on the banks. A platoon in Maude's irregulars consisted of three members. Mildred, the lowlander, was the third member of the platoon and had been charged with aiming and firing the over-baked projectiles. This feat was achieved by having a pair of padded knickers strung taut between the handlebars of two off-road mobility scooters, upon which Gladys and Mavis were sitting. A third scooter sat between them, with Mildred on top, holding a metal hook attached to said knickers. The surrounding banks around Heifer's deep curved in, which allowed enough angle of fire to cover the entire depression. All Mildred needed to do was reverse her steed while angling into her field of fire, and slip the hook. Gladys and Mavis were tasked with ensuring the knicker elastic remained secured to their mobility scooter handlebars. But Mavis wasn't so enamoured with the setup, because it was her knickers holding the rock cakes.

'This is such an abuse of my dignity,' Mavis complained again as they readied to rained down fire.

'Oh, God give us strength,' muttered Mildred.

'I reject the assertion that my underwear is, is… roomier.'

'Mavis, we've been through this,' Gladys said. Unlike the other two, Gladys had a petite bum.

'Her bum is just as big as mine.'

'Bah, it most certainly is not,' Mildred exclaimed.

'Don't you bah me. I demand a retrial.'

'We have already proved your undergarments could hold more rock cakes,' Gladys patiently replied. 'Now can we just concentrate on firing them?' They looked down in grumpy silence as Tancred's posse tried to extricate themselves from the stinking trench, waiting for the moment when they were given the signal to fire.

'Lowlander,' Mavis muttered.

'What did you say?' Mildred challenged.

'The next one to speak gets a rock cake in the gob,' snapped Gladys.

Down below, the liberators were beginning to organise themselves. Rodney had managed to wedge himself into the corner of the trench and was giving the others a leg up. One by one they slivered onto the ground like mudskippers and attempted to free themselves from the scramble nets. Just as a few of them managed to stand up, Maude dropped her arm to signal open fire.

'Here goes,' Mildred squealed as she reversed, pulling the pants taut and aimed into the depression. She released the hook and out twanged a batch of bullet hard rock cakes, each about the size of a cupcake. Her salvo was accompanied by others coming from the surrounding banks.

'Your drawers draw well, Mavis. It must be that Marks and Spencer's heavy-duty elastic,' Mildred said with a mischievous glint in her eye. Mavis nailed her with a rock cake.

The attackers heard the twangs above and instinctively looked up as a hail of cakes descended on them from out of the mist. Lawre and the few others who managed to escape the trench and netting barely had time to register horror before the hard jagged cakes smashed into their upturned faces and bodies, pummelling them back into the stinking, tangled mess to land on the ones below. In the turmoil, the Blatherton pig was knocked off its pole. A granny on a scooter sped in to pick up the head and a bucket was lowered from the roof to retrieve it. Maude whistled and Burt trotted into view. He sat down looking at the pig's head longingly while Maude placed her foot on the snout and searched out Tancred's eyes below.

'Use it as a bargaining chip,' Deirdre said, fearing that Maude had other ideas. By now, twenty-four pleading eyes were looking at the pig's head, but her eyes were planted on the only two that weren't: Tancred's.

'So, this is the fabled Blatherton pig. It didn't take me long to find out about your revolting little club,' Maude said. Barty, wringing his hands in anguish, replied, 'Please don't harm it.' She rolled the head around with her foot.

'Maude, don't do it, you'll only make things worse,' Deirdre whispered.

'Do what?' Maude replied with a cruel edge to her voice.

'Whatever you are about to do.'

One thing that had been weighing on Deirdre's mind all night was sleep, or rather Maude's lack of it. Maude was quite capable of protecting a whole Cornish coastal village from a fleet of Barbary pirates with a mere lash of her tongue, but when she was tired her temper was liable to get the better of her.

Maude looked down on the dejected attackers. 'If you agree to unconditionally surrender, I may just spare the pig.'

'Oh God, please show mercy. We surrender,' Barty spluttered. He gave a sidelong glance at Tancred and wasn't assured by the look on Tancred's face. 'Tancred, tell her that we surrender,' he begged.

For Tancred, the equation was not so simple. Saving the hallowed snout and receiving the eternal thanks from the Blatherton Club wouldn't save him from his father's ire for the failure of the operation, not to mention the matter of some decidedly dodgy arrests. And Richard and his bootlickers would lose no time poisoning the constabulary well. Redemption could only be found in the release of the hostages, even if it did mean the heart-rending loss of the Blatherton pig, even though being chest deep in swampy silage did rather make that a distant prospect. It was Rodney that settled his mind.

'If she touches a bristle on its head, I'll spend my last

breath ringing her scrawny neck,' Rodney growled.

Tancred saw an opportunity to galvanise the troops. 'No we won't,' he declared.

'What!' screamed Barty.

'No!'

'You can't!'

Barty grimaced and rasped in a voice drizzled with menace, 'You better throw in the towel, Punchard.'

'I know you won't honour your word, Appleby, you old dried-out harlot, so go to Hell!' Tancred screeched. And indeed he was correct, Maude had no intention of depriving Burt of a good chomp.

'Oh dear,' Deirdre murmured under her breath.

'Call me a harlot, will you? Why you…'

Listening to Maude's scorched earth response, Deirdre was reminded of an aunt of hers who throughout her life had been pure of virtue and thought. But after a lifetime of hobnobbing with the saints, dementia had set in and her tongue had become an instrument of the gutter. Maude finished by saying, 'There you go, boy,' as she kicked the head towards Burt, who gleefully set to with jaw and claw. After a stunned pause, the reaction down below was positively volcanic. Like bedlamites, the attackers began to squirm their way to freedom.

'Now you've done it,' Deirdre exclaimed.

'Pippa will be here before they can escape.'

'They don't need to escape. All they need to do is take the fort and hold out for reinforcements. Assuming their phones still work.' As it happened, this scenario hadn't actually occurred to any of the liberators down below.

'Best we stop them, then.'

Maude signalled again for her artillery to open fire. It was about this time that Richard and Joan found a vantage point behind a bush overlooking Heifer's Deep.

'Blow me, it's a pitched battle,' Joan said above the yelps and curses from below.

'Tancred walked them straight into a trap,' Richard replied with a grimace. The sky was raining rock cakes. Looking along the bank he could see the artillery platoons as well as snipers using upturned Zimmer frames. He saw Maude directing the attack from the top of the fort.

Richard pointed along the top of their bank. 'I wonder if we could knock out some of these batteries.'

'I think you should honour your promise. Besides, they look like they are running out of ammunition.' This fact was also becoming apparent to Maude and Deirdre. Despite the barrage, most of the attackers had managed to pull themselves out of the trench and were on the point of tearing themselves free from the scramble nets. And because of the bombardment, many of them were now sporting cuts and bruises.

It was Tancred who was the first to pull free. He scrambled up to a bush and waited for the others. Behind him a sturdy branch came out of the bush and clonked him on the head. His eyes spun and he dropped face down onto the ground.

'Time to send in the dogs,' Maude said, and gave the signal. The liberators were all out of the bog by now and sensed the tide was turning their way as the airborne assault waned. But then they heard the skirl of bagpipes followed by the sound of rustling and yapping. Emerging out of the thinning mist came Maude's highland regiment, sporting tartan bows. The liberators looked at the furry wave heading for their ankles with disbelief.

Maude nudged Burt with her foot and said, 'Don't just sit there.' Burt looked at her, then at the liberators below and mournfully down at the pig's head again. 'What are you waiting for?' Maude demanded, poking him with her foot again, which he didn't much approve of, but he recognised her as the alpha boss. Quite why had always alluded him, but packs are packs and packs have their politics. He gave a big huff before standing up and setting off to support his regiment.

What the liberators didn't realise was that Pippa had honed these canine assailants into ruthless bare-paw street fighters. The attackers raised their sticks and stormed forward to meet the challenge. But despite most of them being dab hands with the old cricket bat, the dogs evaded their strikes and went for any vulnerable flesh and bone. The whole scene collapsed into disarray.

From above, Richard and Joan watched one liberator trying to wade in on a Scotty, who was ducking and diving like a true pugilist, when out of the undergrowth sprang three other canine scrappers and set upon the unsuspecting youth. Never again would Richard see a Highland Terrier in the same light. They went about their task with a savage efficiency, attaching themselves to the most painful parts of the human form with eye-watering gusto. An animalistic cry rose up from the Scotty-adorned fellow as he staggered around in mortal danger of being unmanned by one particularly frenzied assailant. Another two liberators, who looked like twins, were fighting back-to-back to fend off other gnashing jaws.

Rodney was surrounded by five of the fluffy monsters, but he was holding his ground. When one jumped up, he grabbed it. The hapless beast sounded like a deflating bagpipe as he dropkicked it into the bushes. The others backed off, but Rodney's grin faded when he heard a deep growl behind him. He turned to see Burt just five feet away from him. When it came to scrapping, Rodney prided himself on his quick thinking. He stepped back to the edge of the trench and just as Burt leaped, he spun out of the way, leaving Burt to sail straight into the trench. Burt howled with rage as he struggled in the scramble nets and silage. Stage left, Barty managed to tear the furry appendages from his person and roared his defiance at the banks. A well-aimed rock cake spun his head one way and before he could recover another spun his head the other direction. He fell to his knees and was engulfed once more in a ferocious furry mass.

Despite the dog onslaught, the liberators were gaining ground and it was clear to Maude and that they might even prevail. Then, as if almost on cue, Maude's eyes were bathed in the sight that she had been waiting for. On the opposing bank to Richard there was a vista to the sky where undergrowth and trees gave way to a grassy knoll. Upon that knoll now stood Pippa, looking every inch the lovechild of Rambo and Miss Trunchbull's bigger, more psychotic sister. Naturally, the sun took this moment to break through the mist and shine down on the towering figure. All eyes turned to her and silence descended. Maude looked down at the liberators and said with a fair degree of relish, 'Now you're buggered.'

Barty gasped. He couldn't believe his eyes.

As Pippa bounded down, the bushes on the bank became alive, shaking and shuddering in a downward shockwave. At the bottom, the Baker's Dozen popped out like grasshoppers with nunchucks at the ready. The liberators backed away from the strange sight before them. By the time Barty had extricated himself and gathered up his leadership skills, Pippa and the Baker's Dozen had them cornered against the fort wall. They all looked bedraggled and were foul smelling. Their clothes were torn and they all were showing cuts, bruises and bite marks from their failed attack.

Rodney was staring up at Pippa with something approaching awe. Without taking his eyes off her, he dropped the branch he was holding to the ground. All the others promptly followed suit.

The last to drop his weapon was Barty. He then spat some fur from his mouth and said with what dignity he could muster, 'We surrender.'

Tancred, who had managed to revive himself and was now hiding under a bush, watched the capitulation of his comrades and knew the day was lost. So he bade farewell to the erstwhile liberators and scampered up the bank under the cover of the undergrowth. A Punchard did not turn and run in the face of the enemy. They made strategic withdrawals. In this case, Tancred was planning to strategically withdraw all the way back to the safety of Wolfestone Manor.

From the bank above, Richard and Joan looked on. Richard scanned around, searching for signs of Tancred. He glimpsed a fast-moving blond mop moving through the undergrowth at the top of the bank flanking the fort, that had to be Tancred.

'Let's get out of here,' Joan said. Richard was inclined to stay. He wanted to know what Maude was really up to and he certainly didn't think it was just to accumulate hostages. Something devious was afoot. Something *else*. The grannies were feverishly searching for Tancred and Maude seemed none too happy that he had slipped away.

'Find him! He can't be allowed to escape!' the grannies' fearless leader shouted. The posse of miserable liberators were being forced back into the silage trench. A very disgruntled Burt was tasked with standing guard along with the other dogs. As Richard panned the battleground, his eyes came to rest upon a finger attached to Beatrix, one of the Baker's Dozen, pointing directly at him.

'Up there!' she yelled.

'Ah, perhaps you are right,' Richard said to Joan. They both rolled out of sight, stood up and legged it.

TWENTY-SEVEN

Thin shafts of sunlight flickered through the trees as they weaved their way through the forest with the resonant grunts of the Baker's Dozen pressuring them from behind. Richard and Joan came to a large clearing with a stream running through it. They looked around for somewhere to hide. Richard pointed to the top of the clearing where an overgrown hedge bank had become a line of trees. When they reached the bank, they launched themselves through the trees and into the ditch behind. Richard landed on something soft that let out first a groan then a string of curses. He looked down to see something shaggy trying to wiggle out from under his body.

'Will'yer get off me yer big lump.'

'Ishmael? Is that you?' The bundle by Richard's feet wriggled to a sitting position and said, 'Just sitting 'ere minding me own business when two ruddy feet land on me from the 'eavens. Don't yer look where yer jumping?' Richard leaned down to offer her a hand up when he noticed a sack next to her which was emitting some suspicious whimperings.

'You let them go right now, you hear me,' Richard said sternly. Ishmael opened her mouth, but the ominous rise of Richard's eyebrows stilled her tongue. With a huff she undid the sack. Two Highland Terriers shot out and bolted into the woods.

'I suppose you're going to tell me they were strays,' Richard said.

'Feral Scotties, a big problem in these 'ere woods,' Ishmael replied demurely as she stood up and smoothed down her frayed layers.

'Shush! Something's going on in the trees over there,' Joan said, pointing to the treeline. They could hear a lot of shouting and crashing around in the undergrowth, interspersed with bouts of wailing and crying.

'Them Baker's Dozen found them fresh meat, I reckon. Hunting they are, closing in for the kill,' Ishmael offered. Richard had a hunch who they were hunting and, a few moments later, his predication proved correct as Tancred, filthy and covered in torn tweed, burst from the undergrowth in a staggering run. From behind him a rock cake flew out of the vegetation and hit him square between the shoulder blades forcing him to the ground. Richard, Joan and Ishmael watched as three of the Baker's Dozen emerged from the treeline. Tancred staggered to his feet, but was forced to his knees by two more rock cakes. In a symbolic act of despair, he arched his back and raised his arms to the sky, before slowly falling flat on his face for the second time that day.

Joan couldn't resist. 'It reminds me of that scene out of *Platoon* where Willem Dafoe staggers out of the jungle, pursued by the North Vietnamese.'

'Huh?' blurted Ishmael.

Joan started to hum 'Adagio for Strings'. It took Richard a second to click why. He couldn't help but chuckle, but he wished he hadn't as the Baker's Dozen homed in on Tancred's position.

'I dread to think what Maude has in store for him,' Richard murmured, cracking a wry smile. Ishmael, ever the one for mischief then started singing, 'Always, look on the bright side, of life, da du…da du…da du, da du, da du.'

'That was not the picture I was looking for,' Richard said by way of reply.

Now the image of Tancred, singing along with a line of crucified convicts, was also in Richard's head. *Platoon* and Monty Python were making a strange cocktail. Watching the dejected figure of Tancred being bound and dragged away left him feeling strangely melancholy. Despite everything, he couldn't help feeling sorry for Tancred.

'At least they're not chasing us now,' Joan proffered.

'Come on. Let's get back to the others before they do,' Richard replied.

Ishmael snorted. 'What, that van down the lane? If they 'aven't already been captured, they soon will be.' Richard was already reaching for his phone. He found Alwin's number and dialled it. The moment Alwin picked up, Richard said, 'Alwin, are you OK?'

'Yes. But please tell me it's you…coming towards us?'

'No, it's not us,' Richard said and glanced at Joan. 'Get out of there, right now. We'll find our own way back.'

'But we can't just leave you.'

'Just do it. Go back to the hotel and wait for us,' Richard said, 'We'll be all right.'

'If you say so, boss,' said Alwin. Richard ended the call.

'Well, we're on our own now,' Richard said to Joan.

'There's only one way yer getting out of this forest now,' Ishmael added.

'Would this involve some grovelling?' Joan said.

'Most certainly.'

'Ishmael, have I ever told you what lovely eyes you have,' Richard said.

'Now yer taking the piss.'

*

Back at Heifer's Deep, Barty and his stinky band of failed liberators had been fished out of the bog one by one, pushed to their knees, tied up and hooded. A local farmer was busy filling in the silage trench. The hooded figure of Tancred was hauled in, causing the guarding Baker's Dozen to kick his hooded compatriots into a standing position so that they could all be roped together. Tancred was placed on the end and they were all prodded into a march. As they were dragged, stumbling back down the track, an unpleasant notion came to Tancred that they were being taken to a rather different kind of trench in the woods.

After a few minutes they were commanded to stop. He could hear a vehicle coming. The person standing next to him whispered, 'Is that you, Tankers?'

'Yes, is that you Barty?'

'The very same. Er, this mob, surely, they wouldn't… you know?'

'I fear the worst, Barty. At least I won't have to face my

father,' Tancred replied, consumed as he was with self-pity. They heard a truck draw up close by. This was followed by some clunking and banging. Tancred imagined a truck with a canvas back being opened to reveal a heavy calibre machine gun. He was just waiting for the cha-chunk to confirm it.

'Barty, this is it, gunned down in the woods by bloodthirsty pensioners. Prepare yourself. Will you see your way to forgiveness while we still have…do you smell that?' Tancred realised Barty was sobbing. Before he could offer any more words of comfort, he felt rough hands upon him cutting his clothes off. A few minutes later all of Tancred's posse were standing blindfolded and stark naked, facing whatever fate awaited them.

'Why have they taken our clothes?' Barty whimpered. Tancred had a ghastly theory involving Pippa, but he wasn't about to voice it to Barty, lest his nose was accosted by Barty's digested main course from the night before. He had a feeling the first course had been foie gras.

Suddenly their hoods were pulled off to reveal the vintage fire engine in front of them. In front of it stood Pippa, holding a fire hose with the Bakers' Dozen off to the side looking on in amusement.

'I think I know why that vintage fire engine was in the woods, now,' Lawre said, not that any of them needed his insight.

'Can't have you smelling of silage, can we now,' Pippa said as she pulled the lever back and began to douse them in freezing cold water. Once she was satisfied that they were nice and clean, the hoods were placed back on and, one by one, they were redressed, although in what Tancred wasn't sure. It felt like he was now wearing sturdy high-top boots and a shirt and tie.

Maude was delighted when she saw Tancred and his crew being led back into Heifer's Deep.

'Don't they look a picture,' Maude said to Deirdre. 'Is everyone ready?'

'Yes. So here it is, the moment of truth,' Deirdre replied. 'How long have we got?'

'Ten minutes. We better start bringing out the others.'

Tancred was cut loose and led to a spot where he was told not to move. He could hear the same happening to the others. It was at this point that he began to suspect his involvement in someone else's cunning plan. His relief at still being alive began slowly to be replaced, by dread.

*

William Hanock of the *National Mail*, who had made a career out of manufacturing dark deeds, was annoyed to see one of the news networks already parked down the lane in the woods. It seemed that his anonymous tip-off had not been as exclusive as he had hoped, which was a shame because the police were there in droves, which suggested something juicy was going down. But his antennae was already picking up something strange.

Hanock was well known to the police and for this reason they were apt to fiddle with their truncheons at the mere sight of him. But this general longing of the boys in blue to cave his head in was not in evidence as they got ready to face whatever was about to go down. In fact, they were showing him an unnatural deference. When he asked what was happening, all they said was that a serious incident was in progress, but they had no more details to give at that time. As the police moved out at a trot, he caught sight of two Range Rovers and an Aston Martin parked along the lane with deflated tyres. Strange indeed. The news network was jogging after police, burdened by their equipment. He soon overtook them, to their annoyance.

★

'Now,' Tancred heard a voice shout. What felt like a stick was thrust into his hand and a deep, menacing female voice that he knew must be Pippa's said, 'Drop it and I'll drop you, got it.'

'What's going on?' Tancred called out.

'Shut it or I'll tear you a new one.' A different voice, harsh and higher pitched. Tancred shut it.

A few seconds later, the hood was pulled from his face. What he initially saw were the backsides of the Baker's Dozen disappearing into the undergrowth. Then he heard someone say, 'Hey.' His eyes were drawn to his boots where, to his amazement, Maude was laying prostrate, looking like she had been trampled by a herd of cows.

'Lift your foot,' she said. Tancred was so shocked that he did as she asked. Then, to his horror, she placed his foot on her head. Before he could react, he heard a male voice boom, 'HO!'

The voice belonged to Police Constable Frank Murphy.

Tancred looked around to see a mob of other police officers pouring into Heifer's Deep. Maude was now moaning under his boot. Indeed, there was a great deal of moaning and wailing going on around him.

'Right, you're all nicked.' This voice belonged to Police Constable George Law. Tancred's eyes passed from his boot to the blood-stained stick in his hand. As his bottom jaw dropped like a brick budgie, he saw that he was dressed in black trousers, a brown shirt and a black tie with an elaborate insignia consisting of two Ts. He looked around to see that all of his posse were dressed in the same way along with other people he did not recognise. The new faces were the kidnapped Temperance Trotters. Nipper wasn't among them, destined as he was for an entirely different fate…far, far away.

'Excuse me,' Tancred turned towards the voice and saw a man in civilian clothing holding a camera. 'Great shot. You're going to be famous,' William Hanock said. Tancred looked down at Maude again and she flashed him an evil expression with her eyes. When the realisation hit Tancred, he dropped the stick and screamed.

Hanock couldn't believe what he was seeing. There were a couple of dozen people dressed in what looked like paramilitary uniforms, all brandishing sticks. But the real gold was the grannies, who were lying about in battered heaps everywhere, not to mention a fair number of small crawling dogs, who were whimpering as though they were in great pain. He switched his camera to video mode and recorded the scene. He zoomed in on a granny holding a limp Highland Terrier in her arms, weeping. He didn't notice the dog open one eye to look around before closing it again. He had to admit that even he felt squeamish when he saw another granny trying to lift herself from the ground in distress, her dress having been torn open from behind. In a particularly touching scene, one dog was howling a plaintive howl above the still body of its fallen mistress.

Hanock saw that the guy with the mop of blond hair was now in the throes of some kind of fit. One of the policemen decided that this constituted some kind of undefined threat and tasered him. Tancred fell onto his face for the third, and final, time that day.

★

The morning drew on with Richard and Joan trudging behind a surprisingly pacey Ishmael through deep forest, which afforded little phone reception. When they eventually came to higher ground, Richard's phone signalled a missed call and a voice message. It was from Chief Superintendent Phillip Barrington and all it said was to call him. When Richard did, Barrington picked up immediately.

'Richard, are you OK?' Barrington asked.

'Yes, Sir.'

Before Richard could elaborate, Barrington replied, 'Good. Now listen to me. I can't go into things at the moment, but hasten to say because of Tancred's actions things are a little delicate. So, I need you and your team to keep your heads down and sit tight until you hear from me tomorrow morning. Are you all together?'

'No. Most of the team is hopefully in Guildbury by now.'

'Call them and tell them the same. Just find somewhere to sit tight until then.'

'Yes, Sir. What is—'

'Just sit tight and wait.' The line went dead.

'Well?' Joan asked.

Richard puffed his cheeks out and replied, 'Seems we need to go to ground until he contacts us tomorrow. That's all he would say. I better call the others.'

He called Alwin again. Alwin picked up on the first ring.

'Boss, am I glad to hear from you. Are you both OK?'

'Yes, we are. Where are you?'

'Back at the hotel. We only just managed to get away from Blackwood and her mob. Where are you?'

'Still in the woods.' The line went quiet.

'Boss, do you want us to come for you?' It was said sincerely, but Richard could hear the trepidation in the voice.

'No. I've just spoken to Chief Barrington. He wants us all to just sit tight until he contacts me tomorrow morning. So, just stay in your rooms and keep your heads down.'

There was silence for a few seconds, with faint whispering at the other end. 'OK, boss.'

'I'll call you later to let you know how we're doing,' Richard replied and ended the call.

'So, all we have to do now is get back to the hotel,' Joan said.

'Where has Ishmael gone?' They looked around but she was nowhere to be seen. Just as they thought she had abandoned them, she emerged from some bushes.

'Call of nature,' Ishmael declared. She then turned and

said, 'Guildbury's thata way. Me cottage is this,' Ishmael said, pointing her finger. 'But the woods will be crawling by now. Maude won't want witnesses. I've a small barn out back. There's a hay loft at top. Yer can stay there tonight.' As it was now mid-morning, that meant the best part of a day and a night.

'We have to get back.'

'I don't reckon Maude means yer no 'arm, but 'arm she will if yer force 'er 'and. Let it be, yer life depends on it.'

'You actually think Maude is a threat to our lives?'

'To the life me sees in yer future. To the life that yer will destroy if yer take that road.' Ishmael was pointing in the direction of Guildbury. 'Trust me, as yer did before,' she added.

'How do you know I did?'

'You're alive.'

'You know what Maude is up to?' Richard said.

'I know that if yer leave now yer'll be caught,' Ishmael said.

'We can't stay here.'

Ishmael tilted her head and smiled. It was a kind smile. 'Just believe me, yer'll thank me in time,' Ishmael replied.

Joan looked at Richard and saw the indecision on his face. She pressed her lips and then said. 'OK, woman's intuition time. She tried to save your life once. I think you should listen to her.'

'That's assuming I believe in psychic abilities.'

'Why take the risk of trying to get back to Guildbury,' Joan replied. 'Let's just wait it out here until we know it is safe. The others will be OK.'

The birds and the trees took over the conversation for the few seconds of silence that followed.

Richard was almost surprised when he heard himself say, 'OK.' Suddenly it was as though a great weight had been lifted from his shoulders. 'We'll stay.'

'Good,' was Ishmael's response as she turned away to hide a smirk and proceeded towards her house. Richard followed her and Joan followed him.

The barn turned out to have a hay loft. Richard gave it an innocent look. Ishmael casually looked at Joan and smiled, as Joan gave the barn a speculative look.

Inside there was fresh hay and it looked as though it had been recently cleaned. It felt cosy and safe. The loft doors were open to glorious views of the rolling countryside. Ishmael left them and a few hours passed as though they were on some rustic weekend break. It was early afternoon when they were both woken by Ishmael calling up to them. They had both passed out on the hay and awoke with their bodies almost touching.

'Want some grub?' They were both ravenous, but they were wary about what 'grub' actually constituted. They suspected actual grubs. Joan looked down to see Ishmael holding a basket with cheese, bread and a couple of apples.

'It looks safe,' Joan whispered.

'I can 'ear yer, yer know,' Ishmael growled as she handed the food to Joan through the hatch before climbing up herself.

'That's very kind of you,' Richard said. Ishmael placed her behind on the side of the hatch and watched them begin to eat. 'Lovely up 'ere on a day like this. Many 'appy childhood memories up 'ere. Would 'ave lost me cherry up 'ere if it 'adn't been for me pa with 'is pitch-fork.' This caused Richard to choke on a piece of bread.

'Dare I ask what the cheese is made from?' Joan said, ignoring Richard's warning look.

'All I can say is that it took me a lot of milking,' Ishmael replied.

'Can we change the subject?' Richard cut in.

'If it makes yer feel any better, it's not from no dog.'

'Strangely, no, that doesn't,' he replied. He became aware that their antics in the forest had left the two of them covered in mud. Ishmael seemed to be thinking the same thing.

'Anyways, things to do. I'll sort the bath for yer later,' Ishmael said and disappeared down the hatch.

Richard frowned, then sunk his teeth into an apple and lay back in the straw. 'I bet you it's a big cauldron.'

Joan smiled as she inspected her grubby arms. 'Why do you think she is helping us?'

'Because she cares, I guess,' Richard replied. 'Or she's looking to expanding her diet.'

'Not that I'm complaining. I just hope we have made the right decision. It feels right.' Joan lay down next to Richard. He filtered the sunlight through his fingers, thinking about what Joan had just said. He didn't want to dwell on their decision and hunted for a change of subject.

'Apparently photons don't experience time. In vacuum at least.'

'Is that so?' came Joan's dry response.

Richard wondered if he could have picked a better

subject, but ploughed on. 'I was imagining the duration of the universe as just a brief flash. And all that will be left to prove that all its majesty ever existed will be life, released like a genie from its cosmic bottle.'

Joan decided he needed some lessons in small talk. 'Are you feeling all right?'

'I just hope it's not called Punchard.'

Joan burst out laughing. 'For a second there I thought you had lost your marbles.'

They ate in silence for a while, before Richard spoke up. 'Despite all his privilege and his low rent narcissism, part of me can't help feeling sorry for Tancred.'

'Yeah.'

'I tried my best,' Richard murmured, trying not to think what the future held for him.

Joan patted his hand and said, 'I don't think you could have done any more. Anyway, all we can do now is sit back and take in some photons and see what tomorrow brings.'

He prayed that they were right about Ishmael.

TWENTY-EIGHT

Godfrey generally wasn't one to dwell on the mysteries of Einsteinian spacetime, but if he had been asked whether or not time was relative, he would have readily agreed. He had spent the last two days fending off an increasingly irate Sir Archibald. And if that wasn't enough of a problem, his unexpectedly romantic decision to take Lillian on a weekend break to Valencia had unexpectedly left her with unusual amorous inklings. Hasten to say, bedtime had become an experience fraught with danger.

It was only once they had arrived at Gatwick that he could dare to believe he really was going to escape. Soon he would be in the sky, with Surrey dwindling in the distance and the rays of freedom beckoning him forward. In a state of nervous joviality, he went through check-in and security after which he and Lillian found a perch in one of the airport cafes. All he had to do now was keep Lillian believing in the fiction until their feet were planted on Spanish soil and he could see nothing on the horizon to prevent that.

'The Mercado Central sounds simply divine,' Lillian said as she investigated Valencia in her guidebook.

'Oh, I'm sure,' Godfrey replied from behind *The Times*.

'What's a cephalopod?'

'I have no idea. Something you don't want to meet on a dark night,' Godfrey ventured from behind the paper.

'That would be a dark sea. It's some type of seafood apparently.'

'Oh. Well, it can't be any worse than octopus.'

'It's called *pulpo* in Spain,' Lillian replied, looking smug.

'What? These cephal-thingys or octopus?'

'Octopus. I'm getting into the lingo.'

'What's cephal-thingy in English?'

'I'm not sure, it's a bit confusing.' Lillian put her guidebook on the table next to Godfrey. 'I'm going to the loo.'

Godfrey put down his paper. He hadn't considered that they would have to learn Spanish if they were going to melt away into the Iberian expanse. He considered it now, while realising there were a lot of other things he also hadn't considered. Now that his fear had subsided, he felt about as prepared as a teenage runaway. Suddenly the whole venture seemed madness. Each time he played out the conversation with Lillian in his head, his imagination of the scene made him feel sick. He saw Lillian heading home through the departure gate without a backward glance. He saw his own lonely stooped figure, probably with a black eye, watching her go. He would become destitute, cut off by Lillian from funds as punishment for his stupid plan, begging for scraps of cephalopod from the gutter. Despair flooded into him as he stared into his Earl Grey.

'Have you read about this attack on the Cartel?

'I know, it sounds terrible. What's this country coming

to?' Godfrey's eyes moved from his tea to the couple sitting next to him, looking at their mobile phones.

'It says the police have declined to comment on rumours that they are looking for the Sugar Tsar Mervyn Nipper, in connection with the attack. It all sounds very dodgy to me,' said the woman.

'And some. The proverbial is really going to hit the fan over this,' said the man. Godfrey sat up and grabbed his own phone from his flight bag and checked the news. There was breaking news of a thwarted vigilante attack – with unconfirmed rumours citing a paramilitary wing of the Temperance Trotters – on the Granny Cartel in Surrey. His eyes widened when he saw an embedded video with a picture of a dishevelled Maude with a microphone pushed into her face. He was just about to play it when his phone rang, displaying an unknown number. He tentatively answered the call.

'Hello?'

'Godfrey, this is Maude.'

Godfrey's heart crawled up his oesophagus. 'Leave me alone,' he croaked.

'Aren't you the sly dog? You nearly caught us out. Anyway, I thought that while you were waiting for your flight to Valencia, we could have a quick chat.'

When Lillian returned, she found Godfrey sitting in an ashen daze.

'Godfrey, what's the matter?'

He turned his face up to her.

'I'm sorry, Lillian, but something has come up. I'm afraid we are going to have to…delay our trip.' Lillian just stood and looked at him until fate's spell was broken. She then slumped down onto the seat next to him and said, 'This better be good.'

'There is some pressing government business I need to attend to. That's all I can say.'

★

William Hanock had rarely felt so frustrated in his life. He had more than enough to sensationalise the story of the Temperance Trotter vigilantes, but he knew that there was something far juicier behind the raid. One of the police officers he had spoken to, who happened to be called Frank, had told him in confidence that the police were looking for Nipper in connection with the attack. If he could prove Nipper was involved then he could liberally spray the government with enough brown stuff to drown it. But so far all he had was the tantalising words of a single police officer, which wasn't enough.

He was just mulling over why Frank and George were such common names amongst policemen when the office phone rang.

'Hanock speaking?'

'Is this William Hanock?'

'Who's asking?' Hanock said and waited. He generally saw it as a good sign when people hesitated before divulging their names. 'Hello?'

'Godfrey Fairtrade.'

'What, as in the deputy assistant parliamentary under–'

'Yes.'

Hanock pulled the handset from his ear and looked at it in surprise. He put it back and said, 'Er, how can I help you?'

'I have some information about what happened in the Surrey Hills this morning.'

'I'm listening.'

'Not on the phone. Face to face. It will be…worth your while.'

'How do I know you are on the level?'

'This goes beyond Nipper. That should be enough.'

Hanock ran his tongue across his top teeth. 'Oookaaay, and just where do you want to meet?' he said, nodding to himself.

'The Lord Nelson Hotel. Waterloo Station. One hour. I'll be in the corner of the bar.'

'I'll be there.' The line went dead. Hanock put the phone down and drummed his fingers on the table. This goes beyond Nipper, that's what he had said. And what is beyond Nipper? Hanock picked his nose with excitement.

*

The Lord Nelson was a sticky-floored Victorian cenotaph to the countless smokers that had passed through its doors and on to the grave over the years. While not the carcinomatous temple it had once been, it still catered for the cult of the cirrhotic, as evidenced by the sombre wreckage cradling their noggin glasses at the bar.

Hanock saw Godfrey brooding at a table in the corner of the bar with a baseball cap and dark glasses. He looked ridiculous. All the other tables were empty, apart from one in the far corner where an old lady was reading a paper. Hanock waited at the bar for the sweaty mound of lipid that was the barman to pull himself off his stool and waddle over to take his order. He bought a noggin of lager then went over to Godfrey's table and sat opposite him.

'William Hanock,' he said by way of welcome and stuck his hand out. Godfrey looked at the hand but made no attempt to shake it. Hanock ignored the snub, set his phone to record and said, 'Have I your permission to record this conversation?'

Godfrey looked startled. Through the tiny earpiece in his ear, he heard Deirdre say, 'Yes he does.'

'If you must,' Godfrey said reluctantly. Hanock smiled and said, 'So, what did you want to speak to me about?'

'This attack on the Granny Cartel, I believe it had the backing of some very senior members in the government and the police force.'

Hanock blinked. 'You've already mentioned Nipper. Who else are you saying was involved?'

'The prime minister and the Metropolitan police commissioner, to be exact.'

Hanock blinked again. 'Are you serious?'

'In my role as…in rural law and order, I have been privy to a number of conversations and correspondence.' Godfrey pushed some email hard copies across the table. Hanock started to flick through the documents as Godfrey continued: 'Although nothing is said explicitly, it is obvious that Nipper and Sir Archibald had been contemplating a far more radical solution to the granny problem.'

Hanock looked up from the papers, 'So you think the PM knew of this?'

Godfrey shuffled in his seat, looking uncomfortable with the question. 'A few days ago, I overheard Nipper saying to Sir Archibald that they had received the green light from up above to crush, as they called it, the grey scourge. When I questioned Nipper about it later, he said that the granny problem would be resolved before the week was out. When I pushed him on what that meant, he said that, as a government minister, I should learn when not to ask questions.'

'And you think he was talking about the attack.'

'I am certain of it.'

'But how can you be so sure?'

Godfrey shuffled in his seat again. Sensing his unease, Deirdre said, 'Get on with it.'

Godfrey sat up and replied, 'Because I was the one who tipped off Surrey Police that an attack was imminent. I knew something was wrong, that they intended to do something illegal.'

Hanock puffed his breath through his lips. 'Wow. And you think it was with the PM's consent.'

'I believe that to be the case.'

Hanock whistled softly. He looked at Godfrey and could see that the man was under considerable stress. Godfrey would more accurately have described it as duress. Deirdre had supplied him the fictitious emails and told him what to say. Maude had given him two options at the airport. The first option composed of the standard romantic play date with Pippa, after which he would be exposed as a sexual deviant with a taste for underage prostitutes. Then he would be painted into the government conspiracy against the Cartel as well as having his attempt to abscond from the country shown as an attempt to escape justice. She assured him that the Spanish police would be waiting for him the moment he set foot in Spain. The second option began with him sitting in a pub with a sleazebag reporter. So here he was.

'And are you prepared to go public with your suspicions?'

Deirdre said into Godfrey's ear, 'You bet you are.'

'Yes. Tomorrow, I intend to resign my ministerial position in protest at this totally un-British behaviour.'

Who's he kidding, Hanock thought.

'As a servant of the people, I feel I have no choice but to follow my conscience and reveal what I believe to be a serious abuse of power.'

Hanock leaned back in his seat with a crooked smile. A politician with a conscience always gave him the willies. If God had wanted politicians to be honest, he wouldn't have created electorates, or the media. But if a government minister wanted to commit political hari-kari, who was he to stand in their way? He had hit phenomenal pay dirt and that was all he cared about. And if things went south, he could always direct any flak back towards the lamb sitting opposite him.

'OK, Fairtrade, I'll run with it.' Hanock said and made a note to buy a lottery ticket later.

Deirdre added, 'Enjoy the ride.' Godfrey thought there was zero chance of that.

TWENTY-NINE

Joan and Richard watched the flames lick around the sides of the cauldron.

'You were right.'

'I was kidding.'

'You'll need these,' Ishmael said, walking into the barn holding a small wooden stepladder.

'I feel we're missing something,' Joan said as she circled the cauldron.

'Root vegetables,' Richard replied.

Ishmael scowled at him and said, 'What do yer take me for?' There was some loud cooing behind them. She picked up a clod of earth and lobbed it at the offending pigeon.

'I'll leave yer to decide who goes first, unless that is, yer go in together,' Ishmael finished with an impish grin.

Richard and Joan's eyes locked in a moment of embarrassment. Richard cleared his throat and said, 'Joan, you can go first.'

'When you're done, I'll bring yer supper. Hope you like jugged 'are and don't forget to kick the fire out before yer get in.' Ishmael winked as she headed out of the barn.

Richard rubbed his neck and mumbled, 'I'll be upstairs.' He made for the ladder.

Fifteen minutes later, Joan appeared at the hatch.

Richard said, 'I've just spoken to the others and explained where we are. They all seem fine, if a little bored. How was the pot?'

'Actually, it was really nice. You haven't got a comb by chance, have you?'

'Unfortunately not,' Richard replied and made his way down the hatch. When he returned, ten minutes later, Joan was by the doors pulling the last of the knots from her hair with her fingers. Her dark skin was honeyed in the warm evening light, its rays exposing the silhouette of her breasts under her blouse. He stood halfway through the hatch, unable to take his eyes off her, unable to breathe, feeling like a fluttering adolescent exposed for the first time to the charms of sexual attraction. She looked around and saw the flustered look before Richard's facade came down like a drawbridge.

Joan tilted her head to one side and said, 'Everything OK?'

'Yes, just felt a bit dizzy for a second. Shame we can't get our clothes clean,' Richard said, avoiding her gaze as he climbed into the loft. 'But at least they are dry.'

'Richard,' Joan said. He turned to her and she was about to speak when Ishmael called up from below that they were ready for supper. Joan sighed and shouted down, 'Thanks.'

'That would be great,' Richard called back. He went over to the hatch and lifted a stew pot from Ishmael's hands. A few moments later, Ishmael was back at the loft steps with plates, cutlery and a hurricane lamp. 'There be a box and two deck chairs at the back down below.'

While Richard went below to retrieve them, Ishmael climbed the ladder up to Joan. 'There's some blankets down there to haul up as well,' she called down before saying to Joan, 'Nice 'aving company from time to time.'

'We appreciate your help.'

'All in a good cause, wouldn't yer say,' Ishmael replied, fixing Joan with her eye. 'I'll see yer in the morning.' She winked before disappearing down the hatch. Joan leaned against the barn timbers and puffed her cheeks out.

As Richard sorted out their improvised table, Joan examined the stew. She pulled out a tiny limb and muttered under her breath, 'They must have very small hares in these parts.' She proceeded to put the stew on the plates, avoiding the more suspect specimens.

'I really hope this wasn't someone's pet,' Richard said as he took the plate. Joan chuckled and said, 'I'm sure it's fine.'

When they had both finished eating the surprisingly tasty meal, Joan went to lie on the straw behind Richard while he remained in his deckchair watching the sun descend below the trees to the sound of cooing pigeons. He wondered how long he would have the liberty of seeing such a view. Joan's voice broke the silence.

'What Tancred said, back in the car park. Was it true, what he said about your childhood?'

'My mother was a junkie, that's all I know.'

'And what about your father, if you don't mind me asking…'

'My father? No idea.'

Joan said no more, not wanting to push the subject.

Richard, feeling at ease, and safe in Joan's calming presence, felt strangely able to converse about the subject that usually made him clam up. He guessed at some point the subject would come up.

'My childhood was spent in and out of homes,' he spoke in a matter-of-fact tone. 'Between foster parents and…' he trailed off.

'Sounds like you had it difficult,' she replied, before raising herself into a sitting position.

'It had its moments. I had my moments. And you?' Richard said, batting the conversation back to Joan.

'I've got family in Britain and Jamaica. My parents moved to Britain when I was five. I have four brothers and two sisters. We're pretty close.' Silence returned and hung around feeling a bit awkward.

'You all knew I was up on an assault charge?'

'And this was your penance,' she said. 'Being blackmailed into helping Tancred by his father. Why else would you have put up with him?'

'Is that the general view?'

'It's my view.'

'My ticket out of jail, assuming I was successful,' Richard admitted. 'I was to make sure Tancred didn't screw up and let him take credit for any success. I agreed only if the scrote I assaulted got what was coming to him.'

Joan saw that Richard had let his guard slip and risked another question. 'Why did you do it?'

There was a long pause before Richard replied, his eyes seemingly lost in the view. When he did reply, all he said was, 'Just a bad day. I let myself down, that's all.'

Joan got up. As she did, she said, 'You are fond of saying that.'

Richard frowned. 'Saying what?'

Her shadow moved across him, leaving her haloed by the evening sun. She was studying him.

'That you have let yourself down. Or rather, you let something you really believe in down.'

Richard looked away. 'I'm an idealist, despite... or because I grew up being let down, I suppose.' That sounded trite, he thought, but his thoughts were smothered when Joan bent down and kissed him. She pulled away and cupped his head in her hands. 'You better not let me down.' She kissed him again, more urgently this time as his arms began to reach around her. He took a breath and said, 'This is totally inappropriate, you know that.'

'Oh, I do hope so,' she replied and pulled him into the hay.

*

Richard heard a cough. In his sleepiness he drew Joan's naked frame closer to him under the blankets. He heard the cough again. His eyes opened the same moment Joan's did. They both cocked their heads around to see a rather unnerving sight. In the grey light of early morning he could see two people were sitting in the deckchairs. The dawn light showed one to be a short lump of scruffiness. The other was a longer length of primness, with a dour face chalked out by the grey light.

'Makes me wish I were ten years younger,' Ishmael said.

'A few decades more than that I think, Ishmael,' Deirdre said.

'I knew it the first time I saw 'em.'

Deidre looked down at Richard and Joan.

'My name is Deirdre Wotheringspot, I don't believe we have met. I'm here on behalf of the Granny Cartel. I apologise for the intrusion,' Deirdre said. Joan pulled the blanket around her neck and sat up, followed by an angry-faced Richard. It took him a few second to realise where he had seen her before. On top of the fort with Maude.

'I guess I misjudged you,' Richard said to Ishmael.

'No love loss betwixt me and this old bag, believe me, but I couldn't leave yer to yer own fate,' Ishmael said.

'Believe it or not, I am really here to help you,' Deirdre replied.

'And just what do we need your help with,' Richard retorted.

'I have managed to find you a last-minute cancellation in Valencia for the two of you. You fly out this afternoon. Two weeks, all expenses paid. We're offering a similar deal for the rest of your team,' she said. Richard was about to speak but Joan placed an index finger on his lips. 'Shush, let's just see what she has to say.'

'Thank you, Joan. It is in the Cartel's interest that you and all of your team are out of the country for the next couple of weeks. I'll need you to talk to the others. When you come back, things will have changed. You will not be facing jail time. In fact, we are quite prepared to arrange a promotion for you, if you want it.'

'You seriously expect me to believe all this...*you*?' Richard said.

'Your future depends on it,' Deirdre replied.

'T'is the path I saw. T'is the path yer should follow, all of yer,' Ishmael said. Richard was tempted to make some pithy comment about Ishmael's supposed psychic abilities, but he let it slide. Besides, his own instincts were telling him that Deirdre was on the level.

Deirdre stood. 'We'll leave you to get dressed and then I'll take you to your offices. I have arranged for the others to meet you there.'

'You have?' Richard and Joan bellowed in unison.

Deirdre stood by the steps and gazed back at the couple. 'There are four other people we need to pick up along the way. Call it a show of good faith. I'll explain things more on the way.'

*

Sir Archibald sat at his desk in Wolfestone Manor with a cold kipper before him and the *National Mail* strewn across his desk. He heard the phone ring again in the hall and assumed it was another reporter. A few moments later he heard a knock at the door.

'Tell them to piss off.'

'Are you sure?' the housekeeper said through the oak door.

'Quite.'

The housekeeper went back to the phone and said,

'Sorry, Prime Minister, but Sir Archibald has told me to tell you to piss off…that's precisely what he said…quite sure…I will.' She put the phone down and went back to the door of Sir Archibald's study, knocked and went in. Sir Archibald had already buried his head in his hands. 'That was the prime minister. He told me to inform you that you are suspended pending further investigations.'

'Did I hear you telling him to piss off.'

'You were quite specific, sir.'

'So I was.' Sir Archibald had taken on a dazed expression.

'Would you like anything else, sir?'

'No, you have done quite enough,' he replied. 'You may take my kipper away, I'm no longer hungry.'

'Very good, sir.' She picked up the plate and left.

Sir Archibald looked down at the picture of Godfrey Fairtrade on the front page of the *National Mail*. After a moment's reflection, he picked up his letter opener. The miniature sword glinted in the morning light as it slowly rose above Godfrey's face.

★

While Sir Archibald was stabbing Godfrey's face to shreds, Godfrey was fending off a verbal assault from his own wife.

'Pressing government business, you said,' she said, pacing around the kitchen, waving the *National Mail* in his face. 'You've just made me a pariah of the coffee mornings. I'll never be able to show my face in Ewell again.'

'Not everything is about you, Lillian!' Godfrey grunted.

'After everything I have done for you, after all those

years following you around from one wretched posting to the next. And this is the thanks I get.'

'Well, I'm sorry I have been such a disappointment for you.'

'You're a fool and always have been,' she spat.

'So, after all these years, what does that make you?'

'I won't stand by and let you destroy my life.'

'I had no choice!'

'You always have a choice!'

Something in Godfrey snapped. He got up and grabbed her by the shoulders and shouted, 'I had no choice.' She stared at him, stunned by his anger.

'Why?' she said in a small voice. Godfrey couldn't hold it back anymore. He sat down and with his gaze fixed between his legs, told her everything. When he had finished, he braced himself for the inevitable and looked up. What he hadn't expected to see was soft, wet eyes. She came up to him and held his head to her stomach.

'I'm sorry,' he heard her say, feeling a tear fall on his bald scalp.

*

The others stood when Richard and Joan came into the office. Richard nodded to Rosie, Mark and Thomas, who all had casts on their arms and Muhammad, who was holding a walking stick. All nine of them looked puzzled when Deirdre walked in behind them.

'This is Deirdre. She represents the Granny Cartel,' Richard said.

'Barrington said nothing about this,' Alwin replied.

'Barrington?'

'He called us this morning and told us to meet you here.'

Richard stared at Deirdre. She smiled and said, 'A conversation for another time, perhaps.' Behind them walked in Chris, Doug, Gail and Rosalind: Nipper's protection duty, all looking a bit dishevelled.

Once Richard had introduced everyone he said to Deirdre, 'Can I talk to them alone for a moment?' He took the others into Tancred's office. Once the door was closed, Alwin said, 'Have you seen the news?'

Richard and Joan looked at each other. 'No, we've been out of the loop, but we have a vague idea,' Richard replied.

'They turned the raid on the fort into a paramilitary attack, made all the Temperance Trotters and Tancred's posse dress up as paramilitaries. Maude's been shouting from the roof tops about how defenceless grannies were beaten and abused and Surrey Police said tragedy was only averted because of an anonymous tip-off about the raid and have linked Mervyn Nipper to the attack but he seems to have disappeared off the face of the earth.'

Alwin took a breath as Jenny threw a copy of the *National Mail* on the table and said, 'It gets better.'

'Thank God we weren't on that raid,' Emmeline said as Richard picked up the paper, which had a picture of an agitated-looking Godfrey Fairtrade on the front. Richard read the first few paragraphs and said, 'Can you all excuse me for a second?' and left the office. He went up to where Deirdre was sitting.

'I don't want Godfrey to get hurt.'

She looked up at him. 'Would it matter?'

'Yes, it would. I can understand what you've done, even if I don't like the way you did it. But Godfrey is completely innocent of anything.'

With some gentleness she replied, 'I know. He isn't in trouble, anything but.'

'I'll hold you to that,' Richard said. He turned to go back to the office, but when he got to the door Deirdre added, 'The police are keen to talk to Nipper, but he seems to have disappeared, presumed on the run. He was the mastermind behind the raid, after all.'

Richard turned back to her and said, 'And the truth is?'

'We've found him a new line of work with lots of fresh air and plenty of sun. It will do him the world of good, I'm sure.'

'He's a high-profile person. Won't he be looked for?'

'By whom? No family, no friends, no power base and a government that in future would much prefer he stayed disappeared. The press will look for him, I'm sure. And they will find nothing.'

Richard humphed and went to close the door.

'You're a good man, Richard,' Deidre added. Richard nodded with a faint smile and closed the door. Everyone in the office stopped talking when Richard came back in.

He looked at them all and said, 'OK, this is our situation.'

THIRTY

The old Dakota dropped through a sky of cotton blood clouds, buffeted by the sultry air, as it descended towards the dusty airstrip cut through the equatorial scrub. There to meet it was one solitary goat. Its passage across the airstrip had been disturbed by the sound of the approaching plane. Its eyes narrowed as the big bird swooped towards it. When it had been a kid, an eagle had tried to drag it into the sky. Ever since then it had possessed a pathological hatred of anything airborne – and the goat now had horns and knew how to use them. It squared up, stretched its neck and flicked a blond tuft away from its eyes. The goat with no name was ready to kick some feathered butt.

As the bird grew larger, it saw its talons come down. It had never seen a feathered foe with three talons before and there was something odd about their shape. They reminded it of the four feet of those noisy beasts who ate the two-legged creatures and then threw them up again. It could talk all day about that. The bird also seemed not to have any feathers. The closer it got, the stranger it became, but all these things were of no consequence. What was of slight concern was its size, as it dawned on the goat that this one was far greater than the one that had tried to lift it off its juvenile hooves.

That concern grew as the bird grew closer. The goat's eye began to twitch. It stomped a hoof in the ground to show it meant business, but still the bird came, with its strange incessant cry further nibbling into the goat's resolve. Only when it hit the ground and started running towards it with a trembling scream did the goat's resolve completely desert it. With a high-pitched 'Naaa', which loosely translated, meant 'Sod this', it fled into the undergrowth just before the plane reached it.

The old C-47 taxied to the end of the airstrip and slowly turned until it was pointing in the direction it had just come. The starboard-side door opened and a large sack was pushed out. Just before the door was closed again, a book was thrown at the sack, hitting the head of the person it held. Then the plane set off again for the sky.

The person in the sack struggled as the sound of the plane dwindled away, until they finally managed to pull their head free. Nipper sat there with only his head exposed and looked around. It took his eyes a little time to adjust, after being blindfolded for so long. His eyes were drawn to a dog-eared book lying next to him on the ground. He assumed it was the thing that had hit his head. He leaned forward to see what the title said. He saw the Lonely Planet logo. Under that was the word: Honduras. Every time he read the word his brain short-circuited. He couldn't bring himself to connect the word with where he was sitting despite the cacophony of tropical sounds assaulting his ears or the foreign scent of the land proclaiming the reality as clearly as if the banking plane had been dragging a banner.

Something in the bushes went 'Naaa'. He turned towards the noise and saw the head of the goat sticking out of the undergrowth. It looked up and down the airstrip before stepping out. Then it looked at him.

This was turning into a trying day for the goat with no name. First, it had been chased away by a bloody great bird and something was now lying on the ground that for the life of the goat it couldn't grasp. The goat wasn't surprised the bird had thrown it up. It had the head of one of those two-legged creatures, the noisy beasts ate and threw up, but it had a body that it could only describe as a turd.

Whatever it was, the goat didn't like it. It felt ill-tempered (and slightly humiliated) after the encounter with the bird and was in no mood for turd-shaped creatures. So, the goat lowered its head, scuffed the ground with its hoof, and, with a malevolent 'Naaa', charged.

Nipper hadn't much cared for the look the goat had given him, which to him had been none too welcoming. When it lowered its head and stamped the ground, Nipper realised with bum-puckering certainty that the animal was going to charge him. As the goat naaa'ed like an Exocet missile, Nipper began to scream. Then suddenly, ten feet away, the goat skidded to a stop, spun round and high-tailed it back to the safety of the scrub.

Nipper felt something hard press into the back of his neck.

'Your...last...request...gringo.'

Nipper slowly turned his head to see a spindly old man standing behind him pointing a gun at his face. He had a tatty sombrero on his head. His trousers and short-sleeved shirt were weather-beaten and unwashed. This was finished off with a gun belt over his chest, and flip-flops.

He pulled the gun away and said with a chuckle, 'I always wanted to say that. I am Ramón Diaz, I have been waiting for you. Lucky for you I was,' he said, pointing in the direction the goat had fled. Nipper said nothing – he had temporarily lost the power of speech.

'I know what you want to ask,' Ramón began. 'You want to ask why Ramón was waiting for you.' The red-eyed silence that met him seemed no handicap to the conversation. 'Pippa sent me to pick you up. You are to be my guest from now on.' Ramón noticed the widening of Nipper's eyes and added, 'Don't worry; the years will fly by.' Nipper's eyes widened further and Ramón saw he was trying to say something. It took him a few seconds to realise that Nipper was trying to say 'years'.

He sat down next to the sack and lent in towards Nipper's face conspiratorially. 'So, you know Pippa?' He pulled back, not waiting for a reply, a dreamy look on his face. 'What a woman,' Ramón said adoringly. Nipper abruptly stopped trying to say 'years' and looked at him with something approaching fear.

'We were fighters and lovers. Never have I met such a woman.' Then sadness enveloped Ramón. 'She was my one true love. I had hoped to see her again.' Nipper was actively trying to pull away from him now, although the sack was proving an impediment to his escape. Ramón absently tapped the sack with his gun and Nipper froze like a rabbit circled by a hawk. Satisfied that he now had his audience back, Ramón recommenced his trip down memory lane.

'You want to know how we met,' Ramón stated. Nipper didn't, but he had the feeling he was going to find out.

'We met in a bar in Tegucigalpa. I walked in and there she was at the bar, fighting six men with foolish tongues. What a thing of nature she was, radiant, graceful as the jaguar, as she danced through the melee of their arms and legs. It was like watching ballet but with lots of brutal violence. I knew at that moment I wanted her scent on my body.' It was all Nipper could do to prevent the meagre contents of his stomach from landing on the sack.

Ramón heard the retching. 'Air sick, you are. It will pass. Anyway, that night I wooed her to my bed, which wasn't hard, for she was a woman of great appetite. Nipper nodded forlornly. We made love until I passed out. From that night I knew my heart could be for no other, even though she had fractured my hip.'

The pair sat there in silence for a while, Nipper in the sack, Ramón savouring his memories. Nipper heard a 'Naaa' coming from the undergrowth.

'In those days I ran a distribution business for the CIA,' Ramón said, holding his gun up. 'She joined me and we became partners.' Ramón turned his solemn eyes to Nipper. 'She saved my life, you know.' Nipper obviously didn't, nor did he care.

'How, I hear you ask?'

Nipper shook his head but Ramón paid no attention.

'One night we were transporting guns through the jungle on a mule train when we were set upon by unscrupulous men, twenty in all. I was shot in this leg.' Ramón pulled his trouser leg up to show a large scar. 'We were surrounded and I made my peace with God, for escape was the thought of fools. But Pippa picked me up and plunged into the forest through a murderous hailstorm of bullets. When we were safe, she laid me down and set a tourniquet to my leg. And then she went back and the hunters became the hunted. That night the forest sung of Hell-bound souls being delivered to their fate. In the morning she returned like the crimson dawn. No guns were lost. In fact, we had twenty more.' Ramón was a man who liked to look on the bright side of life.

'She may have stolen my heart, but I owe her my life. I promised her then that one day I would repay the debt. And so, here you are.' Ramón was touched to see that his story had brought tears to Nipper's face. Then he saw the Lonely Planet on the ground.

'Ah, Pippa's book of travels,' He picked it up and opened the first page. His eyes moistened. Holding the book up to Nipper, he said, 'Look, see what she has written.' In a childlike scrawl were the words:

A Ramón, mi Palillo,
Pippa

'That was her nickname for me, "My little stick". Nipper's eyes shifted from the words to Ramón and back again. Then his eyes darted back to Ramón with alarm, seeing that he was now holding a large knife. He lent away in fear as Ramón began to cut the sack open. All Nipper was wearing was a pair of briefs, which had been shredded into a rather unwholesome thong. Ramón frowned and said, 'You will need more than that if you are to work in the fields,' as he cut the rope around Nipper's hands.

Nipper uttered his first proper word in hours. It was, 'Fields?', spoken in a quivering voice. His face was drained to the colour of concrete.

'Why yes, if you are to live with me you must also work. My days of banditry are no more. I now have a farm, growing sugar cane. Business is good.' Nipper could see the bitter irony in that.

'I am a good master, fair with the whip. My men are fed, sometimes well, and live in the barn with the animals in case a jaguar comes calling. And the hay is changed at least once a year.'

Putting it mildly, Nipper felt somewhat overwhelmed. He wanted to scream, to cry, to tear the living heart out of life. It was as though he had come home to find his future had packed up and taken with it the family marbles. Madness was stalking through the corridors of his mind. There was only one clear thought. To rain hell on those who had brought his life to such a place.

THIRTY-ONE

The fightback started on Monday morning.

The prime minister's private secretary, Florence, had phoned on Sunday morning and completely broken protocol with the prophetic words, 'Houston, we have a problem.' Houston wondered if Florence had just been waiting for the chance to say that. The superconducting properties of bad news never ceased to amaze him. It seemed to skip from one cranium to the next with alarming efficiency. Her call was quickly followed by an avalanche of other messages about Godfrey's revelations in the *National Mail*. Coming on the back of the events in Surrey the day before, he needed no one to tell him how precarious the situation was.

With public opinion turning even further against the government, the prime minister knew he was in the biggest fight of his political career. He needed time to affect an escape and had no compunction about throwing Sir Archibald under the bus to that end. After all, it was Sir Archibald's son who had been at the centre of the whole debacle and was now presiding in Guildbury jail. As for Nipper, he would happily reverse the bus over him for instigating the godawful mess in the first place, and his disappearing act only supported Godfrey's accusations. This and Nipper's disappearance had left Eleanor Houston in an existential quandary as to the future of the Temperance League and a rather lonely figure in the panic-gripped halls of No. 10. Eventually, she just retreated to the flat with a bottle of Glenmorangie in hand.

By the time Monday morning arrived, Houston was ready to come out fighting. In front of the door of No. 10, with the sound of hordes of protesters jeering in the background (bused in by the Granny Cartel), he told the country that the accusations against him were completely groundless and frankly ludicrous. He announced that there would be a full and far-reaching public inquiry into the appalling and cowardly attack in the Surrey Hills on Saturday. He confirmed that Sir Archibald had been suspended, pending an investigation into the attack. He promised that no stone would be left unturned in the search for the truth and that the guilty parties would be punished to the full extent of the law. Then he sent out his heartfelt condolences to the victims and their families and vowed to bring them justice. He refused to make any comment about Nipper's or a serving police officer's involvement in the attack, saying only that it would be inappropriate of him to comment on ongoing investigations.

Sir Archibald also came out fighting on Monday morning. He travelled up to London to find out what had happened to the original police taskforce. Frustratingly, Tancred would only talk to the family solicitor, but if Sir Archibald could find Richard and the team then he had a chance of grasping back the narrative. But when he got to New Scotland Yard he was met with a wall of silence. Barrington said he had no knowledge of the taskforce and that Richard was on annual leave in Spain. Naturally, no one had any knowledge of the Temperance Trotter and Nipper's kidnappings, because Barrington had made sure it had stayed a secret.

When Sir Archibald accused Barrington of lying through his teeth, Barrington ordered him to leave the building. That was when his mother's genes took control. He managed to barricade himself in his office armed with a broken chair leg and some mace. It eventually took SCO19 to winkle him out. Courtesy of an anonymous tip-off, the press got a grandstand view of him being dragged screaming and kicking out of New Scotland Yard, claiming that it was all a giant conspiracy.

On Tuesday morning Houston received a fresh hammer blow, this time from Anonymous. The hacktivists published emails (supplied by Deirdre) which they claimed had been taken from the prime minister's personal email account, showing his complicity in the Surrey Hills attack. This coincided with mass rallies (organised by the Granny Cartel) calling for the abolition of sugar restriction and a clean-up of government. Houston continued to protest his innocence, but by now no one was listening. In the halls of Westminster, the wolves were gathering.

On Wednesday morning Home Secretary Sir Cecil Mandeville-Blythe, who was now being referred to as 'the Submarine' by some members of the press, surfaced and stepped into the fray. On the steps of No.10, before going into a full COBRA meeting to discuss the crisis, he evaded questions about his support for Houston. Instead, he said that he had no knowledge of the events that led up to the attack. He had been aware of concerns about Nipper's growing belligerence towards certain groups and subtly implied that he was uneasy about how this may have influenced policy but wouldn't be drawn on exactly what that meant. Asked if he had any interest in becoming prime minister (a planted question) he said he had not, but jokingly said that if he were, he would repeal the law on sugar restriction, to the surprise of the press.

Sir Cecil's betrayal reached Houston before he did, but his fury proved impotent because of the next betrayal. Led by Sir Cecil, the cabinet unanimously asked for Houston's resignation. An hour later Houston, on the steps of No.10, granted their wish. As he spoke to the gathered press, he heard the crowds outside the Downing Street gates singing 'Another One Bites the Dust'. He then walked off into the shadows of history, vilified and with his cherished chiefdom a distant dream. The next day, Sir Cecil was made interim prime minister. The media hailed it as a popular choice, as Maude orchestrated the hails from behind the scenes. Pop idol Harry Webb released a cover of 'Congratulations' with the words changed to hail the end of sugar restrictions. Celebrations were thrown all over the country, leading to much nausea and tummy aches.

Over five thousand miles away, Nipper was cutting sugar cane with blistered hands under a beating sun. The other workmen kept their distance from him, for it was clear he was a few canes short of a stack.

*

Richard and Joan were enjoying the Spanish sun. It turned out the hotel Deirdre had booked for them was a lovely old world hotel in the centre of Valencia, overlooking a square with a medieval church. They also had more than enough money to do what they wanted. This was fortunate because they had been given limited time to pack, grabbing their passports from their respective homes and meeting at Waterloo Station before heading to Gatwick.

For the first two days they only left their room for meals, yet those two days would for ever be precious to both of them. Their room had a balcony overlooking the square and the sun would play through the curtains in the afternoon breeze. Richard and Joan lost their hearts to the sound of the ancient church bells and the babble of foreign voices down below.

On the third day they ventured out to take in the sights of the city. They lunched in the Mercado Central and relaxed on the beach in the afternoon. On the fourth day, curiosity forced Joan to pick up an English tabloid.

'The PM has resigned…and Sir Archibald has been arrested.'

Richard took the paper from her and put it back on the stand.

'But…'

'Not another word,' Richard said as he pulled Joan away.

*

Tancred looked up at the waning moon through the bars of his cell. Once more he heard his name being called from the other side of the block. The voice was harsh and cruel and the other prisoners had made a game of it.

'Tancred.'

'Ohhh, Tancred,' the other prisoners responded.

'Tancred,' the growling voice came again.

'Ohhh, Tancred.'

'Tancred, I'm going to eat your liver.'

'He's going to eat your liver.'

Tancred had the feeling his father wasn't going to forgive him any time soon.

THIRTY-TWO

The months passed. Sir Cecil made good on his joke. Sugar restriction officially came to an end. The crown prosecution service dropped the charges against Houston and Sir Archibald through lack of evidence. They continued to proclaim their innocence, but it fell on deaf ears. Whatever the rights and wrongs, they were now men of the past. And it was a past the country had no wish to revisit.

Only the charity sector mourned the end of sugar restrictions and, with it, the Granny Cartel. The reason the authorities had never managed to find a money trail from the Cartel's activities was because the Cartel's financial dealing had been hidden under the Official Secrets Act, not that the government had any clue. With help of sweet-toothed sympathisers in MI5, most of the Cartel's money had covertly flowed into shielded offshore accounts, eventually finding its way into offshore trust funds set up for charities across the country. Now the money flow had dried up, but it still left many charities with healthy offshore accounts that over time would quietly filter back into the onshore world. Years later an investigative journalist would write an exposé alleging a link between the Cartel, MI5 and the charity sector. They were branded a conspiracy theorist, despite many believing it to be true. When Richard and Joan read the article, they were both convinced it was true.

In a surprising show of charity, the Granny Cartel dropped all charges against the Temperance Trotters and Tancred's posse, stating that the country needed to heal its wounds. Sir Cecil praised them for their humanity. Again, all those released claimed they were innocent in the first place, and were roundly ignored.

Godfrey was given the chair of the new parliamentary committee scrutinising standards in public office. He would go on to get a knighthood in the New Year's honours list for service to the community and the foreign office, much to the irritation of the foreign office.

As for Richard, for the first time in his life, he felt part of a family, and both he and Joan were working hard to extend it. Joan made inspector and Richard was promoted to detective chief inspector, thanks to Chief Superintendent Phillip Barrington, who was himself moving up to become the new Met police commissioner, now that Sir Archibald Punchard was gone. Whether Richard liked it or not, he was on the inside and so was Joan. Barrington had made that abundantly clear, not that either of them would trust him again.

Years later, Richard would see Tancred across a street near Victoria Station. Tancred had been dressed not to impress. Unsurprising, given the media's interest in what they now called the 'Sugarless Years'. Their eyes had met, only briefly, before Tancred melted into the crowd. Richard had rushed over the road in the hope of catching him. To… he didn't know what. To say something. To even hug the damn guy. He'd looked around, but Tancred was nowhere to be scene. Close by, underneath a covered-up hawker's cart, Tancred had huddled. He had learned a skill. Richard never saw Tancred again.

And the years passed. The death of Jason had made life hard for Molly Willoughby. Maybe she would not have survived, if not for a local priest with a kind eye. Under his wing, Molly had discovered a new self and in time became a respected member of the community, and a dental hygienist.

*

In a bucolic corner of Surrey, a very secret afternoon tea with a very reclusive Maude and her key conspirators was taking place. Since the events at the fort Maude had kept a low profile, feeling it was prudent to stay out of the limelight. It hadn't been easy, with the press trying their best to put her under said light.

Those in attendance represented some of the most powerful people in the land. The head of MI5: the recently knighted Sir Andrew Harrington, was there. As was his aunt, Deirdre Wotheringspot, who was helping Phillip Barrington, the new Met Commissioner, make some useful future contacts. There were over three dozen people in all, representing the great and the good of the nation. A world of men, but not really.

Even the PM, Sir Cecil, had flown under the radar to attend. He would only last three years as PM, stabbed in the back for the role by the dishevelled blond Foreign

Secretary, Horace Karloff, whom Sir Cecil despised even more than Nipper.

The one person who wasn't there was Pippa. She and the Baker's Dozen had taken themselves off to a spiritual retreat in Tibet. At that very moment, the Baker's Dozen were crossed-legged in a circle with Pippa in the middle rotating a mallet around a large singing bowl. Deirdre never did discover how Maude met Pippa or Sir Cecil.

'Are you going to tell me what really happened to Nipper?' Sir Cecil asked Maude in a hushed tone. Maude and Deirdre exchanged glances.

'Let's just say he is cultivating a tan,' Maude replied. As predicted by Deirdre, apart from the press, no one had put much effort into looking for Nipper, least of all the authorities, despite a dedicated vocal manhunt. When the storm hit, his natural disposition meant that there was no one to pine at his imaginary grave. Apart from a few of the Temperance Trotters; but they had their own problems dealing with society's assumptions of guilty. But that hadn't been enough for Maude. Social media rumours began to circulate that Nipper was dead, slain by bloodthirsty renegade Temperance Trotters in an internal power struggle. Slain by his own twisted brethren. Maude was smiling sweetly at Sir Cecil.

'Perhaps it's best I don't ask any more,' Sir Cecil said with a wry smile. He considered Maude to be almost as devious and ruthless as himself.

Deirdre tapped on the table as Maude went into the kitchen. 'We would just like to thank each and every one of you for your support of the Granny Cartel. Maude has baked some exquisite offerings in celebration of our success.'

Maude came in with a tray of cupcakes. Each one of them was a beautifully crafted masterpiece. Everyone started to clap.

When Maude passed one to Barrington, he said, 'It seems a shame to eat them,' just as the chief inspector of Surrey sidled up and jokingly said, 'They're a bit small.' Maude turned to him and placed her hand on his sleeve.

'Everything in moderation,' she replied.

EPILOGUE

A number of years before the events recounted here, the below advert appeared in *The Lady* magazine – a publication historically known in the world intelligence community as *the* global marketplace for assassins – in the classified ads:

> – Do you want to avoid a messy divorce?
> – Do you have a neighbour you wish would just disappear?
> – Is it time for a change of boss?
>
> *I can help.*
> I provide a fast, efficient service with a fifty-year anti-unearthing guarantee.
>
> All replies received in confidence.
>
> PO Box 21
> Bognor Regis
> PO21 1BA

This advert was placed by a certain Pippa Blackwood, who happened to be a driver for a skip hire company at the time.

One of many people who replied to this advertisement was a certain Maude Appleby, concerning a certain restaurant owner.

But another person also took note of the advert, for a rainy day. That same person finally contacted Blackwood shortly after the sugar restrictions came into effect. Soon afterwards, the private secretary and right-hand man of the Sugar Tsar went missing, about the time Pippa Blackwood left her un-consecrated skip burial business to come and work for Maude Appleby.

The name of this other person was Sir Cecil Mandeville-Blythe.